THE WALL OF WINTER

BY PAUL GRIFFIN

PUBLISHED BY LYON AND LAMB

c/o 22 Trevellan Road, Mylor Bridge,
Falmouth, TR11 5NE

First published 2016

Available from www.lulu.com/shop

ISBN: 978-0-9527781-7-2

PART 1 – BEHIND THE WALL

'I beg you, by the drowsy logs of evening,
Before creation settles in the fire,
Now to look hard, regard that liar the mind.

With the dog's sighs, the hissing of the ash,
The drum and whistle of the jamming wind,
 It covers up the facts, the singing streams
And water birds behind the wall of winter.

Unheard and savage by the twittering water,
Their tribes do not disturb your evening rest;
But high as builds the greatest granite builder,
No wall keeps out the water floods of truth.'

I - TOWLE ARRIVES

He walked slowly and cadaverously up the path, his head bent, with the preoccupied air of a boy coming home from school. It was only when he raised his head that I saw his infinitely deep eyes; and it was only in company that the compacted quiet shook out into a set of crazy movements, as if he were seized by the wind-harassed tensions of the trees. There was something not human about him, a visibly intense effort to be normal.

'Good evening,' he said carefully, when I had opened the door. He waited with patience for my conventional reply, as if it were something he was sentenced to hear before the world could go on.

'My name,' he continued, 'is Towle. I am expecting some brown bread.'

There was not a glimmer of humour.

'Oh, yes?' I said, playing for time.

'I wondered if you had it, by any chance.'

'You mean you want to borrow some?'

'Only if it should be necessary. The baker may perhaps have left some, as I asked him; if not at my house, perhaps at yours.'

I was beginning to emerge from the mists. The meeting with him had jerked me out of current events, as subsequent meetings always did. Engrossed in some urgent concern, I would turn a corner and see him standing in that peculiar silence, waiting for me to set aside my affairs and react. His presence had the irritating insistence of a telephone ringing.

I remembered that the Thatched Cottage, on the other side of the High Street, had been sold to a Mr Towle.

'Come in,' I said. 'If you have time, that is.'

Then he smiled for the first time, a curious relaxation of the cheek muscles, like a cat forgetting its dignity. I felt that he had wanted to be asked in more than he had wanted brown bread.

'I'm afraid my wife's out,' I said as he stepped into the hall. 'But you must come up and have a drink, and see my balcony.'

He followed me upstairs and into my study, which was in its usual state of disorder.

'I bind books,' I explained. 'Please disregard the mess, and come through here.'

We were very proud of our balcony, which seemed to us to give Brink its unusual Mediterranean look. It was set like a stage box over the High Street, with seats at the daily and nightly performances of the town's affairs. There were honeysuckle and rambler roses climbing up the support, so that a passer-by might stop and converse, or walk on, pretending that he had not seen whoever was on the balcony. We, on the other hand, stood a sporting chance of avoiding Mr Macready or anyone else not to our taste, by lurking behind foliage till the danger was past.

Towle regarded this for a minute or two. Then he said 'Fair Verona, where we lay our scene!' and smiled again, in the same jerky way.

'Sit down,' I said, lowering the tone. 'I'll fetch some whisky, if that will suit you.'

I gathered from his gesture that it would suit him, and went for glasses.

We talked a lot that evening, in a way I find it hard to describe. Some people are sticky because they will not talk at all, and others are loquacious bores; but here were the two types united in one person. Most conversations with Towle went the same way. You started by chatting merrily, he studying you and answering only with a twitch of his face and the occasional monosyllable; then some topic would excite his interest, and he would begin to talk endlessly about his own affairs, often intimately and embarrassingly, until you searched for an excuse to stop him.

On this occasion he talked of his parents and his work. His parents had let him down in a number of ways, he felt; but from their bad treatment of him he had gathered an immense interest in people generally, a desire to understand and account for their behaviour. He had been a historian at Cambridge. Now, aged about thirty, he had resigned a Fellowship at his College, and was settling down to write a book. The death of both his parents had enabled him to do this, for they had clearly not extended their unkindness to the point of cutting him out of their wills. I asked him what the book was, and he said it was on an aspect of medieval philosophy; not, it seemed to me, the best way of pursuing an interest in human beings.

He talked and talked, and it grew darker and darker. As he poured out his personal life with less restraint, he sank down into his chair until he almost seemed to be lying full-length, with only his head upright. Each paragraph tended to be prefaced by a neurotic convulsion of the body; but always his tone was deep and slow and measured. As the light dimmed from the dying sunset his eyes seemed to grow brighter, as if they were the volcanic walls of some conflagration deep in the recesses of his head. I felt as if I were trapped on the balcony with some creature on the fringes of humanity; yet his voice was kind with a sort of clinical kindness. Fear and distaste crowded in on me, until my heart beat faster with an intense dislike which I admit I did little to resist.

Suddenly he stopped talking and just looked at me. Stricken with an equally sudden panic, I plunged into the gap.

'Look here,' I said. 'I'm keeping you from all you have to do. I know what moving house is like. I'll go and fetch you that bread.'

He twitched another smile in the darkness. 'It doesn't matter,' he said. 'I've only arrived with a few belongings. I was in lodgings before, you see. Now I shall have to gather some furniture together. And I have had my supper; the bread was for the morning.'

Hypnotised into social grace, I asked the question I feared to ask: 'Have you got a bed for the night?'

For the first time, he laughed; it was like an amateur actor trying to render the words 'Ha! ha!' - as if he knew people did laugh, but had not quite fallen into the way of it himself. 'No,' he said. 'I'm afraid I haven't.'

At that moment, nothing would have persuaded me to have such a person under my roof for the night. Having suffered myself, I had benefited greatly from the kindness of the world; now here, facing me, was a brother human being, an orphan, needing, for one night only, a home. I had a chance to repay the world; and I ran from it screaming with revulsion as the rich man might have run from Lazarus. I longed for Tiggy and her comforting presence.

'I wish I could offer you a bed,' I said quickly, very conscious of the empty bed in the spare room; 'but just this particular night I can't.'

A feeling came over me that he would ask to sleep in the chair on the balcony, and I cast about for excuses; but he settled his head back and sighed.

'I shall have to make do with the floor, then,' he said. For a moment I thought he meant my floor; then I saw the absurdity.

'Can I help you in any other way?' I asked, willing to provide anything to have him off the premises.

'Thank you, no,' he replied. 'I have bedclothes.'

I went and got the bread, and waited for him to go. He sat in silence, upright now, with his head hunched on his shoulders, looking out over the badly lighted street. It was nearly eleven by my watch, and my wife should have returned from her meeting.

I realised that if Tiggy came back and met Towle for long enough to talk to him, she would instantly offer him the spare bed.

'Well,' I said, 'I'm afraid I promised my wife I'd go and meet her.'

I had to repeat the lie before he stirred. Then he jumped a little, shook his head as if to clear it, and stood up. He looked over the balcony again in thought. 'Fair Verona,' he said slowly. 'I always blamed Friar Laurence. Do you think he envied the young people? It would have been very understandable.'

It was unfortunate that Tiggy arrived at the front door at the same moment as we did. I had to introduce Towle, and talked hard in the hope that she would ask no questions.

'I was just coming to meet you, dear,' I said.

Tiggy looked quite alarmed. 'What on earth possessed you to do that?' she asked.

I bundled the reluctant but silent Towle out of the house, and returned to explain myself.

'And you wouldn't even ask the poor man to spend the night?'

She was incredulous.

'I tell you he's a horrible man.'

'Nonsense! He looked rather sweet to me. Pale and interesting. It isn't Christian to let him sleep on the floor!'

I finally persuaded her to go to bed, and went up to my study to shut the windows. The street lighting had gone out, and the moon was getting up in the clear summer sky. I went out on to the balcony for a breath before retiring. The scents of honeysuckle and roses were still strong on the summer night air, but there was another smell as well, a curious smell as of musty biscuits. On the table beside Towle's chair were an untouched glass of whisky and a brown loaf.

II- A Visit to Fifield

Denbury Road was the fashionable quarter of our small town. It forked off the main street and gathered greenery about itself for a few hundred yards in a straight shady tunnel that maintained its shape even when the winter had done its best to defoliate it. The bare structure of the trees alone had dignity, matching the dignity of some of our wealthier residents. Here they lived, many of them retired from cities on some Horatian impulse to acquire a miniature Sabine farm. Here among them lived John Macready, a former company director, and also his wife Ethel. Mrs Macready had been directed for so many years that it required quite an effort to remember her existence. She was a dumpy, confidential little woman who sat at ease in her husband's absence, and sprang socially to attention when he entered the room. They had a daughter Juliet, less pliable altogether, of whom there is more to say.

However, it was the head of the family whose figure walked purposefully down the High Street on the morning after my first meeting with Towle. He carried his stick with a carved head, looking as always as if it were destined to be used as a weapon, and he held his leonine head with the self-conscious flourish of an actor entering a public place. Seeing me on the balcony, he nodded and strutted pleasedly over to try out his lines.

'I am going,' he announced impressively, 'to call upon the new tenant of the Thatched Cottage.'

It was no good trying to advance any conversation with Mr Macready. As with so many people, one had to flatten the dialogue and subdue any impulses to poetry or wit; otherwise some misunderstanding was bound to occur. I remarked that it was a kind thought to call on the new tenant of the Thatched Cottage. Like most remarks, it was a mistake. Mr Macready quickly exposed it.

'No,' he said firmly. 'You are wrong. It is not a kind thought, but a social necessity. This new fellow may not like us, but we are here, and he has got to live with us. It has always been my principle to show a new arrival, as soon as is practicable, what sort of neighbours he is going to have.'

'I met him last night ...' I began, in an effort to keep Macready off his principles; but like thistledown I was swept away by the flood of his rhetoric.

'Of course,' he continued, 'once it was different. These things were automatic. I remember my father saying to me, in the days when we lived in Kensington ...' As he talked, I nodded and raised my eyebrows, watching the sun on the walls and gardens further down the street. Mrs Ellerman's Pip was yawning and scratching in his favourite patch of sunshine, and found himself able to watch a motor-bike go by without being stirred to his usual protest. As his tongue curled out for a third consecutive yawn, I felt a great surge of fellow-feeling. Speech was a precious gift, but nobody loved Mrs Ellerman's Pip less for being without it.

Macready usually talked until he made himself angry; then, with a final bitter remark, he would bring the curtain down and sweep off to prepare for the next performance. On this occasion, however, I was saved by my wife's voice from the kitchen, calling me loudly with anguish in her tone. With a quick excuse I cut Macready off in full cry and dived into the house, determined not to emerge until the danger was past.

Downstairs, Tiggy was huddled against a wall of the kitchen, watching a heap of white chips in the centre of the room.

'Old lecher!' she said. 'He made me break a cup. Anyway, I saved you.'

Her eye was fixed hopefully on me, as I started to sort out the exact relationship of the three statements.

'Has he been ...' I started, moving mechanically for the brush and dustpan.

'Yes, of course,' said Tiggy angrily, stamping her foot. 'He always does. Not this morning, I mean. All the time. Filthy old creature!' She relaxed and emerged from the wall. 'Your girl friend rang,' she said. 'She's coming round when the coast's clear. She wants me to see a dress.'

This was her way of referring to Juliet Macready, who was in fact her friend, not specially mine. She was a beautiful girl, though not as beautiful as Tiggy. Both would have fetched a high price in that Baghdad market which women imagine, not unjustly, to be the desire of the male world. If I let the phrase pass, even for the hundredth time, alarm bells would ring in Tiggy's obscure feminine mind.

'She's not my girl friend,' I said mechanically. 'Anyway, I shan't be here. I'm going off to Fifield to see Bone. You ought to come some time.'

'Well, I can't now, can I?'

I left by the back entrance, and circled round to the bus stop up the street. The blinds were shading the shops, and one or two shopkeepers chattered to me out of their doors. When I finally reached the bus stop it was ominously deserted. We were without a car, and I started working out whether I could catch the next bus and still be back for lunch.

'Where do you want to go?' said a voice from a passing car. It was Derek Major, and by good luck he was passing through Fifield.

I settled thankfully beside him, and we sped out into the country, swapping remarks about the hot spell. Our county is undulating, and well-wooded, so on a cloudless day it was easy to talk with enthusiasm. There were stretches of buttercup parkland, and then crops, with orange-stone farmhouses shimmering in the warmth. After that the North Brink Reservoir, with waterbirds flapping slowly over it; then over a higher hill, and far away, on top of the opposite slope, the first sight of the church and castle of Fifield.

'I'm going all the way to the coast to see a client,' said Derek. He was the junior partner in a firm of solicitors.

'A chance of a bathe,' I said.

'No. Not this time. I've got to be back to go to a dance tonight.'

This remark seemed to give him cause for reflection, and we travelled for a time in friendly silence; but he was bursting to confide, and soon broke out again.

'They say women grow more and more like their mothers.'

I admitted I had heard it said.

'They say that if you want to see what your girl friend's faults are, you should study her mother.'

'That's what you said before.'

'Do you find your wife grows more and more like her mother?'

I considered. 'I never met her mother,' I said. 'But from what I've heard of her, and from what I know about her father - my wife's that is - I'd say that insofar as she's like either of them, she's like her father.'

Derek groaned. 'That's not what I wanted to hear,' he said.

'It's the father I worry about.'

I knew what he meant. Juliet Macready and her new dress came into all this.

'I shouldn't worry,' I said. 'Some women always remain themselves, and those that become like their fathers are probably those with fathers they particularly respect, or who, like my own wife, have been rather specially brought up by them. Her father was a Classics don at Oxford, you know, and her mother died in childbirth. The poor old chap didn't know what to do at first; then he decided that if the classics meant anything they would give him

13

sufficient information to enable him to bring up a daughter. So he called her Antigone, and started by considering whether he should follow the ancient Spartan practice of exposing her on some hillside, presumably in the Cotswolds. This was much against his inclination, and, after much study and research, he was relieved to find that there were hitherto unknown variations in the Spartan practice. His closely reasoned work on the subject made his name academically, saved Antigone's life insofar as it had been in any danger, and ensured him employment at a salary amply sufficient for both their needs. He was known after that, rather unfairly, as Hardman the Baby-Killer.'

'And your wife? Did she become a classics don?'

'Derek, it is necessary to remember that the Ancient Greeks regarded women on a level with slaves. It would not have been decorous for Antigone to have an academic upbringing. It is true, though, that what learning she does possess has profound roots in ancient Greece. She inherited, or acquired, her father's very unusual and lovable attitude to life.'

We fell silent, and Derek brooded on the data I had given him until we reached Fifield, where he kindly dropped me at the Castle gateway.

Fifield Castle is not a beautiful building from less than five miles distance. It is an aggressive nineteenth-century bid for glory, bristling with chimneys and lightning conductors and not in perfect repair; but the first owner, however barbaric in other respects, had a deep reverence for learning, and kept sufficient money out of the hands of his architects and builders to purchase (in bulk) a library. Fired by the work, he purchased another library which, with the first, contained sufficient treasures to ensure the world-wide fame of Fifield Castle. These, combined, indexed, and displayed by successive librarians, would have attracted visitors from all over the world; but no librarian had yet succeeded in mastering the flood of fresh acquisitions for long enough to get down to the original work. As any librarian knows, books attract books, often in the form of vast and unsolicited legacies; successive bequests enriched the Fifield Collection to the extent that it overflowed the very capacious room provided in the Castle, cluttering various isolated storerooms and bedrooms with boxes and shelves of books and manuscripts. These were mostly of little value, as far as anyone could tell; but values change fast these days, and in any event there was much careful sorting to be done.

It was at the stage when bequests were at their thickest and fastest that the early twentieth-century owner of the Castle dismissed his librarian for telling the son of the house what happened to little boys who drew railway engines on the title pages of valuable books. No successor was appointed until that very son of the house in middle age was impelled, partly by the pangs of conscience but more by a desire to clear some space to live in, to pay a local enthusiast to spend his days setting matters in order.

Bone might have been specially designed as an instrument of punishment for the wretched Lord Fifield. I remember the first occasion I visited him, when he was at his most courteous and forthcoming. Anyone who cared about books saw his sunny side. He sat me down in a comfortable chair and brought me some of the fascinating treasures it was his privilege to handle. He was leaning over me, his ascetic face softened and illuminated by his beloved subject, when I heard the click of a door opening and saw his features set quickly in a savage tautness. A voice behind me muttered some request, but Bone cut the person off furiously.

'Please leave the room at once,' he snapped. 'Visitors are not received in the Library during the mornings.'

I turned just in time to see a submissive little man nod wearily and close the door quietly on himself.

'Someone wanting to see the place?' I asked.

Bone looked at me, anger still in his face. 'That was Lord Fifield,' he said. 'Some more of his friends are wanting to come and poke about.' The word 'friends' was spoken as if he were swallowing hemlock. 'And they will have to wait.' With which he turned again to the book he was showing me, and resumed his pleasant eagerness.

Bone was my biggest customer. He excavated like a terrier, examining books and manuscripts with swift intensity, and neatly recording what he found. About once a month he called me over to Fifield to discuss his latest finds, some of which I would carry away to repair. Delighted that I shared his enthusiasms, he would often let me take home other volumes in which I was interested.

On this occasion he was excited about a number of vellum leaves of fourteenth-century medical receipts, which he had related to other leaves in the British Museum. He had obtained facsimiles of these, and wanted to consult me about the best way of arranging the whole in a loose binding for his shelves. With one or two other jobs, we eventually packed it into a neat parcel for me to take home.

Bone was fond of telling me about the battles he had to fight in order to keep Lord Fifield and his friends in a proper state of discipline, but he seldom spoke of matters outside the Castle. Today, however, he adopted a deceptive air of casualness, and opened a new topic.

'Fresh arrival in your area, I hear,' he said, watching me closely. I looked puzzled.

'Man called Towle?' he suggested.

'Oh, Towle. Yes, he's just moved in across the street from me.'

'Mm. I never believe all I hear; and I don't recommend you to.'

'I don't,' I said.

'But he's a curious man.'

'He certainly is. How do you know him?'

'He's been living in the town here. He lodged with Mrs Fraser, opposite the church. A scholar, of course, with a proper love of books; but there was some urgency in his departure.'

'Urgency?'

'Yes. I can't quite understand why. Mrs Fraser has a daughter, Elaine, a girl of about fifteen, and I know she was upset by him. She said it was his eyes, looking at her oddly. One day she had hysterics in her mother's kitchen, and said she couldn't stand it any longer. It was difficult for Mrs Fraser, who's a sensible enough woman, but was a bit rattled herself. She'd wanted Towle to use her front door, but he always insisted on coming and going by her back door, through the kitchen. Anyway, she gave him notice; then her nerve seemed to go completely, and she insisted on his leaving the house immediately. Like her daughter, she suddenly decided she couldn't stand him another minute.'

'Women get very worked up,' I said.

'Of course; but you can imagine what people say in a town like this. I'd have trusted him well enough to feel happy about any of my books in his care; but I don't know about my daughter, if I had one. He always reminded me of a figure in an El Greco. He has that elongated, half-starved look, and the deep eyes.'

'El Greco is supposed to have suffered from an optical defect,' I said. 'I've always thought how delightful it would be to suffer from the opposite defect, and see the world as fat jolly men.'

'Nothing could be worse than a world full of fat jolly men. Only the contemplation of miserable people keeps us miserable people going. However, the Frasers don't seem to have appreciated their luck. I hope you will.'

We parted on this, and I caught the bus home.

It was a hot midday journey, and the bus chugged round the villages, dumping silent women with shopping baskets. I put my parcel beside me and soon found my head dipping out of control with sleep. Everybody wanted to talk, I thought ('thump' of the head sideways against the bus window); Towle, Macready, the Brink shopkeepers, even Bone and Derek Major, they all wanted a chat; and I could manage them ('thud' back against the hard headrest); but if I were not careful grotesque humanity would stutter and explode me out of the quiet I needed, would split my head and open up the dangerous past. Noise ... but in Brink there was peace and sleep ... with my darling wife ... my father-in-law ...

Briefly I compromised with the headrest, and was rescued by a Brink resident in time to shake off my sleep and descend into the dusty, dazzling High Street.

Moving like an automaton, I carried my parcel down the street towards home. Then as I reached the front door my eyes fell on the Thatched Cottage on the other side, and the vision of Macready's principles came before me. Which was neighbour unto him that fell among the thieves?

The door of the Thatched Cottage was ajar. I knocked twice, then walked into the tiny porch and shouted. Clearly the new owner was out. Impelled by curiosity, I peered into the first room. It was in an indescribable mess. Books and dirty clothes were littered over the floor, and a solitary chair stood in the centre. Over all, much stronger than I had experienced it before, was the smell of musty biscuits, making my head suddenly swim with the distaste I had felt the previous night.

I walked slowly home, thinking again about what Bone had said. The smell of lunch inside my own front door came sweetly to me, and I dumped my parcel down and made for the dining-room. The first sight that met my eyes through the door was of Tiggy carrying a tray towards the table. 'Hullo, you lovely things,' I said to her and the cottage pie; but a certain primness in her response warned me that we were not alone. Looking round the door, I saw an elongated shape sitting awkwardly in the corner.

'Lunch is just ready,' said Tiggy half-defiantly, 'and I've asked Mr Towle, because the poor man hasn't settled in yet.'

III - THE GYMKHANA

From that lunchtime began a long military engagement. It is best regarded as a military engagement, because just as soldiers plead war as a justification for killing, we pleaded desperate straits as a justification for behaviour inexcusable on any other grounds. We fought, through many local defeats, to keep Towle off our premises. We were not sorry for him, any more than a soldier finds time to feel sorry for the man who is about to strike him down. We made no attempt to help him settle in, or to help him become a part of our local society. Only we were never rude to him, not outright that is. In a small town, you must not be rude to neighbours; anyway, his own behaviour was in most respects unexceptionable.

Somewhere, and with the right people, Towle had a fascination. Tiggy admitted she had felt this on their first encounter; but by the time I had arrived for lunch that day she had felt the shuddering chill that I felt, the desperate distaste that was beyond reason. After I had gone to Fifield he had dropped in on some slight pretext, and had occupied a chair where she was working and talked slowly at her. Not that he was ever the same with her as with me. He spoke more haltingly, and there were more silences. She asked him to lunch because if ever she was to have the meal ready she had to prepare it in front of him, and because she had been brought up in the great Greek tradition of hospitality.

In the presence of both of us together the gates of his tongue remained more or less closed. At that meal he sat with his eyes fixed on the water jug, munching very slowly whatever was put before him. The most trivial of remarks were taken in silence, mulled over, and then carefully analysed before the munching process resumed. Tiggy's enquiry as to how long he had known the county was answered with dates and even times of arrival and departure. We agreed afterwards that in his presence conversation and quiet were of equal horror, but that over meals quiet was the better tactic. He ate so slowly that even without conversation a meal seemed to go on for light years. One sat, eternally taut before empty plates, waiting, waiting for him to finish, while the mastication proceeded relentlessly, and the hollow eyes gazed steadily ahead.

Yet revulsion and rejection run like fire through groups of people, as they do through animals. One sidelong remark, one dismissive shrug, one hostile growl at a member of the pack, and everyone suddenly turns and drives him from the scene. Tiggy and I were on the inexpressible wavelength of a happy marriage. How far was her revulsion mine? Indeed, how far was Bone's attitude Mrs Fraser's? Could anyone say 'Towle is responsible for his own troubles'? or was some accident in him unfairly used by some evil in us to drive him from our lives?

I was almost relieved next morning to hear Mr Macready on the subject.

'Jeffries,' he called, waving his stick at me as he crossed the road, and lowering his voice when he was under the balcony; 'I am very anxious that the town should become conscious of our new arrival.' He indicated the Thatched Cottage. 'This is a very good type of young man, and I want people to realise their duty towards him. You are the sort of person I can ask to help.'

To my pleasure he showed signs of being in a hurry, and the discourse was brief. 'I have asked Towle to dine with me tonight,' he announced as he left, with the air of a Lord Mayor laying on the turtle soup.

Juliet was our main source of information on the Macready household, but we heard nothing about the dinner party from her since she had declined to attend it. Instead, she arrived at our house after tea, aflame with fury and on the edge of tears, and asked if she could spend the evening with us. She was a big girl, strong in personality and, at twenty-one, emerging late from that awkward adolescence in which girls seem to exaggerate their movements in a desperate self-parody. At this moment, restraints had been forgotten, and I was as terrified by the power of her wrath as I was sorry at the sight of beauty in distress. Returning quickly to my work, I left Tiggy to deal with her.

There was a special relationship between the two of them. Tiggy's placid confidence in public, and her genius for dress, contrasted with Juliet's occasional nervous gestures and strained laughs; but underneath the surface both of them had known terrible social uncertainty, Tiggy because of her strange upbringing, and Juliet because for years she had been convinced she was a Gorgon. Even now, after many young men had provided positive evidence to the contrary, any tribute to her looks made her restless with the conviction that she was being teased. Tiggy helped her to grow out of this into grace and peace, and although Juliet and she were neither the sort to need close female alliances, they understood each other.

I soon became absorbed in my display binding for the fourteenth-century manuscripts; or perhaps I should say in the manuscripts themselves. The headings to the medical receipts were fascinating.

'*For bledyng atte nese,*'
'*For to make popilion,*'
'*For ye colde dropsy,*'
'*For speche in slepe.*'

I was moved to decipher more and more of the faded black lettering on the carefully ruled skins. I discovered a compound said to '*gerre ...*' (that meant 'cause') '*... a maydoun loue a man,*' and began unravelling it with the help of a magnifying glass. So absorbed was I that I failed to hear Tiggy come in, and jumped when she put her hand on my collar.

'My dear,' she said, 'do you know what that man Macready has done?'

'Yes,' I said. 'He's asked Towle to dinner. Juliet's missed a new experience.'

'I should think she has! Her father's behaving appallingly. She feels he's driven her from the house. You know that young man Derek Major? Well, he took her dancing last night, and rang up at lunchtime today like any polite partner, to ask after her wellbeing. The pompous old goat told him to ring off and leave his daughter alone; then he told Juliet not to ask him to the house again. Naturally, she was furious, and told him that if he couldn't be polite to her friends she wouldn't bother to be polite to his. Hence she refused to join the dinner party for Mr Towle.'

'What on earth is Macready about?'

'He's got some system of bringing up daughters that involves their being home by midnight.'

'At twenty-one! He must have been reading an eighteenth-century book of deportment.'

'Well, it's not only that. He has something against Derek. He seemed all right to me, but I don't know him all that well.'

'No,' I said thoughtfully, 'nor do I. He seems a normal decent young man, of the athletic sort. Probably the life and soul of the rugby club dance, but not vicious.'

'There was some dark pronouncement about "bad blood".'

'Oh, dear, dear, dear,' I said, moved. 'Oh, poor Juliet! Poor little thing! Is there any way I can help her?'

Rather to my surprise, Tiggy turned on me and spoke quite huffily. 'She can look after herself.' Then she softened. 'It's quite romantic, really. Roman fathers had all sorts of powers over their daughters, and I expect it was just like this. Do you imagine Juliet will simply go off with Derek?'

'Why?' I asked. 'Are they engaged, or something?'

'And you say I live in the past!' said Tiggy crossly.

Juliet was rather quiet over supper. She had rung Derek and apologised for her father, which made her feel torn two ways. Her anger had died, and she was sorry to have missed Towle, whom she had wanted to meet.

In fact, her chance had gone for some days. She had a week's holiday due from the solicitor's firm where she worked, and where she had met Derek. Rather than spend it at home, as she had intended, she avoided an armed week with her father, and went off to an aunt in London.

Towle continued to drop in regularly. He never seemed to have anything to do, other than borrowing and returning books, household implements, and food. He seemed to know by instinct when I was on the balcony, and would pause in the middle of a prowl up the street to offer his careful greetings to me as I lurked behind the honeysuckle. Then he would stand with his eyes fixed on me in an expectant silence which, in my weakness, I never failed to break. Despite my love of working on the balcony in the fine weather, I began to prefer to remain in my study. Even so, he penetrated our defences, and I would find him sitting motionless downstairs, watching my flustered wife cooking; even, in desperation, she would let him get up to me, and there would follow another of those jerky and self-pitying monologues that lasted through mealtimes and other appointments until, forsaking hints, which he never took, I would simply bundle him out of the house.

On one such occasion, remembering his expressed interests, I showed him the manuscripts. He did not rhapsodise, but fingered the leaves and recited some of the headings as if I were incapable of reading them myself.

'There are several of these in existence,' he said. 'It would be interesting to test some of the recipes. I have always thought that too little attention is paid to the older methods of treating the body. In the Middle Ages, when the body was, as they would regard it, under the powers of evil, a surprising realism was shown in some of the remedies. There was none of the wishy-washy approach of modern homeopaths, whereby physical medicine is regarded as only a useful adjunct to mental attitude. In a way, I suppose psychology is a substitute for the old astrology: bleeding during a suitable conjunction of the stars having been replaced by manipulation during a suitable conjunction of the mind. But bleeding seems a more positive step than manipulation; or at least more drastic and irrevocable.'

This was the first time he had ventured into his own subject, and the first time I had been interested by him.

'If disorders of the body are rooted in mental attitude,' I said, 'then a really drastic remedy seems more likely to stimulate faith than a mild one. I imagine anyone would expect some effect to be visible after drinking a potation of toads' tongues.'

'It is not only that,' said Towle. 'Modern medicine and modern man, have ceased to expect results from physical medicine, beyond half a dozen specifics. Doctors in any age tend to confine their expectations to certain sorts of method. In an age of surgery, the cure for talking in one's sleep would be simply to cut one's tongue out, if anyone thought it worthwhile. In an age of physical medicine, like that of this manuscript, one drank something. These days, a course of sessions on the psychiatrist's couch does the job. These three possible remedies arise from three different sets of expectations. There may be others. It is probably dangerous to exclude any sort of method, as long as it does not claim exclusive truth.' And with that facial contortion of a smile once again, he quoted:-

'O mickle is the powerful grace that lies

In herbs, plants, stones, and their true qualities:
For nought so vile that on the earth doth live,
But to the earth some special good doth give.'
I remembered Bone's faith in Towle's treatment of books. 'If you would like to borrow those leaves,' I said, 'I have no doubt that Mr Bone, the Fifield librarian, would be delighted.'

Towle gave a superior smile. 'Thank you,' he said. 'Some time I might accept your offer.'

For some reason I had not taken into account the possibility that he might really know his subject, and the conversation for a moment lifted the extraordinary cloud of dislike which veiled my reason whenever I encountered Towle. The only other point that ever disposed me in his favour was his fondness for my balcony. He had a most extensive knowledge of Shakespeare, and the balcony constantly stirred him to quotation. He seemed to regard these quotations as his party piece, that by which he made himself a social success; for a social success was what I felt sure he thought himself to be.

Our own social life now dwarfed Towle's irritating presence. My father-in-law's summer visit was due, which gave us a good excuse for not entertaining anyone else; so was the annual town Gymkhana, whose approach kept us away from the house for long periods.

The Gymkhana, held on one of the Grammar School's playing fields at the edge of the town, was a carefully planned assault by the Brink Victory Committee on the pockets of the County. The original name of the Victory Committee had been the Mafeking Committee. In the heat of that great Relief a group of townspeople had determined to build a Parish Hall, the full cost of which they had inadequately explored. A large sum was raised, but an even larger one was needed if the building was to be more than a shell. By the time the Great War broke out, the building was acquiring fittings and furnishings, and after the Armistice the Committee felt sufficiently optimistic to acquire a plot of land and turn it into a park for the returned fighting men and their friends and descendants. The park had no swings, seats, or public conveniences, and a farmer's fence had to make do as a boundary. Far-seeing townsfolk spoke of iron railings, a keeper, and a bandstand. All this kept the Committee in need of funds during the post-war years. It was a sort of automatic reflex that caused them in 1947 to build a recreation centre, thereby ensuring their survival in the usual uncomfortable circumstances as far forward in time as the mind could reach.

My own arrival in Brink had coincided with the retirement of the exhausted Treasurer of this monumentally shaky concern. As an ex-Army officer, I was propelled straight into the job, which mainly involved the planning and execution of the Gymkhana. The theory was that in our hunting area, any fund-raising activity that involved horses could not go wrong. Year after year, the theory was proved false, and year after year failure was explained away. The prizes offered in an attempt to attract support had become enormous, the effect being that bad weather or a clashing event elsewhere could make the annual loss impossibly high, and the final completion of the Victory Committee's task inconceivably remote.

The current headmaster of the Grammar School, Mr Arbuthnot, had been a cricket Blue, and was outraged to find on being appointed that once a year a playing field was being galloped over by horses. The tradition having been too firmly established to permit him to interfere drastically, he contented himself with banishing us to a far corner of the area, and ruling that no horses should be ridden on the south or cricketing side of the Treasurer's tent. This tent was pitched annually and very badly by Mr Arbuthnot's surly groundsman Ted, and it was understood that I would personally receive entries and direct operations from it.

The preliminary skirmishings for the Gymkhana were in full swing when my father-in-law arrived. Fond as I am of him, his ways are terrifying. He insists on having heart-to-heart talks with strangers, he has no conception of time, and he acknowledges social conventions only in bits; those bits sometimes being at curious moments.

I took a taxi to the station to meet him, but only managed to arrive five minutes after the train had come in. There was no trace of my father-in-law. I waited for the next train, then went home, arriving there just as the telephone message arrived that a Dr Hardman was waiting at the station for me. He had been on the right train, but had found an elderly lady waiting to be met by her brother, and had insisted on taking her out for coffee and a chat, omitting to leave a message either for me or, presumably, the brother.

When I picked him up, there was no reference to this.

'My dear fellow,' said the Doctor, wringing my hand and looking more than ever like a polar bear with spectacles. 'I am delighted to see you. And how is the family?' He always called Tiggy 'the family', despite our unhappy failure to provide him with grandchildren. I am sure it would not have surprised him to find a couple when he reached the house: he was a man who took things as they came.

The family hugged him when he was delivered to her, and stowed him in the spare room, the study-bedroom we kept for him at the top of the house. He liked to be free to come and go, and spent his time either on reading and writing, or on little trips along the street to find someone who would talk to him. I have often gone into a shop and found him happily sitting behind the counter talking to the owner. Although his daughter and I regarded him as a menace, to be apologised for like a destructive child or dog, the townspeople were in no two minds about him. He was a great man to them all, to be accepted with his eccentricities, and consulted on matters they would not dream of mentioning to each other.

He always kept out of our way unless we demanded his presence, which made him an easy guest. However, Tiggy encouraged me to take him on visits or excursions, because he loved travelling on buses and entering strange houses. Inside ten minutes he would become a better friend of a friend than I was myself.

This year, I thought to ask him to help me in the Treasurer's tent at the Gymkhana. Although he was unlikely to make the ticket and money arrangements anything but more complicated, I had high hopes of his effect on some of the tough characters that entered horses.

The day was unpromising, with a north-westerly gale blowing into the entrance of the tent, already inclined at an ominous angle. Visitors were mostly blown staggering into our presence, and now and again a sudden lurch in our surroundings proclaimed that another body had been driven into the guy-ropes.

I sat the Doctor by my side, gave him some change, and let him take the money while I issued numbers and tried to keep the records straight.

My choice of an assistant had not been wise. Despite my time in the Army, I am very blind to the merits of horsy people. Perhaps because they have to talk to each other at great distances in high winds, they never seem on my wavelength. They make me feel like a regimental *bhisti*; but it was soon clear that they fascinated my father-in-law.

'My dear child,' he said to the hard-bitten hermaphrodite who presented the first entry fee. 'You're not going to ride a horse!'

The creature simpered, looked practically feminine, and admitted that it was.

'Tell me,' said the Doctor. 'How do you feel about it? Don't you ever come over a tiny bit frightened?'

In no time they were off on an intimate chat, probably containing the first consecutive sentences the horsewoman had uttered in any tone below a shout for twenty years.

When she had barely turned away, the Doctor gave me a wicked look. 'You should always tell a woman the opposite of the truth,' he said. 'It's the one remark she'd never dared hope to hear.' These devastating asides of his were regularly made, often in the hearing of their object; yet I have never heard the old chap in trouble from them. At first I found the revelation of the bogus quality of his conversation rather unpleasant; but now I have come to the conclusion that everybody knows about it, and simply nobody minds. The apparent discarding of a pose is itself no less of a pose.

These enthusiastic chats of the Doctor could only slow up the entire Gymkhana, and should by rights have resulted in frayed tempers from judges, competitors, and spectators. One or two people did come along to complain, but the old fellow soon made them forget what they had come about. However, when a brace of children crept under the table and established themselves on his knee, I persuaded Tiggy to take him away for some tea, and handled the change myself.

Two thirds of the way through the events, a far worse delay threatened. The wind increased tremendously, and a pile of black clouds headed for us that darkened the whole scene. For a little we thought the rain would hold off, then a few large spots hurtled on to the forward edge of my table, and a great bustle of rain drops caroused up out of the neighbouring field. In next to no time the whole scene was blotted from my view. I just had time to admit the Doctor back to his seat (he came out of the rain like a muffled Oates who had thought better of his gesture) and lower the flaps over the tiny tent before we were plunged into howling chaos rather as one imagines that on the South Col of Everest. The walls of the tent strained against us, and the rain belted against the Doctor's side, as if

Mr Arbuthnot and all his boys were uniting with buckets of water to push us out of our tenancy of their cricket field. The last glimpse I had had of the spectators and competitors suggested that they had all sprinted downwind to the school pavilion, horses included. There must, I thought, be a sizeable crowd there now.

Then a disembodied voice said in my ear 'Come on; it's dry on this side!' and a body outlined itself on the lee side of the tent. Another body joined it, and a clearly audible conversation started. I wondered whether to loosen the flaps again, and try to get whoever it was inside our sentry-box of a tent. Boxes of trophies were piled behind our chairs, and there were cashboxes and papers piled on the table and spilling on to the ground. It was hard to envisage taking two more bodies. Then something about the conversation outside increased my doubts, and the bodies moved closer together. I coughed tactfully, and glanced at the Doctor. He had slumped forward on to a cash box, head on arm, and was apparently asleep.

People outside tents never consider themselves audible to people inside tents; and, with the turbulence of gale and rain, I might as well have sung the Marseillaise as have coughed. The conversation, in tones I was beginning to recognise, continued.

'Are things all right at home? With your father, I mean?'

'Oh, they're much as usual,' said Juliet's voice. 'Let's keep off the subject.'

'I want to be sure you're all right.'

'Let's talk about something else!' Her voice was edgy.

I missed his next remark - Derek Major's that is, for I had worked out who he was by now. The wind had risen to a new fury, and shook the whole tent till I thought every support must have gone. At least the rain had ceased to rattle against the canvas, and as the spasm died down I saw one of the bodies remove itself from the tent wall. I heard Juliet shouting angrily from further away.

'What on earth has my father to do with ... anything?' she raged. 'Sometimes I could kick you!'

'But Juliet, of course I'm interested ...'

'Oh, go away!' she shouted, and with typical feminine logic went away herself.

There was comparative silence for a moment, and I thought the storm must have spent itself; then the wind built up in a great crescendo and bent the whole of our shelter over towards Derek, so that he withdrew his body hastily from the wall. The tent began to move back towards the vertical, till suddenly a tremendous gust burst in under the walls and picked up the whole canvas. A guy rope gave with a crack, and just as the roof seemed on the point of sailing away the wind dropped completely. The tent sagged further and further over on its poles; then slowly and with dignity the whole affair sank over to one side, draping the table and ourselves and the pile of trophies and impedimenta in a canvas covering. There was silence, and darkness.

Slowly and resignedly, I pushed aside the folds of thick canvas and emerged on to the muddy field. Derek Major was standing over me, holding up a sort of tunnel to make it easier. 'Good Heavens!' he said. 'Were you in there?'

Something was troubling me. I looked towards the pavilion, and saw a startled group looking towards us, with, behind them, a dispersing mass of cloud and a gleam of sun. Then I remembered.

'Derek,' I exclaimed. 'The Doctor was with me!'

We regarded the collapsed tent, in which there was a tell-tale bulge. It made no move. Derek did his tunnel trick, and eventually unveiled the old man. He was in the same position as when I had last seen him, but his eyes were open, and he was meditating.

'I remember tea,' he said slowly. 'Then there was a wind, and darkness, and the smell of the grave.' He lifted his head, and looked round. 'Where is the Ηππ.οδρομιον[1] …?' Then he saw Derek, whom he certainly did not recognise, and gave a sweet smile. 'My dear fellow,' he said, 'how are you?'

'What with one thing and another,' said Derek feelingly, 'puzzled. Distinctly puzzled.'

---

[1] 'Hppodromion' - racecourse

IV - THE BALCONY SCENE

'Quiet people,' said Father Morris, 'are only noisy people who have despaired of attracting attention by shouting.'

He was sitting in my workroom, also known as The Study, drinking coffee and watching the rain doing its best to drive holes in the roof of the house opposite. His cassock was filthy, and his pepper-coloured hair pointed in all directions.

'Is everyone after attention, then?' I asked.

'Yes, probably. Is that so terrible?'

'It must seem terrible to those who believe in humanity. I don't mind the fact myself; but I do mind the way we pretend it isn't there. I mean, no one pretends that men don't lust after women. No one pretends we don't covet each other's property. I covet some of Lord Fifield's books, and if I say so my reputation goes down not a jot. But the desire for attention is too disgraceful to be acknowledged. Suppose I suggested to the P.C.C. that you preached sermons because you had a need for attention, would you admit it?'

'I should have to modify it, or amplify it.'

'But is it true?'

'It is true that preaching sermons, whatever the main reasons for my doing it, helps to satisfy my human need for attention.'

'Well if I were to say as much as that in public, I'd be made to apologise.'

'And rightly. You wouldn't be able to say in public that Mr Smith lusted after Mrs Jones, either, however true it was; there's a lot you're not able to say in public. You could say I coveted that volume there, which I do; but only because nobody would take you seriously.'

I had some of Jeremy Taylor's sermons, in their seventeenth-century binding; and Father Morris loved the book. He was a newcomer to Brink, not well enough known yet, but obviously prepared to continue the old Anglo-Catholic tradition, and beginning to gain the confidence of his people. He was a civilised man, never trying to drive his flock from pillar to post; but he spoke with authority.

'What bothers me,' I said, 'is that we live life at one level, and talk about it at another. If you listen to our words, you receive the wrong message about us. I talk smugly about loving good books, or being happy with Antigone, or enjoying a game of bridge, as if life is a grand and innocent business. In reality, envy, lust, and pride play their part in those pleasures; I sometimes think a major part. Honestly, why does one enjoy playing bridge? To convince one's friends of one's intellectual superiority is one's real aim. Attracting attention again.'

'It is also possible,' said Father Morris, 'to seek attention by exaggeration; but I grant you that good and evil are all mixed up together. You have to buy the whole bundle. It's very hard for a priest to remember this; for a reason which I should have thought you, of all people, should understand.'

'Why me?'

Father Morris looked at my leg. 'Haven't you realised that people go out of their way to be kind to you? The sight of a lame man puts us all on our best behaviour. So does the sight of a clergyman. If life is one great act, as you say, the acting is all the more desperate when you and I are about. I know. I was an ordinary suburban commuter before I was ordained.'

'And I know,' I said. 'I had two whole legs before my minefield was ordained. People certainly talk to me in the street now as they never did before. Perhaps I detect the strain.'

'A minefield, was it?'

'One mine, to be exact. One was enough to blow me out of the Army and into a quiet life.'

Father Morris looked thoughtful. 'Do you regret the Army?'

'Not for a moment. I hadn't started living before I met Antigone and we came here.'

'But ...?'

'I don't think there is a but. I've just been thinking how noisy everyone is, even here. The very ease with which people fall into conversation with me, together with my natural love of silence, on which you have already rudely commented, means that the real kindness they show is generally wrapped up in this bundle with tremendous demands for attention and sympathy.'

'That's rather a different sort of bundle,' murmured Father Morris, obscurely. 'Anyway,' he went on, sitting up in his chair, 'It's as well you're a good listener. We all have our ministries. Perhaps listening is yours. There's a great need for it.'

'Oh, dear! Do you think I've been sent into the world as a sounding-board for Mr Macready?'

Father Morris stood up, looking almost angry. 'We all shrink from our ministries,' he said. 'The Lord knows I do. But John Macready is an immortal soul, whether he and you realise it or not. He cannot be permitted to eat people alive; but nor can he be denied kindness. I charge you to remember that, Michael Jeffries.'

'Thank you, Father,' I said, meaning it.

'And now I see the rain has stopped,' he said. 'I am returning to Headquarters.'

'I'll walk out of the house with you. I have to go and clear up after the Gymkhana. We left everything over the weekend.'

As we stepped out into the street, Father Morris's cassock began the process of acquiring another layer of dirt from the splashy pavements. He paused before we parted.

'Was it a big explosion?' he asked.

'Fairish. You don't hear it that close. It's a sort of concussion.'

'Most of us need a big explosion,' he went on.

'I know what you mean.'

'But in any direction it can blow us, except one of course, it's on the same old ground, you know: human ground. The new ground may feel firmer, but it isn't.'

Seeing he had lost me, he tried again.

'Well,' he said; 'even a good listener needs someone to listen to him.'

'You say that to a happily-married man?'

'I'm saying it to you. If the going is hard, remember me. I have a ministry too.'

As I watched him striding back to the Vicarage, I thought that he was a remarkable person; but I could not bear the talk of explosions. The conversation had been dangerous, and I was relieved to see how much needed doing at the playing-field.

I returned for a late lunch, and went out again afterwards, the Doctor offering to accompany me. Ted the groundsman had reasons against doing anything the way I wanted to do it, and when I finally got through it was past supper time. The Doctor had gone home ahead of me, and I found when I returned to the house that he and Antigone had eaten. He had gone to his room, and Antigone was hovering in the kitchen over my plate of ham and salad. As I finished it up it was growing dark, though I could see that the sky was clear.

It was one of those evenings when Antigone had decided to look her best. She was wearing a fawn-coloured long dress, and every dark hair was in the right place to contribute to the effect. I knew she considered the work I did for the Victory Committee as nonsensical, but she was doing her best to conceal this and be kind to a tired husband.

She had just removed the last of my cheese when the doorbell rang.

'Towle,' I said. 'Go and ward him off, there's a dear. Say I'm having an epileptic fit.'

She came back after some whisperings in the corridor, and began to sweep the crumbs off the table.

'It's your girl friend,' she said. 'She's sorry to hear about your fit. You'd better go up and froth at her while I finish clearing your mess.'

Cheerfully enough, I went up to the study. Juliet was studying the picture over my desk. She turned as I came in, looking flushed and excited, rather as she had a week before. Her eyes were bright.

'Michael,' she said. 'I'm being a perfect pest to Tiggy and you; rushing over whenever … whenever I want to.'

'Nonsense. Sit down, and I expect some coffee will arrive. Or would you rather sit on the balcony? It's a lovely evening.'

'Let's not,' she said. 'If we sit out there we shan't be able to see Tiggy; and she looks so marvellous tonight. Anyway,' she added, 'I'm a bit frightened of your balcony. It forces me into a role, which isn't me.'

'Juliet in the balcony scene?' I suggested.

'Yes. Father called me after a wealthy great aunt, but names drag you with them, you know; like all those people who feel compelled to follow the trade of their names, Slaughter the butcher, Cakebread the baker, and so on. I sometimes feel I ought to be a romantic little girl; and when I find myself on your balcony, peering through the roses into the badly-lighted corners of the street, I don't feel myself at all.'

'Perhaps it's your true self, trying to come through.'

Juliet laughed rather awkwardly. 'Oh, no,' she said. 'I'm a very matter-of-fact creature.' She had that curious gawkiness that descended on her when she was the subject of discussion. To conceal it she pushed the window wider open, and walked out on to the balcony, the light from the room streaming out after her, and resting on her shoulders and golden hair.

'*O Romeo, Romeo! wherefore art thou Romeo?*' she declaimed, and jumped with astonishment as a voice came up from the street below.

'*But soft! what light through yonder window breaks?*
It is the east, and Juliet is the sun.'

'Who is that?' she whispered. 'Do I know you?'

'Not from Adam; but I am not Adam, or Romeo either, alas!'

'But I am Juliet.'

'Ah!' said the voice. 'But a Macready, not a Capulet, I suspect.' And the familiar amateurish laugh floated up from the street. 'Perhaps I should introduce myself. I am Alfred Towle, and if you are the person I take you for, I have been entertained by your parents.'

'Of course,' said Juliet. 'I was sorry to miss you.'

'I wanted to see your host, if he is not too busy.'

'I'll ask him.' She came back into the room. 'He's rather a pet. Can he come up?'

I could not suppress a wince. 'All right,' I said. 'I suppose he can.'

'I'll go and let him in.' She ran off downstairs, very animated and returned shortly with Towle pacing cautiously behind her.

Men of apparently serious demeanour sometimes seem to change character when they are in the presence of an attractive woman. Juliet's father was just such a man. He would forget his duty of lecturing the world and giggle and pirouette before a pretty girl in a way that filled the observer with nausea. Towle was not like Macready, but he too changed his spots with Juliet. One was forced to admire his consummate acting ability and to wonder why he could not put on the act more often. For in truth he now gave the impression of being a quiet, interesting, even humorous human being, if anything rather in need of protection; and Juliet was quite understandably captivated. He sat in the study with the two of us, twinkling at her and talking as if I did not exist. I made a remark or two, was crushed, and remained silent. I was jealous, ostensibly on Derek's behalf, but in reality on my own and on Antigone's. Her beauty had apparently not been sufficient to melt him in this way.

Antigone walked in as the two were talking, and surveyed the scene irritably. With bare politeness, she gave us the three cups of coffee she had prepared and went to make some more for herself.

Towle and Juliet resumed their conversation, she sparkling up at him and he looking at her with frank admiration. When Antigone came back, Juliet turned excitedly to her.

'Tiggy, Mr Towle's wanting to buy furniture, and I love auctions, so I've made him promise to let me take him round the sales.'

'Really?' said Antigone, smiling coolly. 'But I'm sure Mr Towle would rather not be bullied into buying things.'

'Oh, she wouldn't do that,' said Towle, not taking his eyes off Juliet.

'Of course not,' said Juliet. 'Tiggy, why are you so horrid?'

I hastily stepped in. 'Did I hear you say you wanted to see me, Towle?'

'I did, but it wasn't important,' he said gaily. 'Any other time would do as well.'

'Anyway,' I insisted, 'let's deal with it and get it over. Would you like to talk on our own?'

Towle's manner was more as I knew it now. There was an irritable gleam in his hollow eyes, and he spoke more slowly.

'I ... er ...,' he said, transparently casting about for an excuse. 'I ... wondered if I could change my mind, and borrow your manuscript. The fourteenth-century one.'

'Of course,' I said. 'Would you like to take it back now?' I laid as much stress as I dared on the word 'now'.

It was unfortunate that Antigone, who had taken advantage of the change of topic to fill Juliet's coffee-cup, was hovering with the coffee-pot in mid-room.

'I should love another cup of coffee first,' said Towle, twitching his face in a smile. Antigone moved with a set expression to fill his cup.

'Fourteenth-century manuscript?' said Juliet. 'That sounds fun.'

'It's a collection of receipts, or recipes as we call them now, for common and not-so-common ailments, from the Fifield Castle Library,' I told her. 'Have a look.' I reached for the binder and gave it to her.

'Can you really decipher this stuff?' she asked Towle.

'Mr Towle is an authority on the Middle Ages,' I said. 'He is writing a book on medieval philosophy at this moment.'

'Really?' exclaimed Juliet. 'How exciting! But how on earth can you write, Mr Towle, if you haven't any furniture?'

'I have the bare necessities,' he replied. 'But as a matter of fact I haven't got forward with my work since I came here. The business of settling in is proving longer than I expected.'

I wanted to say that the business of settling in as he performed it would require all eternity, and involve a terrible lot of sitting in other people's houses.

We can help there,' said Juliet. 'There's a sale up the road from us on Thursday. We could go to the viewing on Wednesday. I'd better see what you need first, though. How would it be if I brought Mother round tomorrow afternoon? Do say if you'd rather have second thoughts, and tell me not to interfere.'

The chatter continued with very little help from Antigone and myself. Knowing that Juliet had come to talk about her troubles, and that Towle, even without Juliet's presence, was practically immoveable, I wondered whether the evening could ever end. If I excused myself by saying I wanted to work, or by telling the truth, that I was tired out, it would only transfer the problem downstairs, or hurl Juliet with Towle on to the street. Any plan for breaking up the gathering needed to remove Towle without disturbing Juliet. Suddenly I remembered my father-in-law.

'Antigone,' I broke in. 'The Doctor! You've forgotten his coffee.'

Antigone gasped. 'I'd forgotten all about him,' she said. 'I must take him some at once.'

I tried to signal to her as she left the room, but she was gazing ahead with a contented look in her eyes which set my mind at rest.

Five minutes later, the Doctor walked in, beaming happily. Everybody got up. 'My dear,' he said, advancing on Juliet; 'I heard you were here, and of course I had to come down and see you. It always amazes me that other people besides myself can have charming and lovely daughters. What a clever father yours must be!' He turned to Towle. 'And this ...'

'... is Mr Towle,' said Antigone, emerging from behind her father. 'Mr Towle, this is Dr Hardman, my father.'

The Doctor shook Towle's hand warmly, but did not sit down. 'Towle ...Towle ...' he said, apparently rummaging in his memory. 'Tell me, my dear fellow; aren't you a historian?'

'That is so,' said Towle, clearly overpowered with gratification. 'I've heard of you, you know. It's medieval history, isn't it? At the Other Place?'

Towle assented modestly. The Doctor put a paw on his shoulder. 'Of course. I knew the name was familiar. We must have a good chat, you and I. Tell me, where are you living?'

'I've just moved into the Thatched Cottage, over the road.'

'Is that the hideous red-brick thing?'

'No, the orange stone one further down.'

The Doctor displayed great excitement. 'Is that the Thatched Cottage? My dear chap, all my life I've been longing to see inside that wonderful house. What's it like?'

'Very pleasant, when I can tidy it up a bit.'

'I've passed that house time and again, and I've always thought if its inside was like its outside it must be the most perfect house in all England.' The Doctor looked expansively round all of us. 'Do you know,' he said, 'I've a mind to ask this young man to take me over and show me the place before he and I are a minute older.' He turned back to Towle. 'What about it? Would it be too much trouble?'

'Of course not; but let's make it the morning, It's really in no condition to be seen now.'

The Doctor positively radiated charm. 'Humour an old man,' he said. 'Take me over there now, before I go to bed. It will round off my day to have a lifelong ambition fulfilled.'

Towle was beaten. I thrust the manuscript binder into his hand in case he tried to come back to fetch it.

As the Doctor followed him out of the room, he paused in the doorway and looked back at me. 'What's the fellow's name?' he enquired.

Juliet looked puzzled and disapproving, but did not comment.

As the Doctor disappeared, I thought again of Captain Oates going out into the storm. I hoped the storm would not be too much for him.

My hope was vain. We waited up for the Doctor, long after Juliet had gone, but it was after midnight before he returned. When we tried to thank him for his noble rescue, he was untypically grumpy.

'I always did think that house was a monstrosity,' he grumbled.

'And what on earth is all this rigmarole about his parents?'

V - New Light on Towle

I dreamt that night that I was on the stage of the Victory Hall. I had
to put on a one-man entertainment for the whole town, plus a party
of my former brothers-in-arms, in full mess kit. I spoke, but no
words came out. Outside the Hall, I could hear the stars and the
whole created universe roaring and screaming; but inside there was
silence, the boards of the stage were melting, and I found myself
floundering and sinking. No one laughed or clapped or came to help,
except someone behind me, whose hand was supporting me in the
small of the back.

I woke up, and found Tiggy patting me. 'Having a bad time?' she
asked.

'I can't sleep,' I said untruthfully. 'Where are we going?'

'Going? Off the edge of the bed, at this rate.'

'No, where are we going? Where really?'

'Oh, you mean "*Quo Vadis*?" Away from the persecutions in
Rome,' she suggested.

'What persecutions? What is our terror about?'

'There are always persecutions and terrorists to run away from.'

'Run!' I grumbled, cross at the word she had let slip. 'Limp, more
likely.'

'For goodness sake, stop that! Turn on the news.'

Someone had made a major speech about the economy. 'There is
still much to be done, much goodwill needed, before we can speak of
full employment,' said a voice. 'When every able-bodied person is
willing to work; when each contributes what he can to the benefit of

the nation; then, and not till then, will there be a prospect of improvement in the standard of our living.'

'Turn it off again,' said Tiggy quickly; but the damage was done.

'We will pass over "able-bodied",' I said. 'But I now see what you mean by persecutions. These are attempts to make the convenience of the community a worthy aim for a man's life. What do we say of a man in his late thirties, retired from the Army and living precariously on a disability pension and a small book-binding business, demanding the services of a girl of twenty-five, in the prime of her youth and beauty, able to work in a factory or breed citizens if only her husband could give her any? Morally indefensible!'

'Don't,' said Tiggy miserably, gazing at the wall. 'Don't be so unhappy. It's just as likely to be my fault. Anyway, what sort of a world is it for children at the moment?'

'The same as it has always been. Let's not pretend our wishes are other than they are, even if we can't afford their fulfilment.'

'I like Brink,' she said. 'But if you want more ...'

'Sorry, darling,' I said. 'I get the horrors. Let's face somebody else's troubles. How's Juliet?'

Tiggy shrugged a doubtful pink shoulder in a way that made my head suddenly light.

'Do that again,' I said.

'I don't really understand Juliet. Do what?'

'Wiggle your shoulder like that.'

'I was telling you about Juliet.'

'Tell me anything you like, but wiggle your shoulder again.'

Tiggy lay thinking for a moment. Then she turned over and looked at me. Slowly and deliberately she wiggled the other shoulder, and put her tongue out. This made breakfast very late.

'I think I can trust you to concentrate your mind on Juliet now,' she said primly over her coffee. 'You were asking how she was when your mind started wandering - stop it, you'll spill my coffee - and I was saying I didn't really understand her. A sort of running war seems to be going on, but whether it's about what it's supposed to be about, or more a sort of Freudian showdown, I'm not sure.' She told me what she had gathered from the previous evening.

Macready had it in his head that Derek Major was a young man likely at any moment to want to marry his daughter, and was determined to make his opposition clear as a sort of pre-emptive strike. He was not (he frequently maintained) a Victorian father, and his daughter was free to marry anyone she liked; but (he maintained with equal frequency) it was his duty to give her his advice and opinion, and he hinted darkly at private sources of knowledge about Derek. Juliet, returning from work at half past five each day, found herself tiptoeing about the house in the hope of postponing the evening row for as long as possible. Most evenings it came before bedtime, and the old man's remorseless persistence was always too much for an emotional and uncertain, but spirited girl.

'But is she serious about Derek?!' I asked.

'I don't know,' said Tiggy. 'No one seems to know. I certainly don't. Anyway, things can't go on as they are. No girl can live in Juliet's circumstances. I think she may go somewhere else.'

'She wouldn't stay in Brink, surely.'

'No. Somewhere quite different.'

'But what about Derek?'

'I don't believe you can go on working in the next office to a man you're not sure about.'

'Then she's not sure?'

'Men!' said Tiggy. 'Everything has to be black or white. I don't know, darling. Our job is to pick up the pieces, offer wisdom, and await events, like a Greek chorus.'

'Choruses are dreary. I want to be one of the principal characters.'

'So you are in your own play. Not in Juliet's; unless you care to take a hand, and bid for a second wife, with golden hair. But remember, principals usually come to a sticky end. In this case, you could be clawed by number one wife, or mauled to a jelly by the best forward in the Brink rugby team.'

'I don't like rugger players.'

'You don't like much then; they must form half the male population.'

'They drink, and bellow, and scorn the other half. They are valued by the middle-class world as teenagers value pop stars. I knew a very nasty officer once, ill-mannered, adulterous, and coarse. When I suggested the Army would be better without him, it was like shouting in church. "My dear fellow," someone said, "he scored the winning try against the Navy."'

'That finishes Derek Major, then. Juliet will have to find someone more to your taste. You and her father should get together.'

'I suppose there are always exceptions. From what I know of him, I rather like Derek.'

We saw little of Juliet for the next two weeks. The quarrels seemed to simmer down, and the odd and disturbing friendship between her and Towle became established. She took him to sales and had him round to meals. Macready strutted round the town openly approving of the young man, and Derek Major was not reported as saying anything. Presumably he was thinking a lot.

Macready's liking for Towle did not surprise me. As long as he was allowed to keep talking he was utterly imperceptive. But Juliet's view was more surprising. I had to respect it, and yet again found myself questioning my own.

Looked at impersonally, the behaviour of Antigone and myself was open to considerable criticism. A stranger, lacking many of the comforts of life, had come to be our neighbour, and we had given him very little. I felt a violent personal dislike for him, but did the

Good Samaritan pause to ask himself whether he liked the man who fell among thieves? True, Antigone had felt this dislike too, though not from the very first encounter. It was easy to give it a rational status in consequence, but more likely that she had simply caught an irrational feeling from me. What could be said against Towle? He invaded our premises, and took up too much of our time? Bone said that he had been intolerable to his last landlady and her daughter. This was independent testimony, and had much in common with our own. It looked as if Towle was unable to respect other people's privacy; yet I still felt there was more involved.

I went and talked to my father-in-law; but with all his affection for human beings, he was very bad at distinguishing individuals.

His affection was generalised. People interested him not because they were so different, but because they were so alike, all wayward, troubled, wanting sympathy.

'The fellow seemed very sorry for himself,' he admitted. 'I remember not listening to him as closely as I ought to have done: but, bless you, young men are sorry for themselves, and I caught him off balance. There was a lot of talk about his parents not having considered him sufficiently. I used to be furious with my parents, I remember, and I'm sure your good wife, whatever her name is ... the family ... can see the flaws in the way I brought her up, though my intentions, like those of most parents, were of the best, and my principles really very soundly based. No, that historical chap is just an ordinary human being; lonely, of course, but no more than that.' He laughed happily. 'I'm afraid I wasn't strictly truthful with him that night. In fact I told him a good few whoppers. They won't harm him. Nobody's the worse for a bit of praise, as long as he's struggling.'

I had a vague notion of sounding Bone further, but it was some days before I had occasion to visit Fifield. Eventually, one Sunday, I determined to go over the following day. I had finished the work

Bone had given me, but still had to recover the manuscript binder from Towle. Since Juliet took him up, his visits had practically ceased, and I had the impression that he was at last working on his book. After morning service that day I called in at the Thatched Cottage to ask for the manuscripts.

Towle was at home, asked me in rather hesitantly, and showed me to the sitting room, which looked quite respectable, though still short of furniture. There were even flowers on the mantelpiece and in the window - going a bit far for a bachelor, I thought. I wondered if I had interrupted him in a session of flower-arranging, because there were a few orange blooms lying on the carpet, the sight of which seemed to disturb Towle's composure. He bent down hastily to pick them up, muttered an excuse, and took them out of the room. Then he returned, he was himself again.

'I am about to entertain,' he said in his slow monotone. 'So you must excuse the slight disorder. 'Please sit down. Mrs Boswell is coming in shortly to prepare the lunch.'

Juliet had found someone to come in daily and give him a hot meal.

'I wondered if you had finished with the fourteenth-century receipts. I ought really to take them back tomorrow.'

'Yes. I had been expecting you to ask. I wonder if you would mind if I kept them till this evening. I could bring them across after supper.'

'Please don't trouble yourself,' I said quickly. 'I'll call in for them on my way tomorrow. If you're out, perhaps you could leave them inside the front door. I hope you have found them interesting?'

Towle looked suddenly disconcerted. 'Interesting?' he said. 'Yes. Yes, of course. In some ways, that is. I don't think … I mean, they're nonsensical, really, aren't they?'

'I thought you approved of medieval medicine.'

'No, no. Only to a limited extent.'

'Well,' I said. 'I mustn't keep you from your preparations. I'll drop in at about ten o'clock tomorrow to collect the manuscripts.'

As I left it occurred to me that Antigone had wanted to ask Derek Major to a meal, it being likely that he would welcome some comfort; so I strolled up the street to Mrs Ellerman's, where he lodged. Mrs Ellerman's Pip was in his station on top of the low wall in front of the house, and barked amiably at me. I stopped and scratched his ear, partly to establish good relations before venturing through the gate, and partly to savour the glorious summer Sunday morning. My eye moved appreciatively from the miraculously beautiful arrangement of shades of brown along Bob's back to the less natural but effective massing of flower colours in the tiny front garden. Looking further as Pip and I enjoyed the scratching process, I was suddenly daunted to see Mrs Ellerman holding back the lace curtain in her front room and glaring malevolently at me. The sun went behind a cloud, and I was jerked back to the strange world of people. In the hope of placating her, I waved and summoned a smile. To my relief, her features relaxed, and when she opened the door she was her normal self.

'Oh, Mr Jeffries,' she beamed. 'I never saw it was you. I'm keeping a careful watch out, I am. Somebody's been stealing flowers from my garden. What do you think of that?'

'What a shame!' I said. 'It looks so delightful too. Surely it wasn't while Pip was on guard.'

'It was last night, I think. I remember Pip started barking after it got dark. I should have let him out.'

'There can't be much gone. The bed looks fine.'

'No, that's the funny thing. I know some of the marigolds have gone because their stems are broken off. Perhaps Pip frightened off whoever it was. Aren't some people mean, Mr Jeffries? They need only have asked me, and I'd have given them the flowers.'

It was stupid of me, but not till after I had left a message for Derek did I remember the little bunch of marigolds on Towle's floor. The connection seemed clear, but quite absurd. Why should Towle steal a few flowers he could have bought from a florist or begged from half the gardens in Brink? He was not short of money, and Brink was not short of kindness. Was he mad, a kleptomaniac, a compulsive dancer on old ladies' flower beds? Perhaps he was on the verge of a nervous breakdown. Yet something else was worrying me about all this, some piece of information was lurking at the back of my mind, reluctant to be dragged out. My mind tucked this away with it, and I did not even remember to tell Tiggy my suspicions.

Next day I went over at ten to collect the manuscript binder, and caught my bus, comfortably this time. The other books Bone had given me were in a parcel which I put on the luggage rack, but the binder I kept in my hand. As I turned it over to examine the binding I had given it, the volume fell open at a certain point, and I suddenly sat up and read furiously, my mind bubbling with memories of the previous day. It was the passage I had deciphered before, beginning '*Ffor to gerre a maydoun loue a man*'. It began with a list of herbs and one or two rather unsavoury ingredients, but it was the word '*marigoulde*' that leapt out at me. I read on:-

'*If he be gadered in someres tyde*
When he spredes his floures wyde
In the minethe of august it moste be
When ye mone is in ye signe of virgine.'

It was now August.

'Good Heavens!' I exclaimed aloud, and shutting the binder I clutched it to me and rocked gently to and fro.

'In trouble, dear?' enquired the housewife sitting next to me.

'No, I'm all right,' I assured her, opening the binder again by way of explanation. 'It's just something I'm reading.'

She craned over the book. 'I should stick to English, dear, if I was you.'

'Oddly enough,' I said, 'this is English.'

She looked at me carefully, then with a kind shrug of the shoulders she sat back and clutched her shopping basket.

My mind was not on my neighbour. It was trying to accustom itself to the idea that an adult male of the twentieth century could attempt to brew a love potion. The evidence was circumstantial, but it was very strong. Towle had asked to keep the book till after he had entertained, one presumed he had been entertaining Juliet, he had obviously had the binder open at the page in question, and he had some marigolds, which it looked as if he had picked from Mrs Ellerman's garden. He had apparently felt he must gather the flowers personally, which explained his unorthodox manner of obtaining them.

The question was, had he gone as far as giving the brew to Juliet? and if so, what was the result? For a moment, I almost believed in the efficacy of the potion; then I remembered some of the ingredients, and wondered what dire effect they might have on a twentieth-century stomach. Presumably they were not actually poisonous, just revolting.

What ought I to do, if anything? This needed thought and enquiry. It was time I talked to Antigone, and I must certainly carry out my intention of talking about Towle to Bone. I wondered what meal Towle had offered the Macreadys, and whether there had been any after-effects.

Bone turned out to be in a very expansive mood. He kept me almost till lunch looking over a magnificent set of seventeenth-century pamphlets; then it occurred to me to make a copy of the receipt for the love potion, which meant that I missed the bus back. Bone insisted on taking me out to lunch. With the precision that was the keynote of his character he lunched every day at the same time at a small pub just below the Castle. The food was excellent, and any drop below the highest standard was firmly pointed out to the landlord. The landlord was clearly devoted to his exacting client, and spared no effort to meet his needs.

'I should like my wife to see this,' I said.

Bone rapped his knee in self-reproach. 'Of course,' he said, 'Why didn't I think of it before? You must both come over as my guests next time. We could make it the evening, and dine together. I eat at my house when I am alone, but my housekeeper is aged, and I generally entertain away from home. How about it?'

'You have been kind on many occasions,' I said. 'Give us the pleasure of coming over to Brink.'

'I should be delighted to come over on some later occasion. But the point is that your wife should see this place, and perhaps also the Library.'

'Certainly she would like to see the Library. She's been over to Fifield with me before, but has always had some shopping to do while I was with you.' We left it that a joint visit would be arranged next time

Bone had work for me. Over the coffee I was about to broach the subject of Towle, when the task was taken out of my hands. With the same diplomatic air he had assumed before, Bone enquired

'And how is the new arrival in Brink?'

'Towle, you mean?'

He nodded.

I decided it was not time to be frank. 'It's early to say. He seems unusual.'

'Unusual!' said Bone forcefully. 'I now have positive evidence that he is more than that.'

I pricked up my ears. 'How so?'

'In my experience,' said Bone, with the air of a judge delivering a life sentence, 'a man who cannot behave with books cannot be trusted in decent society.'

'But I remember you saying Towle treated books properly,' I remonstrated, mindful of the loan of the manuscripts.

'I thought he did. But I was taken in. When that man asked Lord Fifield for permission to use the Library, I willingly agreed; I explained the rules to him in what I fancied was plain English. You will hardly credit that only last week Mrs Fraser, his former landlady, brought back to me from his vacated lodgings one of my reference works clearly marked "Not to be taken out". In capitals.'

'No!' I said, anxious to sound shocked enough.

'You may well refuse to credit it. I have of course seen Lord Fifield and insisted that that person's borrowing privileges should be stopped at once. That sort of man will finish in prison.'

'His social sense is not strong,' I conceded.

'It is his moral sense with which I am most concerned.'

'Whereabouts is this Mrs Fraser's house?'

'Oh, it's one of the group by the Parish Church, within easy walking distance of the Library. He had no need to break the rules.'

After this, I went back with Bone to look at the new work he was likely to be preparing for me, then wandered down to the town to wait for my bus. I had time to walk over to the parish church, which was on a sort of platform set into the side of the Castle hill. The leafy churchyard, no longer used for burials, was hemmed in on two sides by rows of old houses. I asked a man scything grass where Mrs Fraser lived, and was shown a house in the middle of one of the rows. The front door gave on to a narrow path which skirted the old burial ground and led on to the main road past the west door of the church. Walking round to the back of the row, I found myself in an alley connecting the main road with the backs gates of the houses. It was not a pleasant alley, and it seemed odd that Towle, according to what Bone had previously said, preferred it to the pleasant walk out of the front door and round the edge of the churchyard. Did he go through the kitchen to stare at Mrs Fraser's daughter? Or because he wanted company? Or because of some social clumsiness? Or was it because he disliked churchyards? Or even (but this was fantastic) churches?

Puzzled and fascinated, I went back to ask Antigone.

VI – RECONNAISSANCE

'We guess he was making a love potion,' said Antigone. 'Philtre, let's call it. We guess the philtre was for Juliet. We guess it was to be given to her at lunchtime on Sunday. That's quite a lot of guessing, and even if it's right it only tells us we're dealing with a very silly man. We knew that anyway. If Juliet swallowed the stuff it may, as you say, have upset her tummy; but I don't suppose she's come to any serious harm.'

'Darling,' I said, 'your natural innocence has preserved you from the truth that some substances exist which have what is called an aphrodisiac effect, and which foolish young men may slip into a girl's gin and tonic.'

'Like some extra gin,' she suggested. 'Natural innocence, or not, that works with me.'

'All right, then. Suppose you discovered a young man was slipping extra gin to a decent girl in the hope of catching her at an incautious moment. What do you do, laugh? Stand by and let it happen?'

Tiggy's eyes glazed. 'I'd wish it were me; I love gin. Anyway, Juliet doesn't drink.'

'Try and keep your mind on the situation,' I begged. 'I'm just putting the principle of the thing to you. And not only that; I'm suggesting we're dealing with a very peculiar man. Why did he go out of his way to avoid consecrated ground at Fifield?'

'My dear boy,' she said; 'I've read Dennis Wheatley, and I believe every word. It's in Pliny, anyway. But if this man is murdering chickens and babies in our High Street, he doesn't need a manuscript from you to tell him what to do next.'

'I wasn't thinking in those rather exaggerated terms; but there is such a thing as evil, yes, even in Brink; and something about Towle is wrong.'

'If you mean he's a nasty man, and we ought to do something about it, I agree; but what is there to do?'

'I'd really like to find out more about that meal at Towle's on Sunday. Can't we ask Juliet to dinner when Derek comes, and sound her out?'

'No, of course not. That would be very tactless under the circumstances. Anyway, we ought to strike while the iron is hot. Why not ask her round tonight?'

'We could. Do you think anything's wrong? I mean, she doesn't come in as often as she used to.'

'Trust you to notice that. No, I think she sensed our feelings towards our neighbour, that's all. I'll ring her up.'

'Damn!' she added, cocking an ear. 'There's the front door. It'll be Father Morris, and I haven't told you about him. He wants to catch you for some reason or other, and I said if you weren't on the bus in time for lunch, you'd be in about now. I'll send him up to you.'

Father Morris wanted some advice. 'Do you happen to know a man called Bone?' he asked. 'The librarian at Fifield Castle? Antigone said you did.'

I nodded.

'Well, I want to find out what sort of a person he is; before you answer I'll tell you why. You may have gathered that one thing I can't stand about parish work is archives, and all the fuss associated with them.'

'Father Falkner was the same,' I said.

'So are most parish priests, you'll find. Now I don't have to tell you that Cyril Arbuthnot is deeply involved in the history of his

Grammar School. I let him prod around in the various registers I've got. Now a very important item is a bound volume of records and historical comment, which covers three centuries, and is supposed to be unique. I'm supposed to hold that volume, but it isn't there, and do you know why?'

I thought I did, but held my peace.

'My sainted predecessor never answered letters from researchers and brass-rubbers, but that didn't stop them dropping in on him at all hours, and about a couple of years before he retired he hit on a splendid way of putting them off. This fellow Bone had asked to borrow the volume I told you about - it's called *The History of Brink 1550-1850* - and Father Falkner let him have it. Now Cyril wants me to get it back, so that he doesn't have to drive over to Fifield every time he wants to consult it.'

'It all seems straightforward enough.'

'Yes, but I've a suspicion there was some peculiar agreement between Bone and the Reverend Father. In fact, I believe the old man "gave" him the book. Well, of course, you can't give away parish property like that. It'll have to come back to me, and be a Mecca for every researcher that cares to knock me up. Now you know why I wanted to know how to approach Bone. Is he easily approachable?'

I laughed. 'No, I wouldn't have used that phrase about him. Mind you, once he respects you, he'll do anything for you. Well, anything that doesn't harm his blessed library, and he may think this does. Dear old Father Falkner must have left you with one or two problems, but I wonder if modern science will get you out of this one. Any book can be copied. This might at the same time placate Bone, and divert your researchers to Fifield Castle.'

'That simply hadn't occurred to me. What a wonderful age we live in. But Bone doesn't sound the sort of person to give in easily. Oh, dear.'

'Look,' I said; 'I know him well enough, and as it happens he's shown me the Brink history, though we didn't discuss the ownership. Would you like me to sound him out for you? I'll be visiting Fifield before very long.'

'No,' said Father Morris. 'It's kind of you, but I've got to face up to this myself. I'll make an appointment to see him.'

'The main trouble,' I said, 'is this refusal of his to trust anyone until he knows him. We must hope your dog-collar speeds the process.'

'It may do the opposite,' said Father Morris sadly. 'I'm afraid some of my colleagues are pretty dishonest about property.'

Dishonest, would you say? Casual, surely.'

'Dishonest. That's all you can call it. Half the books missing from libraries are on parsonage shelves all over England.'

I thought of Towle and the reference book. 'You say that, but you haven't had enough opportunity to go through the shelves of the laity. Anyway, hanging on to books is a only a venial sin, though Bone regards it as mortal.'

'Good. That means he won't hang on to ours.'

'Father …' I said, and stopped. Sin had made me think of evil, and I had a question to ask about that. But how to express it?

The priest looked up sharply. 'Yes?'

'Do you believe in evil?'

'Of course.'

'Evil people?'

'I believe in original sin, which these days people translate into "a tendency to evil". That doesn't mean evil people.'

'But we all have this tendency.'

'So I believe. Do you want to keep this conversation on general terms, or would you rather just tell me what you're getting at?'

'General terms,' I said. 'Do you believe there are persons who follow this tendency so far that they come to hate the light; who give themselves over to evil, and come to regard everything we call good as hostile to them?'

'Yes,' said Father Norris slowly. 'I think there are such persons. Not many, perhaps, who act consciously and deliberately, and none whatever for whom there ceases to be any hope; but, alas, quite a number who pursue ends which, if they were defined, would seem simply monstrous.'

'How does one recognise such persons?'

'My dear Michael, I doubt whether it is for us to seek to recognise them. To seek to do so may be a case of the very sin we hope to avoid. People are very diverse, you know, and the world, or what is now known as "society", offers many different opportunities of wrong choice, with appropriate masks to disguise the choices themselves. There are even masks to put on over masks. But the answer to your question is the old one: men do not gather grapes of thorns, or figs of thistles. By their fruits you know men. If those closest to a person are being tortured or destroyed, this may help you to recognise evil from good. But it is not easy, because evil poses as goodness to the outside world; sometimes, it is the saint who has the honesty to present himself as flawed.'

'Suppose a person avoided churches.'

Father Morris laughed heartily. 'Quite a lot do that. The Parish Church is seldom overcrowded.'

'No, I mean suppose he really shrank from consecrated objects.'

'Then he might be on the verge of conversion.'

'Like the Hound of Heaven.'

'Exactly like. At least he's not indifferent. There's no short cut to understanding human beings.'

'Father, these are only exploratory thoughts. More than once I've met someone who made me feel he'd gone very wrong. In particular, I've met someone now.'

'And so have I,' said Father Morris unexpectedly, standing up.
'And, like you, I'm worried about what may spring from it all. But
we'll leave it there, because we are close to the line that divides
spiritual reflection from gossip. Don't let ordinary human dislike
lead you into folly, that's all. Keep your lines open, and never hit
back.'

'I'll do what I can,' I promised. 'But I have to defend other
people.'

'The great phrase that starts all the wars,' he said. 'I have to do it
for the wife and kids.'

'Don't you have to defend other people?'

'Yes, but you have to be very sure they need defending, and that
they can't defend themselves. Now I must go and gather my strength
to defend myself ... against your librarian friend. Don't bother to
come down.'

He was an astonishing man, but he always made me feel restless
after he had gone. I was still thinking about myself when Juliet came
round that evening; then I cheered up in the excitement of her visit.

The subject of Towle came up almost at once, and I made a
remark about him which could by a stretch of the imagination be
taken as critical. Juliet's imagination got there like a flash, and,
calling him 'Alfred', she defended him edgily. Later on, however, the
feminine approach was more successful.

'Tell me, how is Mrs Boswell doing?' enquired Antigone. She was
the good lady who was cooking for Towle.

Juliet rose well to the fly. 'Oh, she's a great help. Yesterday, we
even had a meal with Alfred. She cooked it very well.'

'Plain, though, I suppose?'

'Oh, yes. Roast beef and two veg, with grapefruit to follow.'

It did not sound very suitable for the administration of a potion,
especially as Juliet would have refused a drink. Then a thought
struck me.

'I always think soup sorts out the good cooks,' I said.

'Yes, it often does,' she agreed. 'But people like Mrs Boswell use packets and tins. I think her mulligatawny yesterday was out of a tin; but I can't be sure, because I never touch it. It's much too hot for me.'

That could have been it, then. The strong flavour of the soup would have concealed any addition; but the plan had miscarried. I suddenly wondered who had had the doctored portion, and could not repress a giggle. Antigone frowned at me, and pursued her questioning.

'Did Mrs Boswell do the serving?'

'She helped, but Alfred did most of it.'

When Juliet had gone home, we held a conference.

'So far, so good,' said Antigone. 'He had the opportunity to slip something in the soup, but it didn't work. Juliet's safe for the moment, but there's no knowing what he may be up to next.'

She was beginning to enter into the thing.

'Can't we warn Juliet?' I suggested.

'What against? You can't say to a girl "Be careful what your Alfred gives you to drink, because it might be a love philtre." "Oh, really?" she says. "What makes you think that?" "Because," you say, "there's a medieval love philtre that needs marigolds, and we've seen marigolds in Alfred's house." That would give her a good laugh.'

'Can we tip off old man Macready?'

'Yes, if you want an hour's lecture on the folly of superstition, the necessity for drawing calm and logical conclusions from available evidence, and the advantages of minding your own business.'

'I don't believe he ever listens to anything,' I agreed gloomily.

'Anyway, he is said to be passionately fond of our sorcerer. Perhaps he's already been given his dose. No, darling, it's like Hercules's poisoned shirt. No one imagines a shirt is poisoned until he puts it on. We'll just have to keep quiet, have our eyes open, and wait for some proof about what's going on.'

In the end, we did agree to see if we could warn Derek when he came to dinner the following night.

I had expected him, a lover out of favour, to be on our side. Not a bit of it. His general demeanour was cheerful, and he seemed to regard Towle as an amiable eccentric, not to be worried about for a moment. He had always seemed resilient, but it surprised me that he should not pay more regard to his own interests. He showed no lack of interest in Juliet, and was prepared to discourse about her and grumble about her father. Towle did not seem to interest him.

Very cautiously, as if we ourselves found it hard to believe, I told him about the love potion. He roared with laughter. Abandoning caution, I admitted our belief. He looked at us as if we were demented to bother anyway.

It was quite a pleasant evening in other respects. Derek seemed an amusing person in a straightforward way, keen on his food and drink, able to enthuse about his job, though not knowing us well enough to relax fully in our company. Afterwards we compared notes, without arriving at any worthwhile conclusion.

'Well, we're on our own,' said Antigone, frowning. 'There's obviously something we don't know about going on. Either that, or he really is a very insensitive person.'

'He should make a good country solicitor,' I said. 'Nothing more than that. Did you notice how he shied off general topics?'

'That won't worry Juliet; though she likes an argument now and again.'

'She doesn't argue because she's a logical person,' I said. 'She argues because she's an emotional person, and finds it better to attack things than people.'

'She's a very insecure person; which is why Derek could be absolutely right for her. I don't know. I just don't feel we can see enough.'

We agreed that I should pay a visit to Juliet's father; not with any settled plan, but just to reconnoitre, in case some vital fact or opening presented itself. I had in the study a volume which I had rebound for Macready in the spring, and which I had tried to avoid returning for months. It was necessary to return it personally, in order to collect another volume, about which the sage wished to deliver himself of some remarks. The time had come to face the inevitable.

Summoning my powers of endurance, I set off next morning up the High Street, and turned up the Denbury Road, which was a dark tunnel of greenery on this overcast day of late summer. Mr Macready's house was a villa of modest splendour in outer suburban style, bright pink brick and black and white paintwork. Not a weed dared show its face in the perfectly kept flowerbeds.

A jumpy looking daily woman let me in to the French-windowed sitting-room, furnished with rather too many expensive pieces, where Mrs Macready was sitting sewing. She sprang up as I entered and settled me fussily in an armchair.

'Oh, Mr Jeffries,' she whispered. 'How nice to see you! We don't seem to have seen you for months. How is your wife?'

Poor woman, her opportunities for social intercourse were sadly limited. She spoke as if we must not be heard by anyone listening outside, and I unconsciously fell into the way of it, lowering my voice to declare Antigone in perfect health as if quite the reverse were true.

'Juliet has talked about her so much, you know. She has met such kindness from her.' She rattled on confidentially for a little; then I showed her the binding I had done.

'That's quite perfect!' she enthused. 'John will be down in a moment to thank you.'

Even as she spoke, the master of the house whipped open the door, just as if he had indeed been listening outside, and paused portentously on the threshold.

'I am glad to see you, Jeffries,' he said. 'You have saved me the trouble of delivering you a note, asking you and your wife to a dinner party on Friday at seven-thirty. The note apologises for the short notice, which is due to circumstances beyond my control.' He looked at his wife, who had merged tactfully into the upholstery as soon as he arrived, and who now, her eyes fixed on him with a curiously blank expression, seemed veritably to be taking on the pattern of the cretonne. The effect was so strange that I peered rudely at her, striving to pierce to the emotion beneath that blankness.

'You will come, I hope?' rapped Macready, recalling me to order. I thanked him and consented.

'We are helping Alfred Towle into the swim of Brink society, so he will be there too; as of course will Juliet.'

This sounded interesting; but while it was my cue to speak I launched myself into the business about the books, and was given my fresh commission. Macready now settled down in his chair to impress me.

'Well,' he said, 'what do you think of our garden this year?'

'It is really delightful,' I said. 'You must employ a host of gardeners.'

'Not at all. I employ none whatever. Every inch of that garden is cultivated by myself.'

I registered dutiful amazement at a fact I had been told several times, then, hypnotised into a routine I knew too well, I played into his hands.

'I can't think how you have the time,' I said.

'Time,' he came in on cue, 'is always there if we know how to use it. I am sorry to say that young men no longer understand how to use time. When my mother found us children lounging, she would quote from one of the French writers, *"Who is there who will not have to say 'I have dreamed my life away'"* - and I determined that one at least of her children would not have to make that cry.'

Outside the window the clean flowers, trapped in their impeccable beds and sprayed with washes against contamination, were dreaming their lives away until the next visit from their taskmaster. I suddenly thought with pleasure of a ragged old fritillary I had seen being blown about in a wood once. Then I wondered if some of the moments of true happiness in my life had not come to me as I listened to Macready. He always turned my mind to beautiful things. The last time I had had to endure him came back to me in all the beauty of high summer: the warm morning street, and Pip idly turning up the soft brown hair on his flank; the pink tongue curling up endlessly out of his gaping mouth until I wondered if it could touch one of the white spots on his head. Charitably, I thought it was a white spot on Macready's brown hair that he turned my thoughts into such sanity and peace.

'Can you defend your generation against that?' cried Macready triumphantly, prepared to listen to the word 'yes' before flooding on. I was about to concede some unknown point when I was saved by the telephone bell.

'That'll be Davenport,' said Macready. 'He wants to buy a bit of land from me.'

I rose as he did, and moved over to say goodbye to my hostess before I could be nailed again.

'Brink 2411. Macready speaking,' said the master. Conversation was impossible with that large voice booming, so I waited.

'Oh, is it!' said Macready irritably. 'Well, you can't; I've told you that already ... I don't care how exceptional they are ... I can't stop you doing that, but keep it short; I'm busy.'

There was a pause, in which Macready actually seemed to be listening. The voice at the other end croaked on indistinguishably, with the effect of blowing Macready up like an inflatable toy.

Finally the effort of listening overcame him, and he began to blow back.

'I'll tell you how I feel about it,' he said. 'I think nothing whatever to it, do you understand? You can just get the idea right out of your head for the present! In a year or two I'll talk to you, but I promise no more than that.' Saying which he slammed the phone down, thanked me curtly for my trouble, and stumped out of the room, leaving his wife to see me out. Mrs Macready smiled gently at me, and just for a moment seized my wrist in a surprisingly firm and reassuring grip.

'I do hope we shall see you on Friday,' she said. 'Both of you, of course. I shan't bother to give you that note.'

I suddenly felt there was more to Mrs Macready than met the eye. But above all I was grateful to Davenport, if that was who the caller was. His frustration was my freedom.

VII - DINNER AT MACREADY'S

At a quarter past seven that Friday we found ourselves tacking from door to door up the High Street, in a nasty squall. It had seemed a good idea to face dinner at the Macreadys, if only to observe Towle and Juliet; but I had forgotten we were already committed to six o'clock sherry at the other end of the town. Without thinking about the weather prospects, we planned to keep both appointments, moving smartly from one to the other.

The sherry party was more hospitable than we had bargained for, but it did fortify us for the task that met our eyes as we left it. Gathered clouds were unloading a fitful deluge. Water was pelting into the street and streaming over the pavement to the busy gutters. The wind was gusting against us, premature dusk was falling, and we fought our way, arm in arm, from one sheltered point to the next, pausing to recover breath.

The lights were on in the Thatched Cottage, as we staggered by it and took cover in the alley that separated it from the house next door. A clear light shone from the side windows, across the bit of side garden, and over the garden wall, illuminating the slant of the rain. We gathered strength for the next dash.

I looked at Tiggy.

'Are you very wet?'

'No, all's well so far. Let's wait a minute, though. We're in plenty of time, and it can't go on like this.'

We waited, and the downpour slackened to a sporadic drizzle.

Tiggy loosened her arm from mine, and moved out a little.

'Do you want to go on now?'

Tiggy looked round at me, her eyes dim and dark and thoughtful, like those of a cat not caring about a sparrow. 'Hang on,' she said, and moved along the opposite wall to the side gate of the Thatched Cottage. On tiptoe, she peered over, and I saw her head jerk towards me.

'Here,' she whispered. 'Take a look.'

I joined her at the gate, where the light picked out the drops of rain on her face. She was gazing intently at the window a few yards away. In it was framed the figure of Towle, pouring out of a thermos flask into a glass. He held the glass, and gazed at the dark liquid in it, moving his lips as if he were speaking an incantation. Common sense told me that he was talking to someone in the room with him.

He moved to one side and picked up a soda siphon. As he splashed soda into the glass I put my lips to Tiggy's ear, and nibbled it.

'There's someone with him,' I breathed.

Tiggy nodded grimly. Towle was stirring the concoction, and talking as he stirred.

'It can't be Juliet,' I continued. 'She's at home.'

'Not necessarily. Your nose is cold.'

It was curious, this stirring. What drink does one serve from a thermos, add soda, and stir? And who else but Juliet was it likely to be? Yet why should she be watching a process designed to entrap her?

'Look! He's giving it to her. Do something to stop him, Michael. Go and knock at the door. I'll try and warn her. Go on!' Obediently I moved as fast as I could round to the front door, gave a loud rat-a-tat-tat, then, unable to think of any reason for calling, hobbled across the street and into the first cover I could see, which was the corner of my own house, where it adjoined the entrance to a builder's yard. As I stood there at the yard gate, I giggled feebly, then wondered what on earth the point was of behaving like a small boy. At that moment

I heard the footsteps of someone coming down the street, and P.C. Fellows, our local bobby, marched with measured tread inexorably by. I thought he had probably not seen me cross, and tried to look like a respectable householder waiting for a friend. 'Good evening,' I croaked hopefully. He answered my greeting, apparently without either classing me as an unusual occurrence, or pausing to ask himself why any householder should stand and get wet within a few yards of his own front door. I wondered whether what he saw at the Thatched Cottage would seem as innocent.

I could now reasonably be seen to enter my own house from the Denbury direction, so I emerged from my hiding place, and moved towards my front door. Across the road, Towle was peering out from the porch of the Thatched Cottage and I saw him prepare to hail the policeman. Before he could do so, I heard above the wind the faint crash and tinkle of broken glass. Towle turned and rushed back into the cottage, while Fellows moved towards the house and paused enquiringly at the porch. I heard him say something into the open front door, then Towle re-emerged, putting on a mackintosh, and they both went round into the alley where I had left Tiggy.

I wondered how I could take a hand to save my wife from disgrace. Nothing whatever occurred to me, so I just waited. After a couple of centuries, the two men came out of the alley without any handcuffed girl, and conferred on the doorstep. Then, to my surprise and relief, Fellows resumed his patrol down the street and Towle went into his cottage and shut the front door.

Elaborately casual, I strolled over to the alley, and peered in. A bedraggled figure was tiptoeing towards me. She took my arm and sighed almost contentedly.

'I broke the bathroom window,' she said. 'I think it was the bathroom.'

'How on earth?'

'Earth,' she said. 'You throw earth at the window to attract attention. It's all stones round here though, and anyway I missed.'

'You call that missing!' I said sternly. 'How did you escape arrest?'

'In somebody's runner beans. It was very muddy.'

The light went out in the sitting-room and I judged it wise to move. Taking Tiggy's arm. I steered her across the road to our own side. She was limp and compliant, the girl of action forgotten for the moment.

As we reached the opposite pavement, the door of the Thatched Cottage opened, and two figures left the house and hurried up the street. I held Tiggy back to let them get ahead. There was something familiar about the one that crossed over as they came abreast of our house, and peered at our slow progress along the pavement.

'Oh, it's the family,' he said. 'Shouldn't you be at your dinner party? Towle says he's late, but he's got an excuse. Someone's been playing about outside his house: knocking on the door and breaking a window.'

Holding Tiggy out of the light, I took the offensive.

'You sound very bouncy, Doctor. Have you been drinking with Towle?'

He chuckled. 'Nothing very strong. Only a sort of fruit cup that Towle's made. It's for you.'

'For us?'

'You'll see. Well, I'm going in. Are you coming, or heading for your appointment?'

'I'm not sure,' said Tiggy from behind me. 'You go on in, darling, and Michael and I will consult.'

The Doctor looked hard at his daughter, but made no comment. Then he turned and disappeared into the house.

'We'll have to go in,' said Tiggy. 'I've got some repairs to do. Michael, have I been a bit silly?'

It was the sherry,' I said kindly.

By the time she was ready to be seen again we were very late indeed. Macready, who was nothing if not efficient, had his emergency plans ready, and on arrival we found ourselves handed a glass of sherry and whisked into dinner.

'We had planned to eat a little later than usual,' he said graciously over the soup. 'By rights this should be a warm night, and I asked our young friend Alfred here to compound the base for a fruit cup, at which I believe him to be something of an expert.'

Towle twitched modestly.

'However, it is not a warm night, and events have detained our guests; so it seemed best to keep the cup until now. Alfred, there is cold soda and fruit on the side. Please carry on when you feel like it.'

Tiggy's sherry glass was empty, and she looked much more confident. After the wet pavements, the warm and prosperous surroundings of the Macready household, and the speed with which I had been given sherry and soup, disposed me well towards the world; but they had had an opposite effect on her. She was alert and dangerously aggressive. I avoided catching her eye, and refused to return the faces and little gestures she was directing at me. My expression was that of an older and wiser male, whose wife has made sufficient of a spectacle of herself for one night. Tiggy retorted by twisting her face into a mask of hatred, which I saw Ethel Macready intercept with fascinated horror.

Towle moved to the sideboard, where the contents of two thermos flasks had been poured into a jug of dark brown liquid, and busied himself slowly and deliberately. Tiggy, who was by now meeting comments, pats, and giggles from Macready in his salacious mood, kept a weather eye on Towle's back.

I turned to Mrs Macready who, though her eyes remained fixed on her husband's behaviour, was making one of her rare contributions to conversation.

'Do you plan to remain in Brink, Mr Jeffries?'

'I don't know,' I said. 'It's rather a remote place for a man of my age.'

'Remote from what?'

'Remote from ways of making a living, for one thing; but also rather out of the full current of human ambitions and passions.'

'No!' said Mrs Macready, and I was surprised by the vigour with which she spoke. I looked at her sharply, and saw as her eyes fell again on her giggling husband that same strange blankness I had seen before.

'No,' she said. 'Believe me, it's all here. Human ambition and passion - all the sin and error that stains the pages of history, and what good there is also. Are you a Christian, Mr Jeffries?'

The question surprised me.

'We generally sit in the pew behind you,' I reminded her.

The scorn in her voice was intense. 'That!' she said. 'That piece of play-acting.'

Her husband had the loudest voice in the congregation, and read the lessons unctuously but well. I began to feel uncomfortable. I was being appealed to, but too directly, and at the wrong time.

'You asked ...' I said carefully, wondering when Macready would take his horrible hand off Tiggy's shoulder. Suddenly his wife seized my wrist in that surprisingly firm but kind grasp.

'Don't take any notice of me,' she whispered.

Macready had unstuck his paw from my wife's skin, to assume the role of the jovial host.

'Now, who's for cup?' he roared.

Antigone gave me a weary look, then jumped as Macready addressed her again.

'Antigone?' Christian names, now, was it?

Towle padded softly to her and filled her glass.

'My dear?'

Mrs Macready smiled wanly and was supplied.

'Juliet?'

'No, thank you, daddy.'

'What? Why not?'

'I don't drink, dear, as you know perfectly well.'

'Pooh! nonsense. This is practically a soft drink.'

'I'd rather have nothing, thank you.'

Towle was back at the sideboard, doing something or other.

Macready was showing his dislike of being thwarted.

'Nothing?' he said crossly.

'Hear me with patience but to speak a word,' said Towle unexpectedly. He had wheeled round from the sideboard and was holding up a glass. 'Take thou this vial ... and this distilled liquor drink thou off.' He came and offered it coyly to Juliet. I saw Antigone sitting up, tense and willing Juliet to refuse.

'What is it?' asked Juliet.

'It is mainly lemonade. I have only added a dash of the cup, just to give you the taste.'

Her father looked angrily at her as she hesitated. Antigone was making faces which, had she seen, she would have been hard put to interpret. Mrs Macready was impassively watching her husband; I turned my eyes on Towle, and saw the intensity of his gaze as he looked down at Juliet.

'Thank you,' said she, smiling, and accepting the glass. The tension was broken, except where Antigone was still making horrified mouths and shaking her head at an oblivious Juliet. Macready bent over to her and resumed their conversation. She answered abstractedly cudgelling her brain; then, ignoring Macready, she leant forward and said brightly to Juliet 'Juliet, may I taste your drink?'

'Why? You haven't tasted your own yet,' said Juliet.

'Mine's stronger. I wanted to see what yours was like.'

Looking puzzled, Juliet pushed her glass across the table. I glanced at Towle, and strongly confirmed my opinion that Antigone was making a fool of herself. He had managed to persuade Mrs Macready into conversation, and was taking no notice whatever of events opposite.

Antigone took the glass clumsily and spilt the whole lot on and over the edge of the table. It seemed to me that she aimed towards Macready's trousers, but her own dress was the main sufferer.

'Oh!' she cried. 'How silly! I am so sorry.'

Macready started fussing about with a napkin, and his wife scurried for a cloth. There was general sympathy and assurance that it was of no consequence, and Towle mixed another drink. Throughout the rest of the meal Antigone sat in deflated misery and gazed at the glass as Juliet drank from it. Clearly, she felt she had done her bit, and failed.

We had coffee in the sitting-room, among the shining mahogany and the shelves of Chinese vases that must have made the Macready house a nightmare for any insurer. As the owner told us about a fine new acquisition, I pictured some member of Lloyds saying his bedtime prayers for the safety of Denbury Road.

Towle had excused himself from the discourse, and was sitting next to Juliet. He was behaving as he had on their first meeting, looking at her with that unmistakable admiration and talking with a vivacity quite foreign to him at other times. Juliet's air particularly attracted my attention. She was playing up to her neighbour in every respect, and encouraging him to expand; but there was real strain in her gaiety, and when she looked away her eyes seemed dark and worried.

Later, during a break in Macready's flow of oratory, I heard a snatch of their conversation.

'I'll be ready at half past nine,' said Juliet. 'Outside the house with my luggage.'

'I shall be there,' said Towle, adding oddly 'I hope.'

'I hope so too,' said Juliet. 'It's a big step to take, and I shan't be a lot of use to you.'

Shortly after this conspiratorial exchange, Juliet stood up and excused herself, explaining that she had to pack.

'My daughter is attending a weekend reunion at her former school,' said Macready. 'She leaves in the morning. I consider it a matter of the greatest importance that she should maintain contact in this way. I return to my own school every year as a point of principle.'

I wondered how his old school viewed the matter.

On the way home through the dark and windy street I told Antigone what I had heard. She was tired and depressed.

'Silly girl,' she said. 'Well, I've done what I can, and ruined two skirts in the process. I'm not going to be chased by the police again, for a girl who doesn't seem to care what happens to her.'

'What I don't understand is why Towle should be involved tomorrow morning,' I said. 'He doesn't run a car, and the Macreadys have two. They didn't sound like a couple planning a dirty weekend. He doesn't behave like a man drugging a reluctant girl. I reckon this potion nonsense, if it ever had any reality, is over now. What's it all about?'

Antigone sighed as she waited for me to open our front door. 'It's a man's world,' she said. 'Lechery, lechery. Lock up your daughters.'

'And wives,' she added, with more spirit. She paused in the hall, and slipped a hand round my neck. 'Darling,' she said, and kissed me lingeringly. 'I do need a new skirt.'

VIII - Exit Juliet

My curiosity was not kept waiting long. Next day, after lunch, Macready rang me up.

'This is just in the nature of a casual enquiry,' he said. 'My daughter often visits you, and I wondered if you had seen her or heard from her recently.'

'Since last night?' I asked.

'Yes.'

'Then the answer is 'No'. As far as I know, she's still at her Reunion.'

'Oh, the Reunion,' said Macready, in a voice which did not succeed in concealing a deeply wounded dignity. 'In fact, she decided not to attend that.'

'She went somewhere else, did she?'

'So it seems. Of course, there is no reason to be concerned for her.' For once, he found difficulty in speaking.

I hesitated. 'I may know something helpful,' I said.

'May I come round?'

He said he would set out at once, and I hung up. Antigone was standing in the doorway, excited.

'She's disappeared, has she?'

'It looks like it. I'd better tell him about Towle.'

'Funny she didn't leave a message. But what is the old man thinking about? Twenty-one-year-old girls don't get abducted these days. Things have changed since Paris.'

'I didn't know you'd ever been to Paris.'

'I haven't, worse luck. No, Paris the man.'

Even then, my mind was so full of Shakespeare I missed the classical allusion.

'Stop dancing around,' I said. She was off round the room with a duster, tiptoeing and bending and stretching like a ballerina.

'Life is exciting,' she said, not stopping.

'Vicariously, perhaps.'

She stopped and looked at me. 'Vicariously!' she said primly. I subsided.

Macready was dressed for drama. He had a carnation in his buttonhole, and was prepared to regain his dignity through suffering.

'I must tell you from the start,' he said, 'that I believe young Major to have had a hand in this disappearance.'

'I doubt that very much,' I said; 'but why do you speak of disappearance like that?'

He tried to evade that one, but it became clear enough that Juliet had led him to believe she was going to spend the weekend at her school when in fact she had other plans. Some telephone message for her after she had gone had seemed urgent enough for him to ring the school, and his alarm at the result had been doubled by the discovery from Brink station that Juliet had caught no train from there that morning.

'You indicated,' he said, 'that you had some information?'

'I said I might have. Did you know how Juliet travelled to the station this morning?'

'She went by car. My wife or I would have taken her, but she assured us a friend had offered her a lift. Who it was I do not know, though I have my suspicions.'

'It was Alfred Towle. He picked her up at your gate at half past nine this morning.'

Macready looked relieved. 'Alfred Towle? Then we can soon clear the matter up. I have every confidence in that young man.'

'That may be,' I said; 'but he doesn't own a car. Why should he suddenly offer Juliet a lift when he has no car? Why did he set off with her for Brink station, and never arrive? Where are they now?'

Macready rose. 'These questions,' he said, 'are easily answered by my crossing the road.'

I watched from the balcony as he paced deliberately across to the Thatched Cottage, and knocked on the door. There was no reply

Macready stood for a while in thought on the pavement; then he slowly returned to me. I could hear the indecision in his slow footsteps up the stairs. He came into the study, and sat down again, his eyes focussed on the carpet.

'My wife,' he said, 'is very disturbed.'

'Understandably,' I said.

There was a silence, then he said again 'Very disturbed. Very disturbed indeed.'

He was saying something, but it was not within range of his normally extensive powers of expression.

'Look,' I offered; 'are you certain Juliet was not going on later to this school do?'

Macready nodded, then shook his head, preoccupied with other thoughts.

'Twenty-five years,' he said.

'Twenty-one, isn't it?'

He shook his head again in slow denial, then faster, to clear his brain.

'Twenty-five,' he said. 'I shall just have to see him when he returns. It will be all right.'

'You certainly have faith in him.'

Macready was regaining his poise. 'Why should I not?' he demanded, looking me in the eyes. 'I am something of a judge of people. I was afraid that Major was at the bottom of this; and that would have been very different. That young man is not all he seems.'

'Nor is Towle, in my opinion. I should like to know why he left Fifield.'

'Tittle tattle!' he said angrily. 'I take no notice of that, when I have a carefully formed opinion of a man. It is unnecessary to make mysteries where there are none. As for the car, Alfred was I know intending to buy one.'

I could see he was worried enough, so I calmed down myself, and offered to let him know if Towle came back.

'Mind you,' I added, 'it might be worthwhile getting in touch with Derek Major in the meantime. He may know something. He's certainly very fond of Juliet.'

'My wife has already telephoned Mrs Ellerman,' said Macready. 'Major is away for the weekend.'

'Curiously, Derek and Juliet were quarrelling when I last saw them together; and Juliet has spent a lot of her time with Alfred Towle lately.'

Macready just looked at me, and kept silence. For once, he was keeping something back.

When he had gone, I descended to the kitchen. Antigone was crouched in front of the oven.

'How old's Juliet?' I asked.

'You know that. Twenty one.'

'Funny. I thought he said she was twenty five.'

Antigone reached into the oven and hauled out a cake. 'How much did you tell him?' she asked.

'About what?'

'About our neighbour.'

'My dear,' I said, 'can you really imagine my giving him a blow-by-blow account of the last twenty four hours?'

'Old goat!' she said viciously, jabbing a skewer into her cake. 'Still,' she added, standing up and turning round, 'I wonder why Juliet had to do it this way. She's hurt her mother rather badly.'

'Do what? What has she done?'

'I think,' said Antigone reflectively, 'we may not see Juliet again for a time.'

At tea a thought struck me, and I strolled up to see Fred. Fred ran a garage that supplied necessaries to motorists as its prime object, but that contained a number of other articles for sale. As a filling station it had long been outdated by a smart concern on the Fifield road; but most townsfolk went to Fred to have their cars seen to. He was the secretary of the Brink Victory Committee, with a place in local affairs; but his ruling passion was to collect junk. The yard behind his garage was full of Fred Stirling's acquisitions, either in the rain or under improvised shelters. There were old sofas, primitive radio sets, great white shells, glazed pottery, basket chairs where cats had their families, vacuum cleaners, and pictures of sunset over the Devon coast. I told Fred on numerous occasions that the junk in his yard was as nothing compared with the junk in his garage. He was the sort of person who enjoyed vile insults as a test of his powers of retaliation, grimly humorous, faithful, with the air of an expert and a large black moustache going grey. I found him on this Saturday evening tidying up his yard, with many a pause to turn lovingly over a prized object.

'Look at this,' he said as soon as he saw me, holding up a remarkable three-tiered piece of furniture with legs that curled as crazily as those regrettable pillars by St Peter's tomb. 'Do you know what this is?'

'An aspidistra stand?' I suggested.

'It's a whatnot,' he said triumphantly. 'Thursday I bought it, and only yesterday I had a gentleman in offering me the earth for it. I'd have let him have it if he hadn't told me what it was. I'm going to clean it up and give it to my mother-in-law.'

'That's a gruesome sort of revenge.'

'I'm very fond of the old dear. She's always wanted one of these.'

81

'Fred,' I said; 'turn your mind to the car side of your business and tell me whether you've had any dealings with a man called Towle lately.'

'Mr Towle?' he said. 'Him at Thatched Cottage?'

'That's right.'

'He's toying with the idea of buying a car from me. He had one out today on trial.'

'Is he back yet?'

'He may be, but the car isn't. It developed a fault, and finished in a garage fifteen miles away. I'm collecting it Monday.'

'What was the trouble?'

'There was nothing wrong with that car,' said Fred defensively.

'But it had been on the road a long time. You can't drive them forever.'

'Fred,' I said. 'I'm your friend. Tell uncle.'

'To be quite honest, the steering went.'

'Lots of people,' I said, 'will believe you were trying to get rid of that car at all costs; but your friends know you better. They know you were just doing a customer a good turn. Like breaking his neck.'

'Malicious comment comes naturally to some people,' said Fred impassively. 'I put the boy on that car; now I wish I'd looked at it myself. You can't get conscientious lads these days. Scamp their jobs, they do.'

Somewhere underneath, he was uncomfortable and worried, so I steered the conversation back to whatnots before setting off home. As I came abreast of my house I saw the lank figure of Towle step out of the Thatched Cottage and pause on the pavement outside. I walked over to him and hailed him. He looked very tired and unhappy.

'Good evening,' he said, standing for a moment like a scarecrow as if deciding what to do next. There was no emotion in his voice.

'I believe Macready is looking for you,' I said.

'I was going along to see him at this precise moment,' he said. 'He's worried about Juliet.'

'He must have heard about my breakdown. News travels fast.'

'I think it's more than your breakdown.'

He looked at the gutter and frowned, then looked up at me speculatively. 'I think you had better come in,' he said.

He returned to his front door, pushed it open, and stood aside not watching me as I passed. When we were in the sitting room he asked me to sit down, but himself stood fiddling with his fingers like someone unused to society. He reached out for a cigarette box, pushed it away again, murmured to himself, and gave a nervous sniff.

'Macready,' I said, 'is very worried about Juliet. She has not arrived at her school reunion, and I think you were the last person to see her.'

He sat down on the edge of a chair. 'I took her to the station,' he said unhappily.

'To Brink station?'

'No, no. I drove her to Grilton. It saves half an hour, and the car needed a trial run.'

'Did she say where she was going?'

'If she spoke about it, she gave the impression she was going to the school weekend. But ...'

'But what?'

He drew a deep breath, and shivered. 'I ... had a feeling there was more to it.'

'Why?'

Towle lifted his head, and looked at me directly. His eyes were bloodshot and penetrating. 'There was something very final in what she said.'

'You mean, as if you and she might not meet again for a time?'

His head bobbed away again, and he began clasping and unclasping his hands. 'Or even … even … at all,' he said in a choked voice.

For a brief moment I thought he meant Juliet was going to throw herself under a train; then I understood what had happened. In some way she had tried to put Towle out of his misery - a ridiculous phrase in view of his present state.

'Oh, dear! I am sorry,' I said inadequately.

'Then the car broke down, on top of everything. I expect I'm a bit tired.'

'You must be. Shall I ring Juliet's father? then you can take it easy.'

'That would be very kind.'

As I left him, he sat back in his chair, rested his head, and closed his eyes.

Macready was not prepared to deal at second hand.

'I see,' he said, coldly courteous. 'Thank you. I will see Alfred at once.'

'Really, you know,' I said, 'this is not a good time. He's very exhausted. You can take it from me that he knows no more than I've told you.'

'No doubt,' he said. 'The fact remains that I should like to see him.'

Ten minutes later, from the balcony, I saw the leonine head borne aloft on its way down the street to the Thatched Cottage. With a sigh, I returned to my book.

A few moments later, there was a scratch at the study door, and my father-in-law shuffled through and joined me on the balcony.

'The wish of the family seems to be that I should sit with you,' he explained.

He glanced down the road over his spectacles. 'I understand,' he continued, 'that our charming young friend has taken a weekend off. No suggestions of necromancy this time, I hope?'

'No, ' I said uneasily.

'We must make an effort of understanding,' he said. 'First you find a friendly dog of the largest size, and try pushing it in any direction you like. As like as not, you'll be pushed over in the opposite direction. Then you find a child and put your arms firmly round it. It will scream and struggle to escape. If you had sat there like that, and read your book, the same child would not have stopped trying to climb on your knee.

'I tried to apply that when I brought up the family. I always made it possible for her to do the opposite of what she really wanted to do. It worked reasonably well; not that I'm anything of a bringer-up of children. They need a mother, you know, as that young man across the road kept pointing out to me. He seems to have persuaded himself he never had one, or as good as never had one, for all the good she did him. I expect she was a female version of your friend Macready, a great closer of avenues, so that he always felt bound to explore them, and push her out of the way as he did so. When children like that grow up, they're a mass of unregulated emotions, you know. They hide them under a cold or awkward exterior, but they're always reaching out to regain the affection they've lost. It's bound to be a clumsy process, because they've never had any practice in being affectionate. He wanted your affection, but you were too sensitive not to be put off by his clumsiness. Only insensitive persons, or saints, would give him enough time to make them like him.'

'I can see why Macready likes him,' I said. 'He's the most insensitive person I know. But is Juliet a saint?'

'The term is perhaps a little old-fashioned. Certainly she has been very cruel to her parents; but she may not have intended this.'

'You may be right,' I said. 'You see through other people's eyes: but I did have this feeling of evil with Towle. He didn't seem to me to be really trying to help. He was bad, because he preferred some odd sort of personal self-gratification to the ultimate good.'

'It is curious,' said the Doctor gently, 'how you refer to classical ethics, while I, a man born in another age, talk like a psycho-analyst.'

'True psychology is timeless.'

'It's kind of you to say so; but Aristotle also has a certain claim to timelessness. The real difference between us is that you have an enviable moral energy, which compels you to make decisions about people. I am much too lazy. I sometimes wonder whether I should not encourage you to use this energy of yours more than you do.'

'How do you mean?'

'Leave this rather beautiful place, and resume the way of life you knew before your accident. No, I don't mean the Army; but forgive me of all people for saying it - you might now be able to enjoy wider horizons.'

'It's all here,' I said, quoting Mrs Macready. 'Human ambition and passion, and so forth.'

'I don't doubt it; but I was speaking of enjoyment.'

'Have you said this to Tiggy?'

'No, of course not. I should not expect her to discuss it with me.'

'And had you anything particularly in mind?'

'I know a man at our sister foundation at Cambridge who has an interest in group of bookshops. They are aiming to start a shop in Cambridge. He asked me if I knew anyone with the knowledge and expertise. I said I might.'

'Mm. Well, I can't deny the thought had struck me. At one time, after I fell in with my mine, it was out of the question. The lameness was a problem; but, worse than that, I didn't seem to want to venture anywhere. I'm much better now, and I find myself restless at times.

We're not very well-off, living like this. We want children, and their arrival won't make things any easier.'

'There'd be no need to commit yourself. You could go up to London, and find out about things.'

'London?'

'The head office is there.'

A door opened and shut opposite, and Macready came walking with unhurried pace up the street. The world was not going to see him flustered.

The Doctor got to his feet and moved with surprising speed to the balcony rail. Macready would have been discourteous not to notice him, but he did not check his pace. A wave of the stick and a polite 'Pleasant evening, sir' met the occasion.

'Indeed,' said the Doctor, with the air of a man beginning a long conversation, 'summer seems to be still with us, despite the contrary evidence of last night.' He spoke so slowly that Macready had to halt his career and face him.

'I wonder, sir,' continued the Doctor, 'if you have the time to favour me with some advice. I am, as it happens, in need of the opinion of an imaginative and experienced person on a matter of business. Might I, perhaps, accompany you up the street on your way home? I need not occupy you for long.'

One could not have envisaged Macready's refusing, under any circumstances whatever.

'You are most kind,' said the old man. 'I shall join you at once.'

On his way past me, he smiled with gentle sadness. 'Did I say "imaginative"?' he asked. 'I really think I did.'

He was back in half an hour, clearly satisfied at having performed the task Antigone had now admitted setting him.

'He is certainly a loquacious person,' he said. 'I feel quite tired. However, he is also very worried, and seems to believe his daughter has left home. His state is not improved by his suspicions about that young man who extracted me from a canvas tomb the other day. He had an ominous telephone call from him recently, it seems, and was forced - I use his terminology - to tell him he would not speak to him about his daughter for a considerable time - a year or two, he said.'

The phrase rang a bell with me. 'Fool!' I cried, meaning myself; 'I was there at the time. I thought he was bullying someone about some land.'

My father-in-law frowned. 'Yet,' he said, 'and with apologies to you, my dear family, I could have sworn that I had been talking to a man involved in even more than the temporary loss of an only daughter. I am not fanciful, but I would say that I had been talking to a man on whom the end of the world had come.'

IX - THE FLIGHT OF THE BUMBLE-BEE

My father-in-law's visit ended next day. There was to be a gathering of old cronies at a London vicarage, after which his college chaplain was running him back to Oxford. As I saw him on to the station platform, I told him I would think more about the bookshop idea.

'Of course,' he said, squeezing my arm. 'Think about it. Speaking for myself, I should miss Brink. It seems a place crowded with event. I shall be interested to hear what develops out of the latest one, particularly as it affects that verbose young historian across the road. I have been thinking of him with some sadness. You know, my dear fellow, I have never found these songs about cruel virgins ridiculous; nor, I imagine, does he. He must believe they represent a considerable portion of human experience.'

I left him waiting for his train, and hurried over to the church for Mattins meeting Tiggy at the lych gate.

A succession of incumbents had fought against the love of the parishioners of Brink for 'proper Mattins'. Father Falkner had reached a compromise by which the mid-morning Sunday service was alternately Mattins and a Sung Eucharist. Father Morris was still fighting his way towards the complete victory of the Eucharist, but making very little progress.

The effect of this alternation was uneasy. The older people either came to church on alternate Sundays or came to church every Sunday and did their best to treat the Eucharist as Mattins. The younger people would have seized the opportunity not to come at all, had not Father Morris packed his choir stalls so full that it was

hard to believe any adolescent inhabitant remained out in the streets
and playgrounds of the town.

For all this, the atmosphere was as friendly and joyful as the
personality of the Vicar could make it. Fred Stirling, looking less
harassed, grinned at us as he thrust service books into our hands at
the church door. We walked up the broad nave of the great wool
church towards the thunder of the voluntary and took our usual
seats, third from the front on the north side. The Macreadys
normally inhabited the pew in front of us; but on this occasion only
Macready was there, sitting straight-backed and looking impassively
ahead of him. The show must go on, I thought; and I remembered
his wife's phrase, 'that piece of play-acting'.

The church was fuller than it had been for some weeks. People
had come back from their summer holidays ready for the new school
term, and the early September feeling in the congregation took me
back to my boyhood. 'Lord, behold us with thy blessing,' I thought.
Cyril Arbuthnot, looking bronzed and rested after his summer break,
was sitting opposite us with his wife, a few rows back.

A hymn, the *Venite*, and a psalm were sung, mostly by the choir.
Few members of the congregation attempted to fit themselves into
the immense volume that poured from the crowded choir. As we
reached the *Gloria*, Macready turned to his right, stepped out of his
pew, and headed for the lectern, carrying a bible. I heard a step
behind me, and looked round. Cyril was standing irresolutely in the
aisle. He looked puzzled. Then he glanced at his wife, shrugged, and
returned to his seat.

We settled down to hear the lesson.

'The first lesson,' said Macready, 'is taken from the Epistle of
Saint Paul to the Ephesians, chapter five, beginning at verse twenty-
two. "*Wives, submit yourselves unto your own husbands, as unto the Lord.
For the husband is the head of the wife ...*"'

He continued, reading from his own bible in that florid way of his, much admired, which always stood between me and what he was reading. It seemed curious to have a New Testament reading for the first lesson. In view of Cyril's abortive sortie, Macready must have got it all wrong; unless Father Morris was paving the way for some special sermon. I glanced at him, sitting back in his seat, shading his eyes with his hand. There was something unnatural about his posture.

Macready was winding up. '*Children, obey your parents in the Lord: for this is right. Honour thy father and mother; That it may be well with thee, and thou mayest live long on the earth.*'

He closed the bible, paused, looked up with a slight curl of the lip; then he said 'Here ends the first lesson', stepped down from the lectern, and carrying his head high walked straight down the aisle past his pew.

Father Morris quickly stood up and announced the *Te Deum*. The opening notes of the organ drowned the click of the church door as it closed. I wondered how many of the congregation realised something was wrong.

After the service, Father Morris disentangled himself from a group of ladies, and took my arm. 'I'd welcome a word, Michael,' he said. 'Can you come to the Vicarage?'

As he returned to his handshaking, I put Tiggy on the road home, and knocked on the Vicarage door. There was no reply, but Mrs Morris's voice behind me said 'Checking up on me?' I turned round, and realised she had been following me. She was an acute, relaxed person, fat, fair and dutiful, but wisely standing apart from anything her husband was doing.

'It's all right,' she said. 'I was there, and awake for most of it. Are you coming in for a drink?'

Father Morris joined us after ten minutes, and sailed straight to the point. 'My dear,' he said, 'I'm going to separate you from

Michael and take him off to the study. Bring your sherry, Michael.'
Mrs Morris pouted politely.

'Now,' said her husband as soon as we were settled; 'can you tell me what's hit John Macready?'

'Juliet seems to have left home,' I said.

'Is that all that's happened?'

'All? What else do you expect?'

He seemed about to say something, then he paused.

'He's terribly upset by it,' I added.

'Can you envisage a man,' he said slowly, 'deciding to publicize his affairs in church?'

'No,' I said decidedly.

'One calls banns.'

'Oh, come!'

'Well, I'm used to making public statements myself, and I can tell you the urge to reveal what happened at breakfast is sometimes almost irresistible.'

'Almost, perhaps; but to stick your neck out like that!'

'Brink is a small place. Everybody knows about family upheavals, sooner or later. It must have seemed best to him to make his position clear.'

'He's unbalanced. That positive air of his is a sort of megalomania.'

Father Morris shook his head. 'It may be so; but most people are unbalanced when they're pushed off their perches. Now look, Michael. I'm going visiting. God knows what I shall find, or whether I can help. I need to talk to a very determined person indeed; and I am not referring to John. I'm glad you could tell me about Juliet. Thank you for coming over.'

'For the last few days,' I said, 'everything has been going on in Greek, as far as I'm concerned.'

'It's a good language,' said Father Morris, fastening his black cloak; 'the language of the New Testament, in fact. Now, Anthaea will be delighted to look after you. Forgive me if I rush off.'

The last I heard of him was calling to his wife, whom I found outside in the hall.

'He's a great dasher off,' she said sympathetically. 'Come and have some more sherry.'

The letter came in the second post next morning, postmarked from London.

> *'My dear Michael and Tiggy,' it said, 'I've just posted a very difficult letter home. I hope it's a kind one, but a clear one. Yours isn't easy either, because of all my friends in Brink I shall miss you most, and because I hated leaving you without saying goodbye.*
>
> *'At the moment I'm staying with a friend in London. I shall look for a job and for somewhere permanent to live, and I have promised myself that, barring emergencies, I shall not visit Brink till after Easter. You know how impossible it has been, with Daddy and me quarrelling, and Mummy trying to make the peace. I think she has suffered more than I have, because he has turned on her so often. I hope the two of them will have a better life in my absence. I hate to think of my coming between them after they have lived twenty-five years together.'*

That rang a bell.

> *'I have a lot to think about. Derek, for example. He has taken all this well, and understands how difficult it has been for me, working in his office. We shall meet occasionally, but not more, until I have sorted myself out.*
>
> *'It was no use facing up to Daddy and telling him I was going. It would have meant a terrible scene. I wondered whether to ask Mummy to explain things to him, but it didn't seem fair, when she has already been regarded so often as the source of whatever is wrong. She has acted*

marvellously to him. Even though she has understood what is in my mind, she has always said I must take my own decisions, and lead my own life. So I couldn't make her the bearer of bad news. In the end, I waited for the school weekend, and just left, using Alfred as a bit of a screen in the meantime. They didn't expect me back till Monday, so my letter will break the news to them.

'It's all very petty, I'm afraid. There are thousands of girls living away from home and making the friendships they want. Yet to Daddy, this will be a sort of insult ... an act of disobedience for which I shall be lucky to be forgiven.

'Derek has had no part in this, though of course I've told him what I'm doing. Daddy may not believe this, though I've pitched it strong in my letter. If you see any chance of reassuring him about it, or of bringing the two together, do please seize it. There's something counting against Derek all the time ... a very tiny thing that could only matter to someone who thinks like Daddy.

'I feel guilty about Alfred. He's rather a pet, and I should never have let him feel I was encouraging him. On the way to the station I hinted as kindly as I could that I wouldn't be seeing him again, and he shook me by breaking down. I feel very bad about that ... buying peace at home at any price.

'Bless you both, and thank you for being such a comfort. When I've settled down in London I hope you'll be able to come and see me.

'Much love, Juliet.'

'Cruel virgins,' I said.

'That's what Daddy said to me, too,' said Tiggy; 'but she didn't mean to be so cruel to her parents. She couldn't know she'd be checked up on.'

'It was on the cards,' I said; 'but I suppose some cruelty was bound to be involved. Towle is the unnecessary bit.'

'That was a bit mean,' she conceded. 'But Juliet can be very gawky. Can you imagine being brought up by that cheap orator, that poor man's Cicero, and making a brilliant success with people? She'll learn.'

'If she sees Towle as a pet,' I said, 'she's not done badly.'

Someone shouted from the front hall. Tiggy investigated, and returned with Father Morris. He looked weary, and gratefully accepted a mug of coffee.

'Sorry to collapse on you,' he said. 'It's been a hard twenty-four hours, and not a very successful one. I'm beginning to look forward to our holiday. I didn't want to pass your house without permitting myself the luxury of talking about other people's affairs. It seems they're to be public.'

'Have you spent the night in Denbury Road?' I asked.

'Not quite; but it feels like it. Anyway, it's been to no purpose. She's gone.'

'We know about it,' I said. 'A letter from Juliet to us arrived this morning. Apparently her parents heard too.'

'Oh, Juliet,' said Father Morris. 'Yes, she's gone. I'm not worried about her. It's her mother that worries me. She left half an hour ago.'

'Mrs Macready?'

'Yes. I thought you must have understood what was going on. She told her husband a long time ago that she would stay with him for Juliet's sake. Now she sees no need to stay longer.'

'But she's his wife!'

'Forgive me, Michael, for saying that you are starting at a comparatively early stage in a train of argument with which I have become sadly familiar. Ethel Macready has taken me through it and defeated me at every stage. She is a Christian woman, and not at all the mouse she appears. I would call her very able, and very strong-minded. She has come to the conclusion that she has discharged her duty to her husband, and she looks forward to retirement rather as I am looking forward to my holiday. The Church, it is true, has in the past set its face against this sort of behaviour. It asks couples to promise to remain with each other as long as they both shall live; but it does also ask them to love and honour each other, and after twenty-five years Ethel has come to the conclusion that she has neither been loved nor honoured. Even if this does not relieve her of her promise, she asks, how can the Church possibly expect her to love and honour a man for whose business and personal standards she has come to feel nothing but contempt?'

'God does.'

'You're learning, Michael. Her reply to that is that God does not have to share a house with him in the Denbury Road. It is possible to argue that point in a theological seminary, but I was disinclined to do so under these circumstances. She argues further that a government which manifestly disobeys God's will should be defied. If a government, then certainly a husband. Here again, the point can be argued. Foolishly, perhaps, I had not expected to have to argue it with a woman who knew such a lot about the early Christian Church.'

'Surely,' I protested, 'this must be against everything for which you stand. What about the denial of kindness to Macready? What about the hope that always exists for him? You spoke to me of that only the other day.'

Father Morris looked distinctly haggard. 'I don't know,' he said. 'I have persuaded her that she must return to her husband if he changes himself, though she says quite honestly she does not believe he will do so. She will not continue bolstering up his opinion of himself, and she believes her departure can only be for his good in the long run. That means, of course, that she wishes to believe so; nevertheless, I have to be honest myself. When the Church first began to speak of "irretrievable breakdown" in connection with marriages I was hostile and angry. I have come to feel the need for more thought on the subject; not less after hearing the calm and logical words of that remarkable woman.'

I looked at Tiggy. 'See you in the divorce court,' I said.

She disregarded me. 'Why do parsons make everything so difficult?' she demanded. 'Of course poor Mrs Macready can't stay with that man. He'll have to make do with bullying the daily; and if she won't put up with it, he'll have to look after himself, or starve.'

Father Morris, looking if possible more haggard, plunged his nose in his coffee mug. 'Oh, dear!' said a hollow noise from inside it.

'Macready must have been very sure about what was going to happen when he read that lesson,' I said thoughtfully.

'Not necessarily,' said the priest, draining his coffee, and standing up. 'It could be thought of as a final act of public bullying, an attempt to bring the universe to heel. At any rate, he tells me he wants the whole town to know his position. He is confident that the rightness of his cause will be apparent to all.'

He stood in thought for a moment. 'What's more,' he added; 'in a sense it will be. He will be here, and his wife will not. Of course his dignity will suffer; but he has found a part he can play to his own satisfaction. The town will accept this.'

'Where has Mrs Macready gone?' I asked.

'There is a brother in the Lake District. I shall call in and see her when we drive up there for our holiday.'

'And where will Juliet stand?'

'She is old enough not to have to take sides.' As he left the house, he said to me, almost mechanically 'Be kind to the man. There really is always hope.'

I quoted this to Tiggy when he was gone. 'Not for the first time,' I said, 'I don't understand. What is this kindness we are supposed to show? If it is kind of his wife to leave him after twenty-five years, perhaps it would be kind of us to hurl abuse at him as he weeds his garden, or take pot shots at him with a catapult as he passes our balcony.'

Tiggy frowned. 'Father Morris is very tired,' she said. 'But he's right. We must do what we can.'

All in all, it was that sort of summer. Every time I thought I understood something it transformed itself like Proteus. Towle, the evil genius, had turned into Alfred, the heartbroken pet. Mrs Macready, the mouse, had bared her fangs, out-argued Father Morris, and defeated the lion, her husband. It was enough to make a man think again about himself.

'Darling,' I said, 'I believe it may be time we moved from the hurly-burly of a country town into some quiet backwater. Piccadilly Circus, for example.'

'Well,' said Antigone, looking interested, 'seriously, why not?'

X - A VISIT TO LONDON

I sat in a crowded railway compartment, wondering if I had a headache. No one seemed to be occupying themselves except in sitting and rocking, pretending not to watch everybody else sitting and rocking. A child snoozed against its mother, breathing heavily, as if it had a nasty cold.

Travelling made me feel as if pits were opening all round me. into one of which I was bound sooner or later to fall. The noise of the train revived my love of quiet, and of an ordered world. New surroundings and events tended to drag me back into a past I preferred not to think about, because it contrasted so strongly with the present. In those days travel had seemed a happy adventure. I sat in memory on a Mediterranean country bus, sharing a double seat with an enormous peasant woman, swathed in a shawl and accompanied by a bony son, two upside-down chickens, and a basket of fish. Now and again a great Greek hand patted me from behind, in case I felt lonely. Desperately I hauled my thoughts back to the present, as the sliding doors of the compartment opened, and a coy little man stuck his head in.

'Room for a little one?' he enquired.

Silently, we all shifted except the mother and child, and the little one fitted himself in beside me.

'They resented me asking in the next compartment,' said the man to the mother. 'Resented me. They've no business. I told the ticket collector.'

The child drew a sighing breath and bubbled from the nose. A spasm crossed the coy man's features.

'Got a cold, has he?' he enquired. 'Poor lad.'

'I think he's running a temperature,' said the mother gloomily,

Everyone avoided everyone else's gaze, and watched the autumnal suburbs streaking by. Our pace slackened, and bastions of dirty brick began to appear along the side of the line, plentifully supplied with niches suitable for pantheons of Victorian railway gods.

We drew into the terminus, the train's note quietening to a hollow rumble under the great canopy of the roof. My interview was at two-thirty on the other side of London. I planned to have a snack at this terminus before setting out by Tube.

I limped round the selection of bars, buffets, trolleys and automatic machines, feeling lost and aimless among purposeful humanity, which trotted and dodged round me, harried by a distorted voice from amplifiers. I definitely had a headache.

Selecting the less crammed of the buffets, I went in and found myself in a great multitude, some sitting with plates on their knees worriedly eyeing their baggage on the table, some standing at stalls like horses, blankly champing rolls and reading midday editions of the news. The static queue at the self-service counter contemplated the problems they would have to solve when their turn came. No one was at the cash desk, a fact which seemed to exasperate the West Indian girl at the hot drinks counter more than it did the customers.

Eventually, the cashier edged her way back, and the queue began to move. I selected a cheese sandwich and an apple, and seeing a notice offering soup asked the West Indian girl for some. She rolled her eyes. 'Dunno why dey put soup,' she said. 'Dere ain't no soup here.' Settling for coffee, I moved towards the cashier and offered a pound note. 'I can't do it, dear. I got no change.' Rummaging in my pocket, I found the right sum. 'Oh, you've got it, have you?' It was a confirmation of her view of humanity.

The cheese sandwich was tasteless, and the skin of the apple was like the arm of a club sofa; but the coffee was all right. I was a long way from home.

Sitting in the Tube on the last stage of the journey I felt my head aching rhythmically and wondered if Brink had somehow institutionalised me, so that I would never be able to live outside it.

Victoria hit me physically as I emerged from the subway. Traffic was flooding past the Victoria Palace, buses were roaring out of the terminus, taxi-drivers were shouting to each other, and even the khaki sky was roaring with jet aircraft. I began to feel frightened, and ill in the pit of my stomach. Slowly I dragged my body away from the station and towards Hyde Park Corner. My destination was not far - a terrace house facing towards Buckingham Palace garden. I dived gratefully into it out of the noise, and asked the girl at the desk for Mr Lederer. A message was waiting for me to say he would be half an hour late.

She was sweet, the girl at the desk, with kind eyes, and fair hair resting on her shoulder like Juliet's. I settled gratefully in the armchair she gave me, rested my head, and closed my eyes. Juliet was living in all this, not far from this place; but she would be out at her job, whatever it was. We had heard twice from her lately, and gathered she had joined the throng of London's temporary secretaries.

Her father had not ceased to proclaim his principles and, as Father Morris had forecast, Brink had accepted the situation. Mrs Macready had not been well known, whereas her husband was a sort of landmark. Since nothing had been concealed, there was nothing to gossip about for long.

Juliet was terribly shaken and worried, and was taking time to grow used to what had happened. She knew she was the occasion, if not the cause, of her parents' separation. At least her living in Brink had kept them together; but since living with her father was something she herself had been unable to accept, it was logically difficult for her to condemn her mother for taking similar action. Offspring do not think logically, and she found she blamed her mother very greatly indeed. Whatever marriage means to the old, the young regard it extremely seriously. Cynics may say that this is why so many of them decline to embark on it; and in this case cynics may be right. At any rate, one sets very high standards for one's parents.

Though she had kept in touch with her mother, Juliet had not visited her nor discussed matters in any detail with her. She had written a second letter to her father, to reassure him about herself, but not to tell him where she was living.

It was somewhere not far from where I sat now, gradually regaining my composure. The throbbing in my head had eased, and when the girl moved me upstairs to Mr Lederer's office and gave me a cup of coffee, I was able to look calmly out over London and think with more detachment of the thousands of humans who lived and worked there. Loneliness like Towle's, disharmony like that of the Macreadys, all the big and little problems of Brink were multiplied over an area where cohesion was precarious, where the Church touched only the edges, where the school children were packed into vast complexes under constantly changing staff who did not even know each other. In the bus, the office, the classroom, the flat, order, stability, even contentment might prevail: but they were part of no timeless pattern, threatened by change, by landlord, employer, union, bully, crook, subversive group.

The trees in the squares were just turning yellow, fighting to assert the balance of nature in this barren place. Before the Macreadys had moved to Brink, Juliet had been brought up here; now she had voluntarily moved back. Could human beings retain their natural balance, preserved in smaller, kindlier communities?

'Good afternoon, Mr Jeffries,' said a pleasant voice. 'I'm sorry to be so late. Has Jennifer looked after you?'

I rose and shook hands with Mr Lederer. He was dark, spare, and hollow-cheeked, leisurely in a way I had not expected.

'She's done me proud,' I said.

'Good. I'm very lucky to have her here. Most girls these days spend their time on thinking about their time off; but Jennifer is the daughter of an old friend, who was rector of the parish where I was born.'

We sat down, and he asked me if I liked the view over London.

'To be honest,' I said, 'I've been wondering how anybody survives.'

'One way is to live as I do in the place where I was brought up, and to spend a lot of money on travelling. I have a flat above here, but that's just a game. To live where you are compelled to live can be a terrible fate; yet what a lot of people are condemned to it. Suburbs are concentrations of reluctant residents, not so unlike Buchenwald. Buchenwald had more immediately shocking results, but the suburbs can shock too. Don't ever live in a suburb, Mr Jeffries.'

'The present suggestion is that I should live in Cambridge. Most people seem to enjoy that.'

'Mr Temple certainly does.'

Mr Temple was my father-in-law's friend, who managed to perform a great variety of functions in Cambridge. We discussed the idea in which he had interested Mr Lederer's firm. Among the flourishing university bookshops was room for a shop, or rather a section of a shop, which could resist the current pressure towards a fast turnover of new textbooks and paperbacks, and concentrate on rare books, incunabula, and special presentations, together with the most modern methods of photocopying. Mr Lederer admitted frankly that the firm's interest was mostly in the larger section of the shop which would compete more effectively with the new-book trade than any existing firm; but it obviously gave him pleasure to think that he was helping to restore a scholarly image to a city that was in danger of losing it. It happened that my training and experience since I left the Army had done much to fit me for running the more scholarly side of things. I was also one of those Army officers, now perhaps commoner, who had acquired an arts degree before serving.

The interview was more like a pleasant chat, and I sensed that the final decision about me would be left to Mr Temple. After half an hour, Mr Lederer rang his bell.

'Can Jennifer run you anywhere?' he asked.

'It's very kind,' I said; 'but I need only to visit a supplier in St James before catching a Tube. A walk in the Park will do me good.'

At that hour of the afternoon, the traffic was only just beginning to build up again. I walked past the Palace into St James's Park. The grimy lake was full of birds, some at the edge hoping to be fed, some paddling about dredging up titbits. From the centre of the bridge the stink was almost toxic. It seemed shameful to cut the wings of these beautiful creatures so that they could live in so mucky a Paradise. The human moral was clear enough. I shivered, and passed on across the Mall and through St James's Square to the peace of my favourite suppliers. No one else ever seemed to visit them, and I had my purchases finished in a pleasant half hour.

When I came out of the shop, the volume of the traffic noise had changed. It was bursting and flooding through the cracks from Piccadilly. The single taxis that are normally to be seen driving along Jermyn Street were now in twos and threes, all in a hurry, all driving a little faster than seemed safe. As I walked up to Piccadilly I could feel my stomach tightening again, and the throb behind my eyes centred on that sore spot in my head. When I stepped on to the Piccadilly pavement it was like a full gale on a sea front in Hell; the noise swept at me before I was ready for it, and threw me physically off balance. My head ached and swam, and I leaned against a wall and shut my eyes until I could recover.

Piccadilly Tube station was fifty yards off, somewhere in the worst of the clamour, the highest concentration of carbon monoxide I turned towards it, put a finger in my left ear, and tried to walk; but my legs were not obeying me. My body seemed to disconnect itself from them and fall away, my shoulder hitting the wall again. After a moment I transferred my packages to my left side and began to feel my way along, supporting myself with the palm of my hand wherever I could. Slowly, against wall and plate glass window, I felt my legs moving one past the other and carrying me on. For part of this time I shut my eyes. When I opened them again I saw streams of people swerving to avoid me. No one paused or looked at me directly. It seemed better to concentrate on the texture of the wall or window on which I was leaning. After a long time I found my hand resting on a glass case behind which were pictures of nude girls. There followed the opening of a cinema, across which I had to launch myself as I had across other doorways and gaps. The entrance to the Tube was close now, and I began to feel a conviction that I was going to stay on my feet and survive. As I reached it, a newspaper seller stepped out and said 'Come along, guv.' He took my arm and got me down the first set of stairs. The noise level had dropped, and I began to regain mastery over my legs.

'Thank you,' I said. 'The noise, you see.'

He looked at me undecidedly. 'Can you manage now?'

'In a moment.'

He released my arm, and I squared my shoulders and drew breath. Strength was returning.

'Bit lame,' I said. 'But all right now. Thanks a lot.'

He patted me and nodded. 'See a doctor when you get home,' he said.

The rest of the London journey was dream-like, but the splitting headache was the worst I had to suffer. At the terminus, I found a train was leaving in ten minutes, bought a bar of chocolate, and boarded it. The smaller compartments were filling up, but the open ones were less popular. I found a four-seater to myself, and felt enormous relief as the whistle blew and we began to slide out of the metropolis. As I put my head back and closed my eyes, the sliding door behind me opened and shut, someone put his baggage on the luggage-rack above my head, and a voice said 'Hullo.'

I opened my eyes and saw Derek Major grinning at me.

'Sorry to disturb your rest,' he said, settling in the opposite seat. 'Don't take any notice of me. Drop off.'

I grinned. 'No. It cheers me to see you. You're a figure from another and better world. Have some chocolate.'

He shook his head. 'I've just had a cup of tea. You look as if you could do with one. Shall I go and explore the buffet car?'

'The chocolate'll keep me going, thanks. The worst is over.'

'Had a bad time?'

His broad shoulders and straightforward manner were what I needed, but instinct told me to be cautious about describing what had happened. 'I've been dragging around London, and hating it. Funny, really; I used to love it.'

'I never think about it,' he said, looking out over the grey roofs detachedly; 'though I've every reason to.'

'Reason?'

'After what London did to my father.' He paused and studied a passing gasworks; then he looked at me. 'Do you know how I've been occupied today?'

'Seeing Juliet?'

'No.'

'Visiting the Law Society? Watching a client sentenced to penal servitude?'

'You're nearer than you know. I've been visiting the nick.'

'Already sentenced, was he?'

'Yes, he was already sentenced. He got five years eighteen months ago, for fraud. Only he's not a client. He's my father.'

'Your father! Oh, that's it, is it?'

'That's what?'

'All the fuss ... or have I got it wrong? Does Juliet's father know about this?'

Derek snorted. 'He should. He and my dad moved in the same circles. One's in prison, one's in the Denbury Road. The City can lead to either.'

'That explains the moral indignation.'

'Mine, or his?'

'Anyway, he hasn't gossiped about it. No one else in Brink knows, as far as I'm aware.'

'My senior partner knows; but after this year in Brink I've stopped feeling it's important to hide it. It certainly doesn't help a solicitor for it to be known his father's in the nick; but it's a fact, and people are getting to know me well enough now. It's up to them.'

'You have a mother, haven't you?'

'Yes. She divorced him and married again. I see her now and again, but not as often as I see Dad. There's a house in Bucks I look after for him; and a cottage in Sussex.'

More pieces of the jigsaw were finding their place. Macready's principles were hardly likely to be satisfied by the son of a criminal and a divorcee. In fairness, I wondered how my own would stand up, if Juliet were my daughter.

'Well,' I said, 'this won't go on for ever. Five years isn't really five years, they tell me.'

'True enough,' he said; 'not with maximum remission. On the other hand, life doesn't go on for ever, either.'

'She's only twenty-one,' I reminded him, seeing the point.

Derek looked at me, and smiled broadly. He was a likeable chap, even if he did look as if he had just emerged from a set scrum. If I were Juliet, I thought, with the wreck of a home behind me, and an uncertainty about myself, I could easily turn to someone as solid.

We settled back into our seats, and watched suburbia stream by

'It'll sort itself out,' said Derek comfortably. 'With my background, I haven't much to offer at the moment.'

That was true. Even if they delayed their wedding until Mr Major was back in circulation, Derek would be supported at the ceremony by a motley crew. Even the strongest-looking of us found the sands shifting under our lives. As for the weakest ... a lame refugee from the Army, matched with a Spartan-reared orphan, had no cause to look down on a couple like Derek and Juliet. 'My strength,' I thought sleepily, 'is made perfect in weakness.' No one, not even the most dignified and leonine of citizens, was more than a child whimpering for company in the darkness. It was just that some children did not seem to possess the sense to be frightened.

I closed my eyes on suburbia, and slept the sleep of relief at leaving London. When I woke, the shadows were falling over the Midland fields, and I felt the joy of being back in my own country.

XI - AN EVENING AT FIFIELD

A few months make all the difference, I thought. The book was in beautiful condition, with a well-preserved leather cover, and the title page was indistinguishable from that of the first edition; all but the date, 1601. That was what showed it to be an inferior copy, printed on the Continent, and full of blunders.

I shook my head, and returned the book to the open shelf. A few pounds would cover its value, even though the earlier edition would make a heavy type entry in any catalogue. A few months - nine months it was - made all the difference. A few months in a book's life, a few moments in a man's life; these were what signified in the intricate web of events. I blocked off the road my memory was travelling, and wondered what part that experience in London was destined to play, what significance it had. I had mentioned nothing of it to Antigone, or to anyone else.

The main Fifield library was filling with the thick evening gloom of autumn, and the tall cases were shutting out the remaining light that managed to leak in through the leaded windows. Outside, the steady rush and drip of rain had been audible since we arrived. Antigone was sitting in the librarian's room, being given sherry by Bone, who was in future to be called Richard. He and I were to transact our business before we all went out to dinner.

Richard came into the room, apologised, and switched the light on. His lean features shone with pleasure at the prospect of a civilised evening. All his gentleness was foremost, and he was in a reminiscent mood.

'Monsoon weather,' he said. 'Did you ever get to the Far East?'

I shook my head. 'Never east of ...' I had difficulty in saying it, and started again. 'Never east of Cyprus. Sorry, frog in my throat. You were in India, weren't you?'

'I was a tea planter; or rather a tea planter's assistant, in South India. At one time I thought all my life would be spent keeping back those great jungles in the Western Ghats. In the event it looks like being spent within the space of a few hundred square feet, here in the middle of England. I'll never forget that endless pouring rain, though.'

'What brought you back?'

'Partly health, and partly loneliness. I need my western culture.'

We got down to business, mindful that Antigone was waiting for us. She had been allowed the run of the archives, and was eventually found happily sipping her sherry over an ancient edition of Plutarch.

'Before we go to dinner,' said Richard, 'I wonder if you would enjoy a look round the Castle.'

'If his Lordship doesn't mind,' I said.

'Far from it. He would like to meet you. I've shown him your work.'

The Castle itself was cold and unmemorable, with a few good paintings striving to be comfortable beneath the mullioned frown of the Victorian Gothic windows. Lord Fifield himself was the memorable part of the tour. He was a small, blue-eyed, twinkling man with an immense courtesy, who seemed completely briefed about me.

'I'm not very good at books and things, you see,' he said. 'I'm more of an outdoor sort of chap; but I know good work when I see it, and I don't need Richard to tell me what a marvellous craftsman you are.

'What's more,' he continued, patting Antigone's hand, 'your taste in girls is as good as your taste in bindin's. It's a pleasure to meet you m'dear.'

I glanced at Richard Bone, mindful of the stern check I had seen him give his master; but he was all smiles, content to call a truce while he was off his special territory.

'I tell you, Jeffries, for all I prefer huntin', I'm proud of m'library - yes, and of m'librarian. I hope you'll go on helpin' us with it. I believe you were in the Army, weren't you?'

I nodded.

'Had a spell in it m'self; before your time, though. Still go to Twickenham once a year. Just to see m'friends, you understand, not because I care for these ball games. Did you play rugby football?'

'Not much,' I said. 'I was never any good at ball games, either.'

Lord Fifield grunted approvingly. 'No sense in 'em. They did their best with me at Eton, but I never could see the point of chasin' after a ball when you could chase after a fox. Now tell me, do you know anythin' about fishin'?'

'A bit,' I said.

'Then listen. Next time you come over, bring your rod, and put a fly or two on my river. At the same time, tell me why the fish are so sluggish. That water doesn't look right to me, and no one can explain why.'

'I'll do my best,' I said; 'and it's very kind of you to ask me.'

'No one else'll fish it if you don't,' said the old boy. He turned to Antigone. 'Now, m'dear, I expect you'd rather be havin' your dinner than listenin' to me. It's good of you to come and cheer the house up. It takes a bit of rennin' these days, but there are one or two pretty things in it. I hope you'll come again, and make another.'

'Your effect on the senior citizens,' I told Antigone as we left, 'is explosive. Is he another nasty old man?'

'He's a very nice old man,' she said firmly.

The rain had washed the sky and gone, so we walked the short distance between the Castle and the pub, and were shown into a private room, where an oak table was set with gleaming cutlery and glasses. The landlord had come out from behind the bar to welcome us. 'I think it's all as you like it, Mr Bone,' he said. 'I decanted the burgundy half an hour ago. I'll have to go back to the bar tonight, but the wife will look after you.'

He looked anxiously at Richard, then, seeing his happy and approving state, he relaxed and grinned at Antigone as he fitted her into a seat. The landlord's wife bustled out of the kitchen and took over from him, cooing over Richard as though he were a long-lost son.

'Mrs Merridew is from Yorkshire,' he said by way of explanation. 'She enjoys cooking beef and I enjoy eating it; so we get on well, don't we, Mrs Merridew?'

Mrs Merridew beamed and trotted back to her kitchen, from which a girl emerged with a tray. She was a thin girl in her teens, with long black hair and a spotless overall. The task of crossing a few feet, balancing three portions of soup, while being watched by three hungry pairs of eyes, obviously stretched her abilities to the utmost, and she stopped halfway and gave an odd sob. Richard Bone hastily sat back in his chair, and began a conversation.

'I am having trouble with a friend of yours,' he said. 'An untidy but educated parson.'

'Father Morris,' I said. 'Be gentle with him.'

I saw out of the corner of my eye that the girl had weighed anchor and resumed her journey.

'Gentle!' said Richard. 'That's all very well, but he's trying to relieve me of one of my greatest treasures.'

'*The History of Brink 1550-1850.*'

'Precisely. Bought by me on behalf of Lord Fifield three years ago.'

The soup had now arrived, and was being placed in front of us with tremulous care.

'Good evening,' said Richard to the girl as she gave him the last plate. She jumped like a jerboa, and gave that strangled sob again; then she seized her tray and hurried off, heaving.

'She's living on her nerves,' said Richard. 'I wonder who she is.'

'Bought by you?' I said.

'Eh? I haven't bought her. Oh, you mean the book. Yes, bought by me.'

'From Father Falkner?'

'Yes. First he lent it me, then he said I could keep it, if I made a substantial gift to the parish. I did; or rather Lord Fifield did.'

'Oh, dear!'

'Why "Oh, dear"?'

'I didn't know any money had passed.'

Richard looked at me impassively. 'No doubt the Archdeacon knew. No doubt the income will be shown on the parish accounts.'

'No doubt both those things ought to be so; but no doubt they're not.'

'Dear, dear, dear! Odd standards some of these parsons have. I wonder what he did with the money.'

'I can tell you what he didn't do with it, and that's spend it on himself. He was a good man, something of a saint. He'll probably have used it to help one or two old people to get through the winter without freezing.'

'A book, or a couple of tons of coal. It's funny, isn't it, how topsy-turvy values sound when you equate them like that. How many sports cars to a Shakespeare First Folio? How many loaves of bread to a paperback?'

'Or, as Father Falkner used to say, the average Christian gives the price of half a pint of beer to the Church each week. Anyway, it's Father Morris you're dealing with now. What does he say about it?'

Richard smiled thoughtfully. 'He's a wild man, that. Let's talk about something else. How do you like the soup?'

'You're torturing him,' said Antigone; 'but it's very good.'

'I like eating here,' he said. 'It's English, somehow. Think of the dingy acres of cloth in restaurants up and down the country at this moment: the perfunctory hotel meals, the bored waitresses, the wine waiters who know as little now about wine as they did in the days when the shabby wine list was young.'

'That sort of place is dying,' said Antigone. 'It's all what's called Good Food, now.'

'Ah, yes,' said Richard. 'Good Food. The chuckle of frying scampi while you struggle not to knock over your hock glass with a menu bigger than that 1623 Shakespeare. Cruel head waiters beckoning trays of instruments so that they can torture ropes of spaghetti over a slow flame. Give me the Merridews, and their terrified girl.'

The girl appeared on cue, and removed our soup plates. Then she helped Mrs Merridew bring in the freshly sliced roast beef and all its concomitants. Mrs Merridew's face was red but ecstatic as she served this wonderful food to her favourite client and his friends. When she went back to the kitchen, the girl began to serve the vegetables.

'I haven't seen you here before, have I?' Richard asked.

The child twitched convulsively, and managed to shake her head. 'What's your name?'

Her face went blank, as if she had met an ordeal quite beyond her capacity. Then she put the potatoes down, and gave **a** short, dry cough, twice, like a dog with a bone in his throat. Finally she burst into peals of laughter and ran from the room, passing Mrs Merridew on the way back.

'Oh, my!' said her mistress; 'Elaine's got her giggles again. I'm so sorry, Mr Bone. She's not a bad girl, but you can't look at her without giving her the spasms. Everything she does on her own she does well, but company just puts her out. A pub's no place for her, I'm afraid. She's all strung up.'

'Elaine?' said Richard. 'Is that Elaine Fraser?'

'That's right, Mr Bone. Mrs Fraser's girl. She never had a father to teach her a bit of sense.'

Richard looked at me. 'Do you recognise the name?'

'Fraser?' I said. 'That was Towle's landlady, wasn't it?'

'Mr Towle used to lodge there,' said Mrs Merridew, helping us to vegetables. 'If she giggled at him as she giggles at people here, he must have been glad to move. By all accounts, Mrs Fraser wouldn't hear of it being Elaine's fault.'

'Thank you, Mrs Merridew,' said Richard. 'If you'd leave the vegetables, and give me the decanter off the side, we'll manage the rest. You've surpassed yourself.'

Mrs Merridew retired, and we set about a meal of beef and burgundy that will always remain in my memory.

'She's a gem,' said Richard; 'but we mustn't let her tattle.'

'Of course not,' I said. 'Even so, she's given me a new view of the Towle affair.'

But Richard could not forgive the borrowing of his reference work. 'You'll see,' he said. 'It'll be prison in the end. Have you seen anything of the gentleman?'

As a matter of fact, in the weeks since Juliet left, Towle had completely altered his way of life. Apart from an occasional afternoon walk, or a spin in the car which a repentant Fred had now found for him, he had stayed indoors, and to judge from the constant rattle of typing that proceeded from the Thatched Cottage, was well into his projected book. We occasionally passed the time of day, but there were no more long conversations.

Richard cheered up slightly at the prospect of a scholarly work from a local resident. 'Well, well,' he said expansively, 'if it's a good one, I'll forgive him.'

Over coffee and brandy I looked at my watch. 'We ought to be off soon,' I said. 'The last bus goes in twenty minutes.'

'Nonsense,' said Richard. 'There's lots more to talk about. I'll run you over to Brink later. I still have to pack up the work for you, and my car's handily parked at the Castle.'

'I've been trying to work out,' said Antigone, 'why Michael has always been a bit frightened of you. I can't understand it.'

Richard frowned thoughtfully. 'I do like everything so-so. I don't give people the benefit of the doubt until I know them; and I don't expect them to make exceptions in their own favour; which a man does who sees on a book "For reference only - not to be removed from the library" and then removes it. Adam and Eve did just that. They had access to all the volumes on earth but one; and that was the one they wanted. The punishment was obvious and right.'

'But surely,' said Antigone, 'we all behave like that. I do, you do. And we all have to live with each other's behaviour. Myself, I'm always disregarding notices, not because I care about doing what they say I mustn't, but because people put up too many notices. Did it matter so much that your book shouldn't be taken out of the library?'

'Does it matter if some trinket you wear once a year is taken out of your room without your permission? It's not worth much; you don't need it; yet you would be very angry if a friend borrowed it without telling you. Our world is coming to an end because people cannot see that bewildered obedience is a sort of love. No rule seems sensible when it is closely scrutinized; the merit lies not in disobeying as many silly rules as possible, but in obeying them. I've always thought that the Fruit of the Tree was nothing in itself. It had no magical power; it probably tasted thoroughly nasty; it just stood for all the silly rules men and women were going to have to obey; it was the ultimate test of love. When Adam and Eve ate the fruit, their eyes were open to a world pointless without the glorious stupidity of love. Now they saw their bodies on the same level as that meaningless fruit. What had been a shape full of wonder and rapture was just a paunchy, fleshy mess, replete with the meaninglessness they had brought into the world.'

Antigone looked at him steadily. 'Is that why you are a bachelor?' she asked.

Richard did not flinch. 'You under-estimate the work of redemption, which gives us back the beauty of the earth.

'Anyway,' he added with dignity, 'I am not a confirmed bachelor. Not after tonight.'

Antigone gave him a dazzling smile. 'Thank you; but I still think books are different. They're anybody's game.'

'So people say. So your last Vicar said to himself, no doubt, when he sold me a book he knew he should have sought authority to sell. So your new Vicar implies when he tries to recover it. Do you wonder I frighten some people?'

'Oh, poor Father Morris!'

'Poor, do you think? He's rich intellectually, and he has a lovely parish. Do you know him well?'

'Michael's one of his P.C.C. They see a lot of each other. We're very fond of him.'

Richard looked at Antigone over his brandy, and meditated. 'Mm,' he said. 'I expect he's very fond of you.'

'When are you going to come over and see us?' she asked.

'When do you suggest?'

'Soon; because we don't really know how long ... Michael, have you told him anything about ...?'

'No,' I said; 'but carry on.'

'You see,' she continued, 'Michael's wondering whether to make a move.'

'Far?'

'Cambridge? Well, it's not so very far; but it would mean an end to the bookbinding, wouldn't it, darling?'

'I don't know. It might. The rare book side of it would interest Richard, though.'

'A book business, would it be?' he asked.

'Yes. I had a letter this morning asking me to come over early next week and look at the possibilities.'

'Oh, dear,' said Richard; 'I don't much like change. Isn't it enough to make beautiful things?'

'I was a very active and involved person once,' I said. 'I got blown up in the Army, and I needed a spell of quiet. Now I've had it, there's no excuse for not returning to the fray.'

'What fray is this?'

'I suppose it's a sort of general fight to survive. If I just bind a few books and live on a disability pension I'm being a drag on everybody else.'

'Any artist can say that; but somehow we seem to accept that they play their part. What's the point of straining yourself to make it easier for everyone else to strain themselves?'

'It's a question of finding your capacity. You tried tea-planting, and found libraries. I've tried the Army, and I've found bookbinding; but I don't know whether that's my full capacity.

Richard smiled. 'Well,' he said; 'my motives are selfish, I expect. I need my friends.'

We went back up the hill through a clear autumn night, and waited while Richard made up a parcel of books. Then he drove us back home, and deposited the parcel in our hall.

'Now I shall know where to come,' he said. 'Selfish I may be, but I still hope you stay here.'

When I opened the parcel of books in the morning, the first thing I saw was *The History of Brink 1550-1850*.

XII - The Leaking Dam

I had said nothing to Antigone about my trouble in Piccadilly. Even so, and for all my determination not to look backwards, I knew that somewhere in me was a dam I had built against the past, and that it was beginning to leak. Antigone had done her job well. The excitement of love and marriage, the settling down to our life in Brink, secure in all respects, even, at a pinch, financially; all this had relieved me of any need to look back and assess. I was trying to live like a character in a film, seen for the first time as a grown man walking along a road, with no existence before that moment. Men are not characters in films, and at some point I had to realise it. Antigone, in her wisdom, was on the lookout. She knew that any step I took outside Brink was attended with danger, and that insecurity meant pain which, like any pain, might mean damage and might mean healing. She saw how I behaved when I returned from London. She knew I was beginning to lie awake at night, with trivialities running in my mind, and she guessed that something in me was fighting to stop my thoughts drifting backwards.

Most of us build dams against our selves. Many a man who supports religion, conformity, and modesty is reinforcing a dam against what he has seen of his own selfishness, rebelliousness, and ostentation. Only, perhaps, in moments of weariness, frustration, insecurity, do his inner tides show their power. Aunt Ada Doom, who saw something nasty in the woodshed, had really seen something nasty in herself. Her cure, a trip to Paris, enshrines a great truth. It sounds simple and immoral to say that the cure for lust is marriage, though the Prayer Book says something very like it; or that the cure for covetousness is acquisition, or the cure for hatred physical violence; but each statement has a germ of this great truth. As Blake put it, it is better to murder a baby in its cradle than to nurse unacted desires. The last way to self-understanding is for a man to turn his back on his true nature; and unless we understand ourselves we are comprehensively lost.

As every man has his own nature, so every man has his own past. A man with a past he cannot bear is not so different from a man with a lust he cannot bear. Sometimes the one proceeds from the other.

Myself, I believe help, or grace, as the Church calls it, was coming to me all through those years in Brink. It came in many ways: partly through the wisdom of Dr Hardman and his daughter, partly through my discovery of the Church, and those two successive Vicars, and partly through events. At any rate, the process of breaking down the dam I had built was being made possible. The pain of the final breaking was still to come, and it perhaps inevitably depended more on providence, the grace of events, than on human guidance. One listens so little, and so imperfectly, to words.

The last significant words I can remember were spoken on the night after our dinner at Fifield. On that night Father Morris presided over a meeting of the P.C.C. Knowing he was in the habit of arriving early at the Parish Hall, I too went early, and found him kneeling in prayer at his table. I slipped the *History of Brink* in front of him and retired to my seat. A few moments later he raised his head, saw what I had brought, and exclaimed with pleasure.

'I must spend more time on my knees,' he said, 'and less talking to stiff-necked librarians. But I really am grateful to you, Michael.' He scrambled to his feet, seized the book, and did a little dance. 'I never thought the man listened to a word I said.'

'Thank Antigone,' I said. 'She made a conquest.'

'Talk about the dry stick blossoming.'

'Are you referring to my wife?'

'No, your friend.'

I laughed. 'He's not so dry. I shouldn't be surprised if we got him married off yet. Did you have a good holiday?'

'Fine. Can you spare a minute afterwards?'

'Not if you preach us a sermon on every item.'

'All right. We'll form a few sub-committees and get off early.'

Despite the condition of the church's roof, the noise from the organ, the critical state of inter-denominational relations, and the lamentable breakdown of the grass-cutting contract for the churchyard, we were through in seventy-five minutes flat. Afterwards, Father Morris carved his way through the bruised P.C.C., patting each member as he passed, seized my arm, and steered me off to the Vicarage.

'What a prodigious waste of God's good time!' he said. 'Now tell me, Michael, what sum have I to disgorge for the relief of having that book to show the Archdeacon?'

'No sum has been mentioned, and I recommend you merely to write and say thank you. Assume that any financial loss has been suffered by Lord Fifield.'

'Well, I must call in and tell Antigone she is good as well as beautiful.'

'As a matter of fact, Michael,' he added as we entered his study, 'we are able to celebrate appropriately. There is a malt whisky here, smuggled over the border from Scotland, on which I should like your opinion.' He burrowed in a cupboard among what looked like a miscellany of Mass books and dirty collars, and produced a bottle with two glasses.

'Did you manage to call on Mrs Macready?' I asked when we were settled.

'Yes, I did. She looked extremely well, very happy, and quite unrepentant. I wondered if she'd be worried about Juliet, but not a bit of it. She feels disapproved of, but believes time will heal matters there.'

'What do you believe time will do?'

Father Morris sighed. 'The human forecast is that John Macready will remain as he is, and Ethel as she is. Both are in stable positions that they can sustain. Juliet's position is less stable. She may return to her father. Of course, what God wants and will bring about in all this is quite another matter.'

'You think Juliet will come back, do you?'

'It seems likely.'

'And what does the human forecast say about Derek Major?'

'Only that Juliet's father will find it difficult to object to him much longer.'

'So wedding bells ring?'

'Maybe. I don't know. It's not for me to make that sort of prophecy. God knows what he wants and will bring about. What about yourself?'

'Me? I'm not a candidate for Juliet. I married the brunette.'

'But where are you going to take the brunette? Will you go to Cambridge?'

'I'm going to see about it next week. I went up to London for a sort of interview when you were on holiday.'

Father Morris bent forward, swirling the whisky in his glass.

'Michael, I believe I once said you were to remember me if the going was hard.'

'That's right. You did.'

'How's the going?'

'It's all right.'

'Are you sure? I don't know much of your earlier past except that you were an Army officer and trod on a mine ...'

'Drove on one, actually.'

'Drove on one, then. I do know you are a highly sensitive person, living a more retired life than is normal at your age. Now suddenly, I find you planning to launch out into some sort of commerce. It must be a big step for you, and a very exciting one; but even allowing for that, you're not looking well to me. Is there anything I can do to help?'

'Such as?'

'Anything. Anything. Is it a good thing you're doing?'

'I don't know. I haven't seen it yet.'

'Is Antigone in favour of a move?'

'Yes.'

Something I had said about not being a candidate for Juliet had stirred a memory, which was worrying at me as I spoke. I felt hot in that study, and my thoughts and words were drifting apart. The whisky, instead of relaxing me, had muddled me and stirred me up.

'I'm not very good with traffic,' I said.

Father Morris was looking at me intently.

'It would be all right,' I continued, 'if it weren't for the noise.' I paused.

'London?' prompted the priest.

'Only Piccadilly. It was all right when I got down the Tube. Really it was. Nothing to bother about.'

Father Morris sat back as though he had what he wanted, but was uncertain how to proceed. Then he said 'Have you told Antigone?'

'She'd only worry.'

'Can you tell me?'

'It all hit me - the noise I mean. It was difficult to walk.'

'Symptoms?'

'A splitting headache.'

'Have you seen a doctor?'

'No. I don't have to visit Piccadilly in the rush hour.'

'You ought to see a doctor.'

'Churston would treat me for a headache by amputating my head.'

Our senior local doctor had not developed a gift for subtleties in forty years of practice.

'The headache probably isn't important. Can't you see Cook?'

'I suppose I could. Churston goes shooting every Wednesday, and leaves Cook to do the surgery.'

'Will you? Next Wednesday?'

'Very well; but what am I to say to Antigone?'

'I doubt if you need say much. Just tell her what you told me.'

My head was clearing, and I wondered why Father Morris was watching me so intently.

'I'm perfectly all right,' I insisted.

'Not many men can say that.'

'Not spiritually; but physically I'm all right.'

'Some Christians find that a non-sequitur.'

'There's precious little spiritual dimension to having your leg blown off by a mine. Well, badly smashed, anyway: but the quacks fixed it up in the end. I was to lead a quiet life, until I felt ready to cope again. I feel ready.'

'Do you, now? I'd love to hear more about your life in the Army.'

'It's all in the past. I don't think about it any more.'

'Don't you keep up with friends?'

'Not really. There was one special one, but he's not a letter writer; and he's been abroad for years. My Colonel's a sort of relation, and he's in Germany somewhere. We write at Christmas.'

'You were saying there wasn't much spiritual dimension to having your leg blown off by a mine. You know, I think that would depend on the circumstances. I had a friend once who insisted all physical illness was of mental origin. Someone asked him how that applied to a child run over by a bus, and he disappointed me by saying it was a case of mental illness on the bus-driver's part. That seemed to be cheating. After all, it was the child who suffered. He could have said - and remembering a conversation we had once I should have been interested if he had said - that the accident arose from the child's need to attract attention.'

'You don't drive over a mine to attract attention.'

'No? Perhaps not, if you put it like that. But I don't think I can accept the event as real when you put it in those simple terms. There were other events that led up to it, and more that followed it; plus much talk mixed in. It was you who said that we lived life at one level, and talked about it at another.'

'You're pressing me hard.'

'Am I? Pressing on what?'

The telephone rang. Father Morris looked disappointed as he received a message. 'It's Antigone,' he said. 'Message: she has a queue of people to see you. Can you come before they start fighting?'

I drained the whisky and stood up.

'I'd like to pursue this some time,' said Father Morris. 'Meanwhile do as I said; and take care of yourself.'

There were lights shining all over our house as I let myself in The kitchen being the nearest, I walked in. Towle was sitting at the table, writing.

'Hullo,' I said. 'Are you waiting for me?'

He nodded, and clumsily stood up, checking the paper on which he had been writing.

'I need a neighbour,' he said, and paused, adding 'We live near each other,' by way of explanation.

'You'd like me to help? In what way?'

'This,' he said, and thrust the paper at me. I saw it was attached to a key.

'Would you like me to keep your key for you?'

He nodded again. 'I am going to Cambridge,' he said. 'For a number of weeks, so that I can use the University Library.'

'College putting you up?'

He nodded yet again.

'I shall be visiting the place myself on Tuesday.'

Towle swallowed, and there was a glint somewhere in the hollow depths of the eyes.

'Lunch,' he said, as if he were regurgitating the word.

'I beg your pardon?'

'Lunch. I should be pleased to give you lunch in my college on Tuesday.'

'That's very kind, but I'm lunching in another college, with my potential employer.'

Towle looked politely interested, but asked no questions.

Tiggy stuck her head inside the kitchen door. 'Oh, there you are,' she said crossly. 'Why didn't you give me a shout?'

'I was doing what came to hand.'

Towle edged towards the door, and appeared to be leaving.

'I'll look after the key,' I said after him. 'Would you like me to do anything more?'

Towle shook his head, thanked me, and departed.

'Why on earth did you leave him down here?' I asked, puzzled.

Tiggy sighed. 'I do my best. I don't imagine he or your girl friend would thank me for throwing them together.'

'Juliet! Is she upstairs?'

'She is, and so's dear Richard. They've been gazing at each other for half an hour or more, and their eyes are all stars. It's a kindness to leave them alone. Richard said he'd missed a book out of your parcel last night, and had brought it over to drop it in but when he saw Juliet he changed his story and insisted on waiting to see you.'

'And she?'

'She's staying the night. She'll explain why later.'

I groaned. 'Surely you could have avoided this. Richard is much too mature for Juliet.'

'Indeed, yes,' said Tiggy sarcastically, stung by my unfairness. 'There must be fourteen years between them.'

I winced, but persisted. 'And what about Derek?'

'My darling, you and I are not the arbiters of other people's fates. I have done and said only what I had to do and say. Things happen as they happen. I did my best to discourage the last man that flung himself at Juliet in my house, but it made not the slightest bit of difference.'

'All right,' I said, making for the stairs; 'but they must be chaperoned.'

Upstairs, Juliet was sitting looking London-y, smart, laughing, and poised, her fair hair tossing and gleaming in the light as she talked. Richard was laughing too, his lean features alert and twinkling. They looked a magnificently handsome couple. I thought of Derek, the incarnation of rugged, easy-going decency, and feared for him. There was no justice in love.

Juliet sprang up and kissed me. 'Michael,' she said; 'forgive me for descending on you.'

'Like a shower of gold,' I said, fired by the moment. 'Zeus must have said something similar to Danae.'

Tiggy took my arm firmly. 'He's all I've got, Juliet darling. Don't take him from me.'

Juliet laughed and turned to Richard, who had risen behind her. 'Richard's been promising to show me his library,' she said.

Tiggy squeezed my arm convulsively, and sighed.

'I've brought a book I forgot last night,' said Richard, grinning rather fatuously.

It was another half hour and my second whisky of the evening before he left and I was able to hear about Juliet.

'I'm going back to Daddy,' she said when she was alone with us. 'Do you think he'll have me?'

Father Morris had been right, then.

'Yes, of course,' I said. 'Will it be possible for you, though?'

'It will if I make my terms clear from the start.'

'And they are?'

'I look after his house, make him comfortable, but live my own life in my own way.'

I looked at Tiggy. 'What do you think?'

'He's no alternative,' she said. 'Anyway, to the outside world the erring daughter will have returned, and that will satisfy him.'

'Have you put out any feelers?' I asked.

'No,' said Juliet. 'He can be so rude on the phone; and I couldn't put it on paper: so I thought I'd just walk in tomorrow, and get it over.'

'Good idea,' I said. 'Especially if it brings you to us.'

'You see,' she continued, 'he's got to have someone looking after him. He's completely helpless in many ways.'

I fidgeted uneasily. 'But it's easy to say you're going to lead your own life in your own way. How will you be able to? What about your job, and your marriage, when the time comes?'

'I've thought about that; but it's no good just looking ahead and imagining difficulties. The difficulties will just have to be overcome. Things never turn out as you think they will. They're always jinking backwards and forwards, and there's always something unexpected on the point of turning up. I often wondered how Mummy stood her life; but never for a moment did it occur to me that she was just waiting to go. I'd have sympathised less if I'd known. Then again, I knew Alfred was a fan of mine; but never for a moment did it occur to me that he was going to be so unhappy. I'd have treated him better if I'd known. How is he, by the way?'

'He was in this house an hour ago.'

'Was he indeed? It was kind of you not to bring him up. I don't quite know how to face him when I see him.'

'You won't have to for a couple of weeks. He's going to Cambridge to work on his book.'

'Well, I just hope it's a success. I shall order copies for all my friends. Tiggy, darling, will you forgive me if I retire now? Bed seems a very good idea.'

'That's what Danae said to Zeus,' I said wistfully.

Tiggy seized my arm again. 'Mightn't Danae have had dark hair?' she enquired. 'After all she was a Greek girl.'

'So was Aphrodite,' I said. 'The one who married Hephaistos, who limped.'

'How lovely!' cried Tiggy. 'I've never thought of Aphrodite as dark. Was she really?'

Poor Tiggy. She caught me when I was tired, and my dam was beginning to leak badly. I lowered my head and muttered 'Her hair was neither dark nor fair. There was a sort of reddish gleam in it.'

Tiggy looked at me appalled for a moment, then in front of the puzzled Juliet she rushed from the room.

When I was able to follow her I found her face downwards on the bed, crying bitterly.

'Oh, God!' she sobbed. 'Darling, let's stay in Brink!' But there was no talking to me. I was going to patch that dam if it killed me.

XIII - CAMBRIDGE

The journey that I made on Tuesday was the last stage of what I thought was a journey into the future, out of the inconsequentialities of my own and other people's lives. The anti-climax of Juliet's easily accepted return to her father was inconsequential in a way I was determined to avoid; yet my determination was sapped from the very start of the journey. The sight of the orange stone houses and Midland fields glowing in the autumn sun as I embarked on the first of my trains reminded me too sharply of my relief at returning from London. It was a cold, beautiful day, too still to attack the remaining leaves on the trees and hedges, but dry enough for the tractors to be out in the fields. Each had an attendant train of the gulls which roosted on North Brink Reservoir, and attracted the scorn of all good seafaring birds.

Just as before, my stomach felt as if it were on a Big Dipper. Perhaps, I thought desperately, approaching forty was too old for change. Perhaps I really was unwell. Despite what I had said to Father Morris, I had not yet told Tiggy I was visiting the doctor, nor had I referred in any way to my experience in Piccadilly. I had spent three happy and ambitious years in Cambridge, and knew every corner of the place, so there seemed good hope that I would stand up to it better than to London. Yet I was not looking forward to a Cambridge surrounded by so much uncertainty.

The night had mainly been passed staring into the darkness, trying to pray, and summoning up pleasant days from the remoter past. Then I found myself fishing up a mountain stream with Bob Atherton, and had to switch my thoughts to those days of convalescence and the old don's sweet daughter, whose kindness and comfort were now always at hand. Sleep would not come. The fact was that I feared change and turbulence, and did not know whether to fight my fear or accept it.

It was not that Brink was a paradise; more that it was a limited theatre of events, a place where there was leisure to follow the drama in the lives of other people, a balcony overlooking the street. I wanted to be a spectator; that was the truth behind my portentous tale of ministry. I did not want to step on to the stage, especially knowing what a crowded and competitive stage Cambridge was.

By the time I had got out of the second train, trekked along that endless station, and hailed a cab, I was moving mechanically. There was an hour or more before I need report for my College lunch, so I asked the cab-driver to drop me in St Andrew's Street, meaning to do some shopping in the big stores. It was a mistake. The traffic past Emmanuel and Christ's had always been heavy, but now it was twice as bad as I had ever known it.

The centre of Cambridge was in the process of reconstruction to some master plan born of desperation. Buildings I expected to see were being swept away, cranes peered over new skylines, and diversions, catwalks, piles of breeze blocks and concrete mixers imposed themselves everywhere. I dived into the nearest store with my heart thumping. What was it I needed? Green baize. Looking about for help, I saw only customers. Then I realised from their attitudes and absence of overcoats that the young people standing about the place were shop assistants, arrayed as I had never seen them before, disguised for some reason.

I asked my way to the materials department, and bid 'Good morning' to a bespectacled middle-aged man.

He eyed me warily, like a County Surveyor being asked to pronounce instantly on a request for planning permission. 'And what can I do for you, sir?' he asked.

'I want some green baize,' I said.

'Green baize!' he scoffed. 'That's the first time I've been asked for that in years.'

'Is it? Well, have you got any?'

'They don't make green baize these days, sir,' he said, with a gusto that confirmed my dislike of him. 'I can do you some felt.'

'I don't want felt. I want green baize.'

'There used to be a shop that stocked it, in Sussex Street; but that's been closed for years now.'

'I'm sure it's still made.'

'Well, *if* it is, sir,' he said; '*if* it is, *we* don't get it.' He said this so proudly that I wanted to clout him.

'Why on earth,' I asked irritably, 'are your assistants dressed like customers?'

'As to that,' he said slowly, 'you'd have to ask the management It might just be something to do with the amount of pilfering.' He looked at me keenly, as if wondering whether to hand me over to the police.

I turned abruptly on my heel, and left the shop. Outside, on the pavement, an elderly and depraved-looking creature was studying a racing edition. I remembered him from years before.

'*For Cambridge people seldom smile, Being urban, squat, and packed with guile,*' I thought savagely, studying the passers-by. There did seem something very unhandsome about the hurrying and shapeless forms that humped shopping baskets along past strolling students, scruffy, bearded, jeaned. The Backs were all very well, but what objects populated them?

I walked on up what was left of Petty Cury, jostled by people in a hurry, and feeling increasingly savage. The town was bulging at the seams, and the shops were changing to meet a whole new culture. Record shops abounded, travel agencies, branches of quack cults: was it here that I was to join the scramble? For a moment my determination failed; then I reminded myself how unfair it was to go by this sort of impression.

The Market Square was its usual chaos of stalls and taxis. I forced my way through the crowd past the cinema and tried to head for Sidney Street, but found an entire road had been replaced by a cat walk. This was packed with what passed for humanity, queuing for the privilege merely of moving about the town.

As the time for the appointment approached, my state was deteriorating. The noise of the crowd, the traffic, and the building operations was affecting me physically, making my heart thump harder. I felt an unreasoned hatred of everyone around me, and by the time I had moved with the throng for a few yards along the cat walk, I was digging my nails into my palms to prevent myself from striking out at someone.

It was bad luck on the young fool behind me who suddenly shouted to a friend ahead, and launched himself forward without considering his position. He cannoned hard into me, looked down at me with glazed eyes and no apology, and lunged forward again.

His new greeting to his friend was choked as I seized him by the arm, pulled him back, and swung hard at his ear.

He half-fell, steadied himself, and looked up at me, surprised. 'What the ...!' he said. Then he pulled himself upright, and looked hard and purposefully down at me. 'Now look, mate,' he said.

But I had let go of his arm, and despite the local reaction of the crowd to what was going on he was swept away out of reach. He was shouting abuse as I turned and made my way like a porpoise back to the Market Square. As I regained the pavement my breath was coming with difficulty, and the faces of passers-by danced in front of my eyes. I was aware of people dodging out of my way.

Then I saw, over the road, a girl standing with bowed head by a stall. She was small, and alone, and uncertain.

'Helena!' I shouted. Whether or not she heard, she looked up, and the eyes were pale blue. Then she turned away.

'Helena! Helena!' I cried again, and stepped off the pavement. The taxis were sweeping by, adding their noise to that of the crowds and the concrete-mixers: then suddenly, out of the sky behind me came the deafening attack of a pneumatic drill, shaking the earth beneath me, and returning in waves of echo from the Town Hall and Great St Mary's. On and on and on it thundered, till my knees turned to water, and I stretched out a hand to prop myself on the wing of a swerving taxi. Then my body was spinning in a mist of pain, thudding against the road, and seeing in the gathering darkness only a pair of hollow eyes, from which a slow voice said 'It's all right. He's a friend of mine. Leave him to me.'

He was sitting over me in the ambulance when I came round, and next day he was there by my bed in Addenbrooke's Hospital.

'You're all right,' he said. 'They say I can take you home tomorrow.'

'Alfred,' I said, using his Christian name. 'I'm very grateful to you. You were there at a moment when I needed someone who knew me. It would all have been much nastier without you.'

He looked at me silently, swallowing now and again. There was an air of pride about him.

'Have you spoken to your wife?' he asked eventually.

'Yes, briefly. She rang me, after you'd told her what happened.'

'How are you feeling?'

'Sore, that's all; and there's a lump on my head. But all in all, I feel tremendously relieved.'

'Relieved?'

'Yes. I didn't want this job, and now I've withdrawn from it.'

'Perhaps there will be something better.'

'Perhaps. But I think I'll stay in Brink for a bit.'

'Mm,' he said, looking preoccupied.

'Look,' I said. 'Don't you bother to drive me all that way. I've had offers to take me, from the don I was due to see yesterday, and from a very worried taxi-driver.' I omitted to say that I had refused both of them.

'As a matter of fact,' he said, 'I need to fetch one or two things from the cottage. I may even stay a night or two, and do some typing.'

'All right,' I said. 'I give in. You're very kind.'

There was still something on his mind. He was sitting convulsing his throat like a frog.

'It's funny being back in hospital,' I said. 'I've seen a lot of this.'

'Yes,' he said.

'Anyway, it's not serious this time.'

He frowned. 'No,' he said slowly. 'At least ...'

'At least what?'

'Don't you think you ought to have a thorough overhaul?'

'Yes,' I admitted. 'I do. Not here, though. They're all right, but they don't know me.'

He stood up, looking relieved. 'I'll see the Sister,' he said, 'and arrange when I'm to call for you.'

He must have said quite a lot to the Sister, because when I eventually got home to a distressed Tiggy I found she had arranged for Dr Churston to see me in the morning, fully briefed by the man at Addenbrooke's. I was installed in bed, told to stay there, and given the pills that had already allowed me two nights' straight sleep. Tiggy was full of self-reproach, and commanded me not to talk about what had happened. She wished she had never encouraged me to leave Brink, and had had a long talk to her father about it.

'He wants to come and see you, darling,' she said. 'He feels very bad about having suggested this silly plan, and he's hoping to call in and say so. Be nice to him.'

Churston came in the morning and gave me the usual lot of tests. He was rather an appalling old man, breezily offhand and insensitive, but the older people liked his ways, and I suppose he was sharper than he seemed. When the hammering and thumping was over he started asking me questions, but soon tired of listening to my replies and started answering for me.

'Nothing wrong with you,' he said. 'You've been under stress, that's all. Haven't you? You been well enough while I've known you. Haven't you? Of course you have. We must just make sure you make a quick return to normal now the cause of stress is gone. Mustn't we?'

It surprised me that he had heard of the word 'stress'. Perhaps I had used it myself at some point. Anyway, I had told him all about the job, and all I could remember about my visit to Cambridge, which at that point extended only to the scuffle. It was obvious enough that I had stepped into the road, though I could not recall doing so.

The doctor told me to stay in bed, and promised to return in a couple of days' time.

That afternoon Tiggy looked into the bedroom at about half past two. I had slept after lunch and, half-drugged, was peacefully counting the patterns on the curtains.

'Are you in a fit state to see your preserver?' she asked.

'Alfred Towle? Yes, certainly.'

'Mrs Morris has asked me to tea, and I thought I might go for a walk and finish up at the Vicarage. I wouldn't stay long; but would you be all right for a bit if I left you a tray?'

'Of course.'

Alfred Towle duly sidled into the bedroom and sat in the armchair while Tiggy put my tea ready.

'When are you going back to Cambridge?' I asked him as she left.

'I thought I might go tomorrow.'

'I hope you enjoy it better than I did.'

'The academic part is a world I can manage. The rest is a little bewildering.' He sat and masticated thoughtfully, then he said 'There was one thing I wanted to ask you before I went.'

'Go ahead.'

'It may seem impudent.'

'Ask anything you like.'

'Who's Eleanor?'

I was completely relaxed, and my pulse barely quickened; but I had to keep silence for a bit.

'Why do you ask?' I said eventually.

'How much have you remembered about your accident on Tuesday?'

'Not much. Why?'

'Did you know you were shouting Eleanor's name as you crossed the road? There didn't seem to be anyone called that on the other side.'

I lay back on the pillow, and peered into the mists of Tuesday. Slowly, they began to clear, and I recalled what had happened. I drew a deep breath and spoke with only a slight quiver in my voice. 'Helena,' I said. 'Not Eleanor. Helena. Helena. Oh, God, it's a long story!'

Alfred Towle stirred almost animatedly in the depths of his armchair. 'I'd like to hear it,' he said; 'if you could bear to tell it, that is. It's important to tell things, and you've always been reticent about yourself.'

I smiled to myself as I remembered the hours I had spent listening to him. Then I felt the past flooding over me in torrents, and I smiled again. 'If we only lived our own lives,' I said, 'we should be less than men; but the temptation is always to do so, to shut ourselves in with ourselves. Perhaps the more we do so, the more dishonest we become. Do you ever feel that Brink, with all its gossip and prying, enables one to lead a dozen lives, that in the end all become truly one's own?'

'If that's so,' he said, 'perhaps you should be generous with yours.'

So I lay there and talked. While a feeling of great comfort stole over my body, and that curious angular man twitched in my armchair, I did what I had been unable to do for so long, and told the whole story of Helena.

PART 2 – THE SINGING SONG

'I beg you, by the drowsy logs of evening,
To listen hard. Behind the unbreathing stone
The living truth is carolling the spring.

Only what happened is the singing song;
No use to look with envious lying eyes
On laughter, grand times, past and lovely times
That never were, and dam the troubling facts.

For dam them all, they'll filter trebling back
To crack the winter with their sweet spring water,
And wake the dog, and douse the fire and wind
With such a voice as turns the earth to singing.'

The Wall of Winter

XIV - THE KYRENIA SCHOOL

It would take a long time to describe all that the Greeks meant to me, an educated Englishman. They meant enraptured teachers declaiming lines of Homer; they meant the humour and dignity of an old Athenian, feeling the poison taking his life; they meant great leaps of mind, unassisted by the long accumulations of culture, the penetration of Zeno, the power of Plato, the singing and the pain of Sophocles. Even the modern Greeks were surrounded by the haloes of Byron, Shelley, and the wartime Resistance.

Cyprus never ceased to mean this, despite all that happened. The sheer timelessness of the villages and fields, the stringy old farmers, the rites of birth, betrothal, and death, made you feel that two or three millennia were as nothing, that the Great Idea lived on. The Greeks are expert in remembering, and expert in forgetting. They remember what they need, but the centuries of alien rulers, whether Egyptian, Assyrian, Persian, Roman, Arab, Lusignan, Venetian, or Turkish, rolled away from their minds; so that the rule of the British had an obviously temporary nature that made it almost, but never quite, tolerable to them. *Tha perasi*. It will pass,' they said, but when the crops were in, the question inevitably arose of what to do to hasten the day.

That September, the battalion was encamped on the Kyrenia pass, which led through the northern range to the sea from Nicosia. We were one of the many battalions brought in to meet the wave of

EOKA[2] terrorism. We had had briefings in Cypriot ways, but honestly Greek and Turk looked all alike to us. The gunmen and bombers that killed our friends worked quietly and efficiently behind our backs, at a shade temperature that alone would have exposed us to enough strain. Life was a baffled search for a suitable reaction against brutes who emerged from the darkness, shot down innocents, and were gone again. Occasionally we succeeded, and found a counter-measure; but for the most part our lives were hot, bitter, bewildering, and often boring.

Many of the officers were married, and disappeared as often as possible to the coast with their families. Bob Atherton and I were bachelors, and not allowed to keep cars at camp. We managed to circumvent this by keeping a joint car in the Turkish village a few hundred yards from the camp. Bob was a tall, languid, good-looking man, who had joined the battalion on the same day as myself, and who had led with me the uncomplicated life of the infantry subaltern, through post-war Germany and northern England. We had walked up trout streams together, shared girl-friends at times of short supply, gone through various fads and fashions, for shooting, low life and high life, but never for riding horses. Except in water sports, he was always physically ahead of me, and always in a better position to choose his girls; but we worked to an agreed code and though he dominated the relationship I never felt uncomfortable about it.

Bob had discovered a new interest that summer. Among the journalists that had been lured to Cyprus by the troubles was a statuesque blonde called Barbara. She was an independent girl who developed her own channels of political intelligence by living in a Greek village house on the northern coast. She spoke Greek and

---

[2] EOKA - Ethniki Organosis Kyprion Agoniston or the National Organisation of Cypriot Fighters

some Turkish, wore clothes like a fashion model, and though her features were too aquiline for beauty, her body was of the sort that acts on a man like Everest to a climber.

The CO was not keen on his officers wandering around the villages, even with the protection of the Press. At the easiest times they had to dress in mufti, carry a pistol, and avoid certain routes; at times of greater danger Bob had to exercise considerable ingenuity to meet Barbara under propitious conditions, without exposing himself to physical danger or the risk of court-martial. This often meant that I had to act as an armed guard while Bob, in the shade of some oleander, coaxed Barbara into a helpful state. Unless I could manage to find a companion for myself, or unless their friendship cooled, I faced long spells of contemplating acres of carob and olive with no occupation more exhilarating than breathing the languid air.

The Cyprus heat is never insupportable, but it can be very powerful from May up to the time in the autumn when the first rains come. Whereas in our temperate English climate clothes are needed for the protection of the health as much as for decoration or modesty, in a Cyprus summer modesty is the only motive behind wearing any at all. This tended to ease Bob's problems, though I never had the impression he was working against the odds; but it did create a longing for a bathe which frequently tortured me. I would sit gazing at the distant glimmer of the Kyrenia sea, and long for its intense blue depths. Sometimes when Bob and Barbara felt sociable we all visited the beach and spent the afternoon drifting over the sand and the rocky submarine gardens, in a watery element so warm and clear as to be almost indistinguishable from the air. At other times, I had to be content with a quick dip after more urgent matters had been dealt with. Then in the evening, saying goodbye to Barbara, towelling and shaking out her golden hair behind her car, we would drive back up the still, hot air of the pass among the clacking cicadas; and there at the top we would look down on the Mesaouria plain, still white in the late sun, stretching away as far as the capital and the Troodos mountains beyond.

One morning when the CO had decided our state of fitness left much to be desired, I marched a platoon by a devious route down to Kyrenia, and halted to rest on a patch of waste land towards the edge of the town. A fence divided the area from a school playground, and I could hear the buzz and chant of Greek children being taught, proceeding from the modern school building beyond the playground.

Even a shortish march in such a temperature had justified the CO's fears, and the men lolled about panting, their uniforms soaked with sweat, in the shade of a half-helpful jacaranda tree. To my annoyance, we had no sooner settled down to our ten-minute break than a bell rang, and the playground began to fill with Greek pupils. There were a few girls in one corner, but the majority were boys, some looking as if they must be in their early twenties, and all talking and gesticulating with eyes fixed indignantly on my exhausted troops. A great boy with long sideburns started to harangue the rest, his arms working like windmills. I called the platoon sergeant over, intending to give the word to move on. He took some time to arrive, time enough for the large boy to organise a chant of E - E - Enosis[3]. They were moving on to E - E - EOKA when a schoolmaster rushed out of the building and shouted something. I was impressed to see that not a boy spoke further. Then the teacher, a smart moustached Greek, turned to the building and shouted '*Eh! Kyria Eleni.*'[4] Another teacher, a woman, had come out of the school and was standing hesitantly at the steps. She now came forward and said something to the master, who indicated me. Then he turned on

---

[3] Enosis - the re-unification of Cyprus with Greece, the declared aim of EOKA

[4] 'Hey! Miss Helen.'

the pupils who were all standing silent and baleful like a dramatic chorus, and barked out *'Mesa!'*[5] At first nobody moved. 'Costa,' said the schoolmaster, looking at the boy with sideburns; and he rattled off a paragraph of Greek like a machine-gun. Costa turned decisively on his companions. *'Mesa!'* he said, and all turned and filed silently into the school. Costa looked at the school-master and nodded. *'Malista, kyrie,'*[6] he said. Then side by side they walked off.

The platoon sergeant was at my elbow. 'You wanted me, sir?'

'Yes,' I said. 'Get the men on their feet, and march up the road towards camp. I'll catch you up.'

'Sir!' barked the sergeant, and delivered himself of a paragraph in English at the same rate as that we had just heard in Greek, and no doubt in the same vein. The men scrambled up and resumed their equipment.

I walked towards the fence, where the woman stood waiting for me. She was small and young, dressed in a severe blue blouse and darker blue skirt. Her eyes were screwed up against the sun, and she seemed to find the task of speaking to me distasteful.

'It would be better,' she said, looking through me, 'if British troops did not come near Greek schools.'

She shaded her eyes with her hand and looked directly at me for a moment; then she turned her head away, and her hair caught the light. It was soft brown, with a glint of red. Her English was perfect, except for a slight regional burr.

'I really must apologise,' I said. 'We thought you were all in school. Do you teach here?'

---

[5] 'Get inside'

[6] 'Yes, sir.'

She ignored my question, and went on hurriedly. 'You see, one of our pupils was tortured in a British jail last week. That makes the children very angry, and your position impossible.'

She stood very upright, and accentuated what she said with movements of her head and body.

'You're English,' I said stupidly.

'My own position is not the point.'

I suddenly wanted to make her laugh, to see her face not twisted up in that absurd way. Her waist was slim, and her impatient wriggling somehow delivered the wrong message.

'I said I was sorry. Look, my men are off now; and you can't really believe that torture story. It's straight off an EOKA leaflet.'

'I do believe it. Now please go away.'

'No. How can I just walk off in the knowledge that an English girl is encouraging Greek children to believe such nonsense?'

She was angry. 'Look. We have prevented our children from making fools of your soldiers. Now go, before they make a fool of you. They are all watching you now.'

'May I know your name?'

'My name is Mrs Demopoulou.' (She pronounced it 'Thee-mop-ou-loo'.) 'If you have any complaints, you should address them to Dr Lazarides, my Principal.'

'I have no complaints. I just did not know that there were any English teachers left in the Greek schools.'

She stamped her foot, opened her eyes wide, and looked straight at me. The eyes were an unusually light blue, and there were tears in them. 'Go!' she shouted, her voice breaking. 'Go, go, go! Every minute we talk is proof that I am a British spy.' It had not occurred to me that she was frightened. 'Forgive me,' I said. 'I simply hadn't thought.' And I turned on my heel and left.

As I slogged up the hill, I thought of her small figure standing there, caught between two opposites; and I wondered how she came to be in so unhappy a position.

XV - THE FOREST BARBECUE

My parents had been due to come out shortly and spend a holiday at the Dome in Kyrenia. Although Cyprus was an unhappy and dangerous place politically, it was still surprisingly easy and pleasant for tourists, and I felt no qualms about encouraging them to make this autumn visit. As long as they behaved as tourists, visitors would meet only warmth and friendship.

However, the British Press was in full cry, every incident was reported in accurate detail by the better papers and in lurid prose by the rest; so I was disappointed but not surprised when my parents cried off. A year later they were both killed on the A1, when a vast lorry drove into them from a side turning. Road accident figures are a very ineffective form of terrorism. Two or three deaths a week in Cyprus did more to alter people's plans than a hundred a week in Britain.

My parents' non-arrival did seem to cut us off even more from the outside world, and encouraged me to be obsessive about the island's troubles. That a pretty little English schoolmarm, married to a Greek, should accept a propaganda horror-story was not really surprising; but it was as annoying as the easy assumption of some of the politicians and voters at home that the British were always wrong. Even my civilian friends in Cyprus were occasionally scornful of the droves of police and troops who were applying their methods to the islanders. They urged us to do all we could to match the natural friendliness that existed between Greek and British.

We were not unsuccessful. Buchan, a friend in the Forestry Department, had a clerk detained in his own village for several days while it was curfewed and searched by a British battalion. The other clerks retailed stories about troops knocking on people's doors and hitting them on the head with clubs when they emerged; so Buchan suggested that when the missing clerk returned he should be asked for his version of events, with no more gossip until then. On the morning the man eventually arrived back in his office he found Buchan and all his colleagues waiting for the news.

'Now,' said Buchan, 'tell us what happened when the troops searched your village.'

'Why,' said the clerk, puzzled, 'they came and knocked at my door, so I went out and ...'

'Yes?' cried the other clerks triumphantly. 'They hit you on the head?'

'Hit me on the head?' said the man. 'Why should they hit me on the head? They gave me a cup of tea.'

It was Buchan who arranged a Forest Barbecue to bring everyone together. These barbecues had been great events in a peaceful Cyprus, with everyone from the local Commissioner to the lowliest woodcutter meeting on friendly terms over plenty of meat and wine, Greeks, Turks, and British singing and dancing the local dances in a forest clearing. There was still enough friendship left to make such a barbecue possible, though some Greeks felt unable to attend. The battalion was invited to send a party of officers, and Bob and I were among the half-dozen who accompanied the CO We two picked up Barbara in Kyrenia and headed east, along the forest road that followed the ridge of the northern mountain range, till we reached a clearing near a forest station, where the young pines clustered on a spur jutting out over the coastal plain, three miles inland. There the foresters had fixed up rustic tables and were roasting lambs on spits over a long charcoal fire. Great demijohns of wine were circulating, and I recognised a number of Kyrenia residents of all races and shades of opinion, sitting at ease and laughing over the old jokes about Cyprus and the Cypriots, jokes that came out at every feast and could stand telling a hundred times over.

It had been the intention to have an evening barbecue, but with terrorists in the hills this seemed to be inviting trouble, so the meal was arranged as a late lunch and started in mid-afternoon, so that guests could leave just before that time when the hot sun sank behind the range, and the air took on a kindlier temperature. The amiable Cypriot vagueness about time works both ways, so that some had been sitting and drinking for a couple of hours when we arrived, while even when most people were leaving, newcomers were arriving hopefully.

Bob settled Barbara at a bench, found a demijohn and some tumblers, and went off to investigate the prospects of food. I chatted to Barbara and my other neighbour, a Turkish Forestry Assistant, then when Bob came back I went across the clearing to pass the time of day with some friends. Before I reached them my master's voice hailed me. The Colonel was sitting with the local Greek Mayor and two others.

'Michael,' he said, 'you're an educated man. I want you to meet two local schoolteachers. This is Captain Jeffries, Mrs D ... D ... here, my dear, you pronounce it.'

'Demopoulou,' said a voice I recognised. It was the girl. She was still in skirt and blouse, but this time of a more fetching variety, the blouse white, edged with lace, and drawn tight in to the trim waist.

We shook hands, and I saw that the light blue eyes were flashing an urgent warning. 'How do you do,' she said formally. This time I rose to my responsibilities and gave no hint of prior acquaintance.

'And this is Yiorgo,' said the CO 'At least, that's the only name I know him by.'

It was the schoolmaster with the moustache, nearly too pie-eyed to shake hands, and unable to get out his full name.

'He is Mr Demopou.os,' said the girl. This time it sounded like Thee-mop-o-loss. I made a mental note to ask my Greek teacher whether this change of accent was a universal custom.

'Your husband?' I asked.

'My brother-in-law.'

'Where do you come from?' I asked the brother-in-law.

He gave a slurred grunt. I turned to the girl.

'Our village is Ayios Iakovos,' she said, 'but we work in Kyrenia.'

The brother-in-law grunted again, and said something that could have been 'Ayios Iakovos'; then he stared at me, crossed his eyes, and mumbled something at length.

'He asks if you have not learnt any Greek,' said Mrs Demopoulcu; 'you who are an educated man.'

I wondered whether to break into the few verses of Homer I could summon, or to try the slender store of modern Greek I had so far achieved. While I was deciding a paw like a bear's appeared round Yiorgo's neck.

'Eh, Yiorgo!' said a loud Greek voice; *'pou pame?'*[7]

Yiorgo's sullen face lighted up, and he hauled himself round. *'Ti tha paris?'*[8] he enquired, and joining a large sozzled friend he staggered off a few yards. Then he recollected himself and lurched back, looking intently at me. *'Signomi,'* he said solemnly; and to the CO and the Mayor, who were intent in conversation, *'Signomi, kyrii.'*[9]

As he regained the support of his friend, Mrs Demopoulou sighed. 'Oh, dear,' she said, 'I'm sorry about that.' She had a way of sighing that expanded and contracted her in some delightful places.

I sat down on the bench next to her, and looked at the golden light that seemed to hang about her, in her hair, on her cheeks, and

---

[7] 'Where are we going?'

[8] 'What will you have?'

[9] 'Excuse me, gentlemen.'

along the softness of her forearm. Then I thought back to our last meeting.

'Is this all right?' I asked. 'I mean, will it cause comment if I talk to you?'

She had not smiled yet, and I felt her hesitate. 'There need be no comment,' she said at last. 'We are all trying to be friends today. Of course, my brother-in-law will not remember much; but even for those who will, I may speak to whoever I wish.'

'Is your husband not here?'

'No,' she said, without offering any further explanation.

'I have been thinking about what you said the other day. May we talk about it?'

She sighed again, protestingly. 'You mean about the torture? Oh, this is not something to talk about today. You must understand that there is war; otherwise why should you be in Cyprus? Also this is the Middle East, not a London suburb. Things are happening on both sides that it is better for both of us not to know - yes, even for you.'

'I can't get used to the idea of a girl like you being torn apart in this way.'

'Who is torn apart? And who is tearing? This is not a personal war. I am a Greek by marriage, and believe me, the Greeks love the English - in their place.'

She was sitting looking sadly at the ground, talking to herself rather than responding to me. I wanted to pull myself and her away from our anger and sadness, and cast around for something to make her smile. A tall shadow fell across us.

'Michael!' cried Bob. 'You are the limit. I take my eyes off you for a minute, and you settle down with the prettiest girl in the show.'

Then at last she looked up at him and smiled, and it was like a Mozart aria. I was half-furious that Bob should dance in yet again and do better than I could, and half-exalted by the result.

I introduced them, and Bob took over. In two minutes the whole thing was on Christian name terms (her name was Helena), and Barbara had been whistled up to join us.

'What fortunate chance, my dear,' Bob said as he worked his long legs under the wooden table, 'enables us to steal you for lunch in this way?'

'Helena's brother-in-law is here somewhere,' I said, 'but he's not at his best today. As for her husband, he's …' I looked at Helena.

'Away,' she said.

'Away from these parts completely?'

'Yes. I'm with his parents in Ayios Iakovos.' This was obviously not a subject she was keen on pursuing, and she quickly turned to Barbara and asked her about herself.

I think Barbara's professional instincts were stirred. Like any journalist she was able to see both sides of the Cyprus situation, and she knew what to say to a girl like Helena, whose position fascinated her. The girls got on well, and now and again Bob put in a remark that kept Helena relaxed and happy. As we worked our way through the chunks of lamb and the tumblers of village wine, her reserve melted and she even began to laugh and answer Bob back.

'Helena,' he said suddenly; 'can you swim?'

'Swim? Yes.'

'Of course you can; so come and have an evening dip with us after this party's over.'

I saw Barbara's eyes gleam with amusement as she watched Helena without jealousy.

Helena shook her head. 'I wish I could,' she said. 'I often look at the sea and want to go off and enjoy it; but married women in Greek families don't just seize a bathing costume and run off. It would scandalize the village. Anyway, I've got no costume here, and there's Yiorgo to think about. I wonder what's happened to him.'

'I'll go and have a look for him in a minute,' I said, reaching for a bunch of grapes. 'There's coffee brewing just at the moment.'

The sun was sloping towards the mountains now, and the smell of wood smoke was stronger and sweeter in the late afternoon air. No longer needing the shade of the pines, we took our grapes and coffee cups to the spur that looked out over the sunlit Mediterranean. Below us was rock rose and scrub, then a few fields, dotted with carobs, running down to the coast road. Ayios Iakovos, a largish village, lay a mile or two to the east, up the coast. Helena sat and looked at it, her honey-coloured skin glowing with youth, more like a Sixth Former than a married woman; then she shivered and turned her head towards me. Her eyes were not on me, and there was a return of the guardedness to them.

'You're cold?' I asked. As she shook her head I heard what sounded like two shots 'Twok-dong, twok-dong' echoing in the far distance below us. People were beginning to leave the barbecue, and cars and land rovers were rattling along the track that wound below and behind us. The noise might just have been from one of them.

'I'll look for Yiorgo,' I offered, and climbed off my rock.

There were groups sprawled over the clearing, chatting, and some of the foresters were putting out the fire and collecting crockery and cutlery. A small party of Greeks were shouting and waving their arms at each other, among them the loud bear-like man. I asked him if he had seen Yiorgo. He looked at me amiably enough and paused, summoning his glazed senses. '*Sto aftokineto, kyrie*[10],' he said eventually. 'Hee-ees-een-hees-car.' This brought a round of applause from his friends. He beamed, made a gesture of sleep, and shrugged his shoulders.

---

[10] 'In the car, sir'

I walked down to where the cars were parked, and found an old Morris with a moustached body in the back. Yiorgo had well and truly passed out.

The news did not please Helena. 'Wretch!' she said. 'How can I drive him back to his parents like that?'

'I'll tell you what,' offered Bob. We'll take you both down to the sea, and dip Yiorgo in it until he feels better. Meanwhile you can have your swim. Barbara will lend you something to wear.'

Helena smiled faintly. 'No. I think his friends will have to solve this one.' She got up, and walked back to the clearing. When she returned she looked relieved. 'It's all right,' she said. 'Stavros is going to clean him up and drop him back at the village.'

'Is Stavros the bear?' I asked.

'That's right. He comes from the next village.'

'Good,' said Bob. 'Now you're free, and we can have that swim. Coming?'

Helena shook her head regretfully. 'No, I can't. Greek married women don't go round in mixed parties without their husbands.'

'It would be interesting to hear of something Greek married women do do,' said Bob.

Helena sat down and wiggled her toes. 'Greek married women do a great deal,' she said. 'They clean the shoes, carry water, do the shopping, do all the rough work around the house. They haven't time to go out and racket around.'

The CO's vehicle lurched up the track below us and stopped. His wireless operator jumped out and addressed me. 'Excuse me, sir, but could you please call the Colonel? It's urgent.'

'I'll have a look for him,' I said, scrambling up.

'Someone want me?' said a voice behind me. The Colonel, burly and businesslike, was already on his way. He clambered down the slope, and listened to what his operator had to say; then he came slowly up to us, meditating.

'I'll have to be off,' he said. 'No hurry for you two, but if you're going to be out late telephone the duty officer and make sure it's all right. There's a bit of trouble.'

'I thought I heard shooting down there,' I said.

'You did. They've winged Corporal Davies; ambushed his truck coming back from Akanthou. Sounds as if he's all right, but 'C' Company's gone out to search the village.'

'What village?' I asked.

'The ambush village. Ayios Iakovos yet again. There's a curfew there at the moment.'

An open carload of Greeks swerved to avoid the jeep, on their way down the hill, and bounced joyously over a rock. They were loaded to the gunwales, an insensible Yiorgo being supported by two friends in the back. As they passed below they shouted and waved to us, and the driver hooted 'E - E - Enosis' in the familiar rhythm of provocation.

The Colonel leaned over his walking-stick. 'It is to be hoped,' he said, 'that that little lot don't run into 'C' Company. They won't be in the mood to put up with much.'

'I should have stopped them,' said Helena, distressed.

The CO turned and looked at her for a moment, puzzled but twinkling. 'Well, my dear,' he said, 'you'll just have to concentrate on keeping these two in order. That's hard enough, believe me.' He looked back at us. 'I must go. Just behave yourselves.'

'But enjoy yourselves,' he shouted over his shoulder as he dropped down the spur, climbed into his jeep, and roared away.

Bob stood up. 'That settles it,' he said. 'Listen, Helena. The troops won't allow any movement in and out of your village until they've finished their search. Come and spend the evening with us, and we'll see you back when the fuss is over.'

156

Helena frowned. 'My poor parents-in-law!' she said. 'Please, please, can you not persuade your men to let me go back through the curfew?'

'I could,' said Bob. 'But see here, my dear: can you look me straight in the eyes and tell me why I should? No, we don't want you with us under duress; we enjoy your company too much as it is: but this is a sort of war that our country's having to fight, however much against her will; and favours can only go to people we're absolutely sure of. Give me one really good reason why I can be sure of you, and of your relations, and you shall go straight back home to Ayios Iakovos.'

He was standing over Helena, seeming more than a foot taller than she was. She looked up at him with her head thrown back, her lips pursed, and her eyes blazing. Then, suddenly, all the fight went out of her. Her head dropped; she turned aside and looked at me, and I saw the tears coming.

'I'll stay with you,' she said; 'just for this evening.'

She sat down quietly by me while Bob and I discussed plans.

XVI - MIDNIGHT BATHE

We took the two cars back along the coast to Barbara's house and
cleaned ourselves up, then sallied forth to Kyrenia and ordered
ourselves an omelette and the local champagne. During this time
Helena became more and more a part of the group. She was graceful,
compact, quiet at first, but in reality alive like an intelligent child.
Although Bob was in charge of the party, and she obviously liked
him and laughed at his stories, it was I to whom she turned eagerly
for information, sometimes about our lives, sometimes about myself.
It was as if I had reinforced some doubt in her mind that had been
present even at the time I faced her anger at the school; it seemed
also that only I could settle it.

By the time we reached Kyrenia harbour, she was talking
animatedly, to the obvious amusement of Bob and Barbara, and to
my complete bewitchment. Although her rather stilted manner of
speaking had changed, so that a trace of colloquial East Anglian
hung about her words, her appearance could have been Greek or
English. Helena's was the classical beauty of the Cyprus-born
Aphrodite, in the light and shade of her features, the slightly
upturned corners of her eyes, and her serene and full mouth; only it
was all in miniature, perfectly scaled.

After we had eaten we all fell silent in the half-lighted restaurant.
Bob was relaxed, with his head resting against the side of a seat,
holding Barbara's hand and occasionally whispering to her. Across
the table, Helena and I sat side by side, watching the reflections of
the boats in the flawless waters of the harbour. The moon had risen,
and was making a path of light out at sea.

I looked at Helena, and saw her eyes flicker at me. It seemed incongruous to think of this girl as married. Nothing separated us; the champagne and the place had lifted us into a shared world of peace and contentment.

'You understand,' she said quietly, 'this is not the Cyprus I see.'

'I understand,' I said.

'In all these weeks I have seen only the school and the village.'

'They are Cyprus.'

'But they are not your Cyprus, Michael. This, now, is the English Cyprus, and I would love it if it were mine. I have tried to be Greek, but I cannot leave England behind.'

'How long have you been here?'

'Nine weeks. I met Xenis in London when we were studying together. He finished last year, and asked me to come out when I had graduated.'

'Were you married in Cyprus?'

Bob stood up and drew Barbara with him. 'Going to look at the harbour wall,' he mouthed over his shoulder as they moved away.

Helena began to laugh helplessly, her hair falling forward over her bent head. She leaned against me, warm and shaking.

'Why do you laugh?' I asked, thinking she found the other two funny.

'You said 'married',' she said. 'I can't marry a man who isn't there.'

Suddenly my heart leapt. 'Helena, are you not married?' She shook her head, and sat still.

'Why, then …?'

'The Mrs Demopoulou? This is Xenis's idea. We are supposed to have married in London.'

'Why? Why?'

Helena looked at me. She had stopped laughing. 'Aren't girls supposed to marry from their homes?'

'Well, why didn't you?'

'Oh, all sorts of reasons. My father and mother, partly. We're not on very good terms. And Xenis is very proud. He told his parents what he thought they would expect to hear. They have been very sweet to me.'

'But where is Xenis?'

'That I can't tell you.'

'Is he interned?'

'No.'

'He's in the hills, isn't he?'

'Michael, I don't know where he is. A year ago, he came home to Cyprus and told his parents he'd married an English girl. His letters after that were postmarked from Kyrenia. In May he sent me an air ticket, and when I arrived Yiorgo met me at the airport.'

'Does Yiorgo know where Xenis is?'

'I don't know. Michael!'

'Yes.'

'I think I've gone a little mad to tell you this. Nobody else knows, and nobody else must. Will you promise me not to say anything?'

I promised. It would already be known that Xenis was missing, and the obvious conclusion would have been drawn. Other young men were missing, here and there in the island. I wondered how obvious the conclusion would be to Helena in her isolation.

Bob and Barbara were back, and leaning over the table.

'Look here, you two,' said Bob. 'Barbara and I feel it's time for that swim. Are you coming?'

I turned to Helena, who protested weakly. 'At this time of night? I haven't even a towel.'

'It's all right, Helena,' Barbara reassured her. 'I've brought a pile of stuff. We can go to a cove we know in a Turkish area. There'll be nobody there now.'

Helena turned helplessly to me. 'You say.'

So I did, wondering where the resolute schoolmistress was that I had seen at our first meeting.

There were military vehicles buzzing up and down the coast road. Bob rang the camp, and gathered that the search of Ayios Iakovos was proceeding according to plan. The curfew would be lifted at midnight.

Bob and Barbara led the way, and Helena drove me in the old Morris. Just outside Kyrenia a section of 'C' Company were stopping cars. We had to wait while two angry Greeks were searched from top to toe; then a corporal I knew stuck his head in the car. 'Sorry to hold you up, sir. Captain Atherton told us to look out for you, but I didn't recognise the car. He's gone on.'

We drove through and turned off along a bumpy track to a deserted soft drinks kiosk on a point above the sea. Our car was parked by the kiosk, but there was no other sign of Bob and Barbara. I shone a torch into the back seat. 'They'll be down in the cove,' I said. 'The towels have gone.'

Helena got out of the car and stood in the moonlight, looking at the vast path on the sea. There was no night wind tonight, and the air was warm enough for her to stand as she was, in her white short-sleeved blouse. She drew a long, sobbing breath, and turned to me.

'What was that you gave me to drink?' she said. 'I don't understand what's happening.'

'I'm a-nother fel-low's girl !' she added, emphasising her point by hammering me on the chest with her fist, three times.

When I kissed her, more or less in self-defence, she moved towards me and clung for a moment. 'It's just that I don't feel like it,' she explained. Then she put her cheek against mine and whispered 'This is not to have any consequences of any sort, you understand.'

This seemed to call for no particular comment, so I kissed her again, and we walked hand in hand down to the cove. Bob and Barbara, uncostumed and giggling, were picking their way into the water. Barbara had considerately put a costume for Helen on the pile of towels.

I removed myself round the point, stripped off, ran in, and plunged. When I came up and swam back to the cove I saw Helena standing on a rock below the point, with her arms poised to dive. She had not put on the costume, and her white body in the streaming moon had the perfection of Aphrodite herself. Just for a moment I saw her, wondering if the goddess of the island was grinding her teeth with jealousy; then she dived into the warm sea with hardly a ripple, and when she surfaced her shoulder flashed at my side. I stretched out a hand for her, but she drew away until I overbalanced; then she splashed water into my face until I launched myself forwards and swam towards her. Her body gleamed as she turned and dived, disappearing in a swirl like a fish rising. I paused, baffled, till she emerged in the shallows and ran from my pursuit, plunging and swimming again as I laboured after her. I was no bad swimmer, but she easily held me off as I chased her all over the bay. This was her element, and not once in those breathless minutes did I lay a finger on her.

Finally, she swam into the shallows, ran out, seized a towel, and wrapping it round her lay on the sand. Bob and Barbara had disappeared. I walked up the beach, and looked down at her as she lay there, her eyes shining and her body heaving as she gasped for breath.

'Pax,' she said quickly. 'Get yourself a towel, for goodness sake.'

The wind was blowing now, off the Anti-Taurus and across fifty miles of sea. I collected a towel and sat by her, wondering. 'Where did you learn to swim?' I asked.

'Cromer,' said Helena prosaically. 'Then London. It wasn't much like this, really.' She started to laugh, and then laughed more and more until she was helpless. I kissed her salty face hopefully, but was pushed firmly away.

'No, Michael,' she said. 'If you'd caught me in the water … well, fear of what might happen lent me wings, didn't it? I used to win free-style competitions once, but you're not so bad yourself; and Holborn baths never presented this sort of problem.' She laughed again, weakly.

Bob clambered down, wearing a white sweater.

'Listen, you two,' he said. 'Barbara's a bit off colour. I think I'd better run her home.'

'All right,' I said. 'Come back when you're ready.'

'Is that what you really want?' asked Bob, the soul of tact.

I looked at Helena. She squeezed my hand and nodded.

'Yes, Bob,' I said insincerely.

'All right. See you later.'

'Now, Michael,' said Helena firmly, when he was gone; 'we've got to be sensible. We met a few hours ago. It's cold. There are two reasons for getting dressed and in our right minds. Please, my dear, don't make it hard for us.'

I was beginning to face a problem too great to be solved by a part and struggle on the beach. I stood up and went round the point to find my clothes. When I came back she was back in her blouse and skirt, with a dry towel round her shoulders.

'Let's go and talk in the car, out of this wind,' she said. We need to talk.'

So we sat in the car, with the moon's light on her head as it lay on my shoulder, and we talked about ourselves as young people do, while the minutes drained away of our first hour alone together. Bob had dawdled, bless him, but it seemed no time at all before we saw his lights turn back off the main road. Then Helena sat up. 'Now,' she said; 'when Bob arrives you have to go back to your camp, and I to Ayios Iakovos. Don't come with me. I'll be all right. Now remember, no consequences. I've got a bit to think about, Michael, and some growing up to do. Please don't write to me, or try to see

163

me. I'm going to write to you when I've shaken off your immediate effect, and that'll take a week. You know what my letter will have to say.'

'This is like an unsuccessful interview for a job,' I protested.

'Don't write to us; we'll write to you. Remember, Michael, I have no vacancies; not even for this day. That I had to steal, my dear; but it's for keeps for both of us.'

Bob drew up alongside us, and switched his lights off. Helena leant towards me and kissed me lightly on the cheek, slipped out of the back of the car, and got into the driver's seat. As Bob drove me away the last sight I had was of her waiting patiently at the wheel for us to regain the road.

Bob was silent until we reached Kyrenia. Then he said 'Do you want to talk?'

'What's to be said?' I asked.

'Only that it's been a jolly evening.'

'Barbara all right?'

'Oh, yes. She sent her love; but she's got to get up early. No, it was a jolly evening.'

'You're very anxious to stress the point.'

'It needs stressing, old boy. You've caught the moon. She's a lovely girl, and wow, she can swim; but she's a married woman. Her husband's a Greek, of some unknown political complexion. It's best left there, with thanks for a jolly evening. How jolly, as far as you are concerned, I shall not enquire.'

I knew he meant well, so I said nothing.

XVII - THE WANTED MAN

'One week. Aren't I a reliable girl?' said the letter. 'An odd week in which nothing has happened except thoughts, of the glimpse I had of the world outside my world, and of your sweetness to me. Since I left Norfolk I've often felt lost; first of all in London, when Xenis was so very gentle with me, and charming in a way you don't often meet in England; then in the village here, where his parents are bewildered but so kind; then a week ago, seeing Cyprus through the eyes of what were my own people. It is not the true Cyprus, that I can see; but it is a pleasant extension of a pleasant age that is passing, and I am so grateful to have seen it.

'I got back here that night before Yiorgo, who had been taken home by Stavros. Our village was buzzing, but the troops were gone. Memnakis next door was displaying a bruise on his head he said had been caused by a rifle butt, but I think he hit it on an olive tree dodging round the houses. As I expect you know, they found some ammunition down a well, and two men have been taken off; but nobody tells me more than that.

'There is still no word of Xenis. Yiorgo occasionally gives me a message he says is from him, giving me his love and assuring me he is safe and sound. It seems a long time since I last saw him in London.

'What else must I tell you about this week? Just that there was some growing up to do, as I thought. Growing up seems to mean discovering what you can have and what you can't. Or rather, since you can have most things, discovering what the prices of particular items are. I have chosen Xenis, and the price is to be a Greek. Since he still wants me I must pay the price, hard as it sometimes seems to a girl who never before left the shores of England.

'There is also a curiously heavy price in remembering the other evening; but I am sure it is even heavier if we try to falsify the record and forget it. So do not quite forget me, my dear Michael. Bless you, and goodbye, Helena.'

It was 'no consequences', then, the letter I had expected, postmarked Kyrenia, and no doubt posted outside the school gates. What else could I have expected, after just half a day of accidental companionship, eased by wine and youth and the island of the great goddess? Everything in this place was violent, sudden, brightly coloured, doomed. Even Bob and Barbara had quarrelled since that midnight bathe, and were having a break from each other. Two 'other ranks' had been killed in an ambush down the coast, and a friendly Greek lad who brought fruit up to the camp gates had been stood against a wall and brutally shot six times by masked men. Barbara had accepted an invitation from an anonymous visitor at the door of her house in the village, to visit Nicosia at a certain time and certain place and report on a 'spontaneous' demonstration in which half a dozen British soldiers were injured. This was one reason for Bob's annoyance with her.

This letter seemed all part of it, even though I only half-believed it meant not seeing Helena again. Nothing could extinguish my hope that we should come together again, for she was as vivid to me as my next-door neighbour in the Mess, and her voice as clear. She was daily working only three miles away. In an island where every day brought a fresh turn of events, and where her situation was so uncertain, there must be hope.

Bob had been very tactful, and had only once again mentioned what he knew occupied my mind. We were sitting in the Adjutant's office waiting to see the Colonel, who was lengthily going through promotions with Eric, the Adjutant, in the next hut.

'You see, Michael,' said Bob a propos of nothing; 'life is very simple as long as you don't complicate it. There are two sorts of girl, those you marry and those you don't. Those you don't marry come in two kinds: the ones you don't want to marry and the ones you can't marry, even if you want to. Look around you, and you will see much of the world's misery caused by people who get these categories confused. You know me, old boy. I'm no moralist, and if I'm selected by a married girl for a tumble in the hay it hurts me like hell to refuse. Generally speaking, I do refuse, because I value my men friends. But if I ever make an exception, I don't try and shift the girl to a new category. I don't get all wound up about her.'

'Don't you?' I said.

'No, I don't. Damn it, I'm not even worked up about Barbara. I haven't lost a wink on the subject. We've been very good friends, and we understand one another. She knows very well what to expect from me, and what not to expect.'

'Does she?'

'Yes, she does. Of course, she's in a different category. I don't say one never gets worked up about a girl. It's bound to happen sometimes. But one has to exercise a bit of self-control.'

'Does one?'

'Yes, one does. I can't make you out. You really worry me. We've had our moments, you and I, but I've always thought of you as a level-headed bloke.'

Eric came in, bearing a great sheaf of paper and looking haggard. 'Go on, Bob,' he said. 'Your turn.' He selected a poster and set about pinning it on the board.

'Just in case you come across any of these,' he murmured. 'Horrible-looking lot!'

I inspected the poster, which contained a new series of photographs of wanted men. Three had been crossed out in red to indicate the successful outcome of a battle in the Troodos mountains.

A thought struck me, and I ran my eye along the names. Under the photograph of a personable young man, clean-shaven, with a curious grey streak in his hair, it read 'Xenakis Demopoulos (Ayios Iakovos) - wanted in connection with the murders of Dr John Parry at Evrykhou in Jan 1956 and P.C. Agamemnon Roussos at Kakopetria in April 1956.'

'Good grief!' I said.

'Found a friend?' enquired Eric.

'Not quite. Can you tell me any more about this chap?' I indicated the picture.

'Yes, I certainly can.'

He opened a filing cabinet, and dug out a card. 'Here we are. Aged 24. Degree at London School of Economics 1955. Disappeared from village October 1955. Probably went to Greece, returning in December by caique. We had a bit of info about this chap the other day, so we know more about him than you'll find on the poster.'

'Any idea where he is now?'

'Troodos, I think; but they get around, these chaps. He's got an English wife in Ayios Iakovos ... Ah, now I understand! The Colonel introduced you to her the other day, didn't he? Pretty thing, wasn't she?'

'Not bad,' I said. 'Put I didn't know who her husband was.'

'Curious taste she has.'

'Very curious. How long have we known about him?'

'Rather vaguely, for some time; but we got a new photo, and some new ideas about him, when we curfewed Ayios Iakovos last week. There was an ex-girl-friend of his who seemed very anxious to be helpful.'

'What sort of a girl?'

'Her name was Androulla. She seemed an ordinary sort of village girl. Quite a beauty. There's jealousy there somewhere.'

This was very complicated. How much of all this did Helena know? She must suspect some of it, living in the atmosphere of a patriotic Greek village. It seemed to me that in the intellectually rebellious atmosphere of London university she might have come to take up a position which in practice she would want to repudiate. It was one thing to believe that her husband was a glorious freedom fighter, but another to be faced with the shooting in the back of decent, kindly fellow-countrymen like Dr Parry, or innocents like P.C. Roussos. I believed with all my heart that she would be disgusted with these acts. Beneath the exterior I had seen at our first meeting was a sensible Norfolk girl, quite unacquainted with anything outside her county and her hall of residence. Even Barbara, a fairly cynical citizen of the world, was revolted by terrorism. Helena would be shattered by its reality.

Bob emerged from the CO's office, and waved me in. I had promised Helena to keep from him the details of her true position; but I was interested in his reaction to the notice, so before I left I stubbed my finger on the photograph. 'Have a look at that,' I said.

He looked, uncomprehending. Then he whistled. 'I see,' he said. 'That's where the husband is.'

'You met this femme fatale too, did you?' said Eric curiously 'What's she like?'

Bob turned to me, winked reassuringly, and nodded me towards the CO's office. 'Nice lass,' he said; 'small, fat, and bewildered.'

'Stupid bitch!' said Eric venomously as I left.

'Helena is not fat,' I protested to Bob after lunch.

He laughed. 'Cheer up, old boy,' he said. 'Eric's idea of beauty is not ours. Look at his missus.'

'Anyway,' I continued, 'you begin to see why she hardly falls neatly into those categories you were telling me about.'

'She falls right in them. Helena is not for you, Michael. She's the wife of an EOKA terrorist, even if she is only dimly aware of the fact.

Man and wife are one flesh, and the law does not ask one to give evidence against the other. I hold no brief for that bloody young man, but he's all she's got between her and a very nasty end. I am saying, my friend, that unless she keeps away from the likes of you, Helena's expectation of life can be reckoned in hours. Even in peacetime the murder rate in this island was distinctly high. In the present situation, Helena's in danger twice over. She has to support the right side, by her husband's standard; and she has to be scrupulously faithful, again by her husband's standard, not yours or mine. Remember that village girl that met Sergeant Sempill behind a well? They emptied a barrel of tar over her, and put a match to it.'

There was undeniable force in what he said. Even with Helena's status not having been legally tied up, the family regarded her as married. Anyway, one does not travel two thousand miles under a man's name, to live with his family, unless one acknowledges a sort of ownership. Bob was right, and I was moon-mad. Helena's letter had told the truth. I must not hope to see her again.

'Bob,' I said, 'this is a bloody island, and I don't know why we bother with it.'

'That's the stuff,' he said. 'Of course it is. As a matter of fact, I shouldn't be surprised to see us bothering about Egypt and Israel before long.'

As I stepped out of the Mess into the fierce sun, one of the Sergeants from the duty company stepped out of a patch of shade. 'Excuse me, sir,' he said; 'but I came by this yesterday in Kyrenia Police Station. It's for you.' He handed me an official envelope of the Cyprus Police.

'They're after me at last,' I said. 'Thank you, sergeant.'

I took the envelope into my tent and opened it. Inside was a scrawled note in handwriting I did not know.

'Michael, something has happened,' it said. 'Forgive my bothering you like this, but if you can help me I shall be at the gate of

St Hilarion Castle from two to half past two each school day this week. Better not to greet each other. Helena.'

St Hilarion is the Lusignan castle above the Kyrenia Pass, perhaps the most spectacular of all the Cyprus historical sites. I reflected for a moment, then went to see Bob.

He looked at me for a moment. 'Helena, isn't it?'

'Yes.'

'Michael, don't go. Don't ever see her again.'

'I've got to,' I said. 'She's in trouble, and she's asking for help.'

'Of course she's in trouble. She'll never be out of it ; but you don't have to be in it too. She's got a husband, Michael!'

'I've got to go,' I said.

Bob sighed and tapped his leg restlessly. 'Oh, God! Well, Hilarion's safe enough. It's what will follow that worries me. Do you want me to come?'

'It seems a good idea, if you will.'

It was just short of a quarter past two. We arrived at St Hilarion Castle on the stroke of half past, and saw the old Morris parked by the entrance gateway. As we parked, I saw Helena leave the Morris and enter the Castle, buying a ticket from the custodian. At this siesta hour there was nobody moving, just a recumbent picnic party visible inside the castle wall, and two cars parked near us, probably belonging to the party. Bob and I bought tickets and climbed up the path towards the peak. It was hot going.

We caught up with Helena at the first saddle. Bob was leading.

'Hullo, Bob,' she said. She was dressed in her school clothes, and she looked tired and strained.

'Hullo, my dear,' said Bob. 'I'm going to admire the view and keep an eye on the path. You take Michael over to the tank.'

Helena looked at me then, hesitantly, searching my face. Without relaxing her expression, she turned and led the way over the saddle to where the Lusignans had stored their water. This is a great tank in the mountainside, below the final climb to the Queen's Window at the top of the crag. Below the tank the mountain falls sheer away to the coastal plain and the indigo sea.

We found a pine tree, sat down with our backs to a wall in its shade, and looked out over this breathtaking view. A dog barked a thousand feet below, and we heard the bells of far sheep moving over the scrub.

'I did this on the spur of the moment,' said Helena primly; 'and I don't want to involve you in any trouble, really I don't. It's just that I simply don't know what to do.'

'Tell me, then.'

'It started when I had a note from Kyrenia Police Station a few days ago, asking me to come and see them about my driving licence. I was expecting this, so I went along after school yesterday, and got things fixed up. When we'd finished, they told me to go in and talk to an English police officer, from something called Special Branch. He was polite enough, but I didn't like him. He asked me if I knew who my husband was.'

'And did you?'

'Not really, but I'd more or less guessed. This policeman said he didn't want to ask questions or come between husband and wife, but he had a feeling I'd come out without knowing what I was coming to, and if at any time he could be of assistance I had only to let him know.'

'An invitation to rat on your husband. That's pretty rough stuff, if he really believes you're married.'

'I don't think he's any reason to doubt it; though he did tell me something else. Xenis was engaged to a girl in the village.'

'Androulla,' I said.

She had been looking out over the sea, talking in a flat, matter-of-fact voice. Now she turned her head and looked at me, her eyes wide open. She was breathing quickly, as if she had been running.

'My God!' she said. 'You're all in this together, aren't you?'

'Of course we're all in it together. There are only a few Greeks and English trying to hold the middle ground, Heaven help them. Most of them will be murdered. Some have been already, like Dr Parry and young Roussos. There's not much room on the middle ground, Helena. You're either Greek, English, or condemned to death.'

She scrambled up, and looked away from me. 'I'm going,' she said. 'I thought I could talk to you.'

She had not lost her power to turn my heart over, but I knew I was saying the right thing.

'You can talk to me any time you like,' I said; 'but remember you're engaged to an EOKA murderer, and I'm a British officer. There's no bridge across that gap. With all my heart I wish there were.'

'Is there nothing you can be but a British officer?'

'No. I can't think of any human kindness that a British officer won't give you.'

I stood up, and brushed the dirt from my hands. She was still looking away from me, over the plain and the sea.

'So,' I added; 'I can only say to Xenis's fiancée: break it off and go home to mother. If you want to take that advice, let's talk some more; but if you're to be an EOKA Greek, have the courage to go through with it. That's the safest course, incidentally. Any other means grave danger. You'll be safe enough in Ayios Iakovos.'

She stood there without moving, in that absurd navy-blue skirt, and all I could hear was the noise of the midday cicadas surging up the mountain side. Then she made the slightest movement of her shoulders, and I knew she was crying.

She turned round, and bent her head. The tears streaked her cheeks as she gave a deep sobbing sigh.

'You don't give me a chance, do you?' she said.

Bob coughed behind us, and I looked round. He was leaning in a gateway.

'The picnic party are coming up,' he said. 'Very fat: Cypriots of some sort, and complaining every inch of the way. I doubt if they'll reach the top.'

'We'll go up higher, then,' I said. 'If they get beyond here, just yell my name.'

I seized Helena's hand, and took her up that astonishing path through the stunted pines to the top of the crag, where the Queen's Window looks down on to the old jousting meadow. She followed obediently, and I sat her down in the ruined window. The light was thick up here at over 2,000 feet, as if a cloud was forming.

'It's all right,' I said. 'Tell me the rest.'

'What is there? Xenis was engaged to Androulla. Some money had passed, which had to be refunded. He told the village the story of how he had married me in England, and because of his status as a freedom fighter, the village accepted what happened.'

'I see now why you could hardly arrive in Cyprus as his fiancée.'

'Exactly.'

'And if it were known now that you were not married?'

'I don't think my position would be possible.'

'And ...?'

'And that Special Branch man told me some of the details of the two murders. I hope they weren't true.'

'It was you who told me this was war, my dear. I'm afraid they were probably true.'

Helena put her head back, and closed her eyes. 'Xenis was so kind to me. He was so kind.'

'The Greeks are a very kind people in some ways; and very cruel in others. You should read Kazantzakis.'

She might have gone to sleep, she was silent so long. Then she said 'I couldn't marry a man who ... who ...' She leant slowly out towards the mouth of the window and heaved in convulsions as if she was going to be sick. After that, her body sagged, and she hammered on the stone with her open hands, and uttered a screech like a terrified child. 'What am I to do, Michael? What am I to do? I can't go back there ... I can't ... I can't ...'

I patted her, and said nothing. She put her cheek to the stone mullion and moaned two or three times, and was silent again. Then she opened her eyes and sat up, staring at the ground and talking rationally.

'I'll have to go back. Now, or they'll wonder what's happened to me. Yiorgo's away for a week, and I've got the car; but I'm sure they're keeping an eye on me.'

'Where's Yiorgo gone?'

'Yiorgo?' She sat up and tidied herself. 'Paphos, I think.'

'What's he doing there?'

'We don't ask. The school lets him off now and again on visits to elementary schools; but we don't take children from Paphos.' She hauled a mirror out of her bag, and tut-tutted at her reflection. A quick servicing followed; then she jumped up.

'Captain Jeffries,' she said. 'You have been most kind. Please forget the spectacle you have just witnessed.'

Her flushed eyes appealed to me to support her courage, and even the Greek schoolmarm's kit could not mask her beauty. I did my best.

'Miss Rose' - she had told me her real name - 'it has been a pleasure. Please allow me to accompany you to your car.'

She shook her head. 'Better not. I'll say goodbye here.'

'Till when?'

'Can you manage tomorrow? I think there may be one or two things I shall have to ask you to do.'

'Tomorrow, at the same place and the same time?'

She looked doubtful. 'I suppose I can visit the castle again. To see what I didn't have time for today.'

'All right. Let's leave it like that; but take my telephone number, and tell me if you want to change things.' I scribbled the number on a piece of paper, and gave it her. 'Now what about Bob?'

'Bob?'

'Yes. May I tell him the real position?'

She hesitated. 'As long as I'm Mrs Demopoulou I'm safe. I'll have to leave that thought in your mind. Indeed, Michael, I am very much in your hands, aren't I? If you feel you have to tell Bob, please don't let it go any further.'

She kissed her hand to me and hurried to the top of the steep path. I watched her walk down it, framed between the pines against the distant shimmering plain.

XVIII - Plan of Escape

'So you think she wants to get out,' said Bob thoughtfully. I had told him Helena's true position, and we were sitting on a rock dangling our legs in the water after an evening swim.

'She must,' I said.

'Then surely you ought not to be handling it. Our Security boys will love extracting a gunman's girl friend from the island. She can probably tell them one or two things on the way.'

'She wouldn't want to. After all, she was in love with the man. Anyway, she came here of her own accord, and there's nothing to stop her booking a passage on Cyprus Airways and returning to Britain. She's not a prisoner.'

'She is in a way. I mean she can't just pack up her baggage, tell the Demopoulos family she's off, and go.'

'No, she certainly can't. There's got to be an element of secrecy.'

'And that's where you come in?'

'She needs someone to help her.'

'Why? What's to stop her booking a Turkish taxi-driver to pick her up at the school in Kyrenia? She walks out of school, climbs in, is driven to the airport, and flies off. End of story. Why do you have to come into it at all?'

'Because so much can go wrong. She has to find fifty pounds, book the air passage, fix the taxi, choose the moment, all under the beady eyes of the Demopouloi. Suppose the taxi-driver lets her down, or there's a curfew at Kyrenia at the vital time, or the school is shut that day. Schools are shutting all over the place. The moment the Demopouloi get wind of anything going on, that girl is in grave danger.'

'But if they find she's having daily powwows with British officers, she's as good as dead anyway.'

'They mustn't. I've been thinking we can hardly go on inspecting St Hilarion. The custodian will smell a rat, or someone will see us. We must find somewhere safe to meet.'

'Somewhere safe! This is Cyprus, Michael. Everybody knows what everybody else is doing. Even with thirty thousand British troops, there isn't anywhere safe from observation. You could kidnap Helena tomorrow, of course, and to hell with observation; then you could put her with a military family at Episkopi, and arrange her journey at leisure: but that means telling Security. Why don't you, for goodness sake?'

'I'll talk to her about it,' I promised.

Next afternoon I drove straight up to Helena's car, below the Hilarion gateway, and spoke to her before she could get out. Then I took the car up the forest road until I found a suitable place, parked the car round a bend, walked back, and stopped Helena further down the road. Bob waited in our car, and I took Helena up to a fold in the hillside under a scrubby pine tree.

'It's not tourist stuff this time,' I said; 'but it's reasonably secure.'

We sat and talked, and were uninterrupted except by an old shepherd who passed with his flock.

Helena was now determined she must leave the island; and her practical problems were much as I had thought. She had brought her passport, and asked me if I could lend her the money for a flight, and book it for her. She did not like or trust the Special Branch, and would not hear of my trying to make her exit official with them. She believed with some justice that this would make her a source of danger to Xenis, which she simply would not be.

There was one more day's school before the weekend, and Yiorgo had not yet returned. It seemed reasonable to appoint the place we were in for a rendezvous on the following day.

When she was gone, I took the car off to Nicosia, and booked a flight in the name of Miss Rose for four o'clock in the afternoon of the following Tuesday. Looking back on my actions in those few days I can see the gaping holes in my security; but even Bob offered no comment on what I was doing.

Back from training in time for lunch on the Friday, I found a telephone message waiting for me in the Mess. The lady I expected to meet would be unable to keep the appointment. This was the first hitch. I had a date, a passport, and an airline ticket, but no contact with my passenger. I hoped she had not run too great a risk in telephoning, and wondered whether she would be able to put through another call.

After lunch, I sat in the Mess anteroom and pondered. I needed only the very briefest contact with Helena, enough to fix an appointment for me to pick her up on Tuesday. The passport and ticket were safe with me till then. A short telephone conversation would be enough; but how could I perform my duties and remain on the end of the Mess telephone? Finally I left a note with the Mess staff saying when I would be about, in the hope that Helena could choose her time to get to a phone box and make a call.

Friday passed, and Saturday morning. I began to make desperate and absurd plans for driving to Ayios Iakovos, for telephoning the Kyrenia school, for stopping the old Morris on the road on Tuesday morning. All these devices could be avoided if only I could speak to Helena for half a minute.

Then at lunch on Saturday I was given a message that had come in during the morning. The lady would be shopping at Constantinou's at about three o'clock.

Constantinou's was a Kyrenia shop that sold snorkels, spears, bathing costumes, rope, anchors, any of the kit likely to be needed by the bathers and boaters who in the best of times swarmed to the harbour and beaches. I took up position in the lounge of a hotel across the main street at half past two, and watched Constantinou's entrance. Bob was on duty that afternoon.

At a quarter past three the old Morris drew up opposite, with Yiorgo driving, disgorged Helena, and drove on down the street. She was dressed in yellow and white, an outfit very unlike her school gear. Standing uncertainly on the pavement, she looked around her before stepping into the shop, and for a moment her light blue eyes seemed to look directly into mine; then with a swing of skirt and click of heels she was gone.

I strolled out of the hotel, crossed the road, and entered the gloom of Constantinou's. The proprietor was talking to Helena, but when I entered he looked up and flashed his teeth.

'Good afternoon, Captain,' he said. 'I will not keep you long. Excuse me.' He dived round a corner and started fetching down boxes from a high shelf.

Helena looked up and wrinkled her eyes at me. She looked cool and triumphant.

'Good afternoon, Captain Jeffries,' she said.

'Good afternoon,' I responded cautiously.

'We met at the barbecue, you remember,' she continued.

'Of course,' I said. 'Are you having an afternoon's shopping?'

'Yes,' she said. 'I am buying a bathing costume. I have an hour or so to spare, so I thought I would swim in that cove just east of the Castle.'

'It's a good afternoon for it,' I said, walking up to her and dropping an envelope into her shopping bag. 'I hope you enjoy yourself.'

Constantinou was now hovering with boxes of his wares, so I retired to the other end of the shop and selected a face-mask. By the time I returned, Helena had completed her purchase and gone.

The moment I was out of the shop I hurried to the car, drove down to the Castle, parked, changed, and walked down to the water's edge. There was a sort of lagoon here, guarded by a string of rocks that stretched out to sea, perhaps on the line of some old Hellenistic harbour. As always on a Saturday afternoon, there were a number of British civilians basking and swimming immediately below the Castle wall; but further to the east, on my right, the company was more cosmopolitan. I could see Helena walking down to the beach over on the far right. As she reached the sand, I entered the water and swam out to the line of rocks. Here a corpulent Colonial administrator was disporting himself, followed everywhere by a springer spaniel, swimming joyously with its ears floating out on the water. The master greeted me, and I watched fascinated as he climbed out on to one of the rocks and poised his considerable carcass for a dive. The dog also hauled itself out, had a shake so comprehensive that it showered me with water ten yards off, and waddled up the rock after its master. As the administrator's frame entered the water with surprisingly little splash, the dog walked forward, peered at him, lowered its head and shook it; then, without further ado, it jumped clear into the sea and paddled faithfully after.

Across the bay, Helena was swimming out to the far end of the line of rocks. I clambered out of the lagoon on to my nearest rock, crossed it, and lowered myself into the open sea on the far side. Here, the water temperature was ten degrees lower, there was a marked swell, and the water stretched down several fathoms to a dark rocky bottom. I was now hidden from the shore, and could swim along the string of rocks to the east without being observed.

After a quarter of a mile I came upon Helena, sitting alone on a rocky shelf, curled up like a mermaid and gazing out to sea. She looked down at me and smiled dazzlingly.

'Foam-born,' I said, hauling myself out of the water and kissing her. She turned her head sharply, so that my kiss arrived askew, and tasted salty. Her skin was cool and soft. She turned her head back and leaned into me, kissing me on the lips.

'Aphrodite,' I said again.

She shook her head. 'No,' she said; 'not a Greek, and not a goddess. Just silly, and English. That's the trouble.'

'Did you read my note?'

'Not yet. What does it say?'

'Tuesday. The flight leaves at four. I ought to pick you up outside the school just before lunchtime.'

She nodded and thought. 'Quarter past twelve, then. I have a break that makes that easy. I can just walk out.'

'Good. I'll keep the ticket and passport till then. Will you go to your parents?'

She nodded again. We sat silently for a bit on that natural seat in the rocks, watching the sea heaving and dancing out to the horizon, and feeling the sun's kindly warmth on our shoulders.

'All that way,' she said. 'Sometimes, when a plane comes in, I think of the London dirt still in its cabin. Sometimes, when a ship sails by I think of the people sitting there at the Captain's table - decent carefree people who walked up the gangplank at Southampton or Liverpool; but mostly I look at that horizon, and think that England has sunk down below it forever.'

'Forever, till Tuesday,' I said.

She shivered and looked at me. 'Maybe,' she said, and, bending her head, she swung her feet in the water. I touched a freckle on her neck comfortably.

'You haven't told me what you're doing here.'

'Haven't I? Yiorgo came back a day early; so we went to school together on Friday. That was why I couldn't meet you. Then today he said he had to go to Lapithos, so I asked him if he'd drop me in Kyrenia to do some shopping and have a swim.'

'How long have we got?'

'He's coming to pick me up from the cove here at around five o'clock.'

'It must be four now. Can you stay for a bit?'

'I don't see why not. There's nowhere else we can talk safely.'

The Fireflies were racing out at sea, in what wind there was. Somewhere in the heat haze, fifty miles away, lay Asia Minor, full of dirty little towns with names out of St Paul's missionary journeys. Behind us was a world in which men were shot, hanged, bombed, interned, set on fire, hunted through the mountains. Somewhere in that world Xenis was camped with his terrorist group, thinking perhaps of the girl he had half-casually brought out to set against her own people.

We were on the borderline between this mad world in which we lived and that workaday world ahead of us where physically a man wakes up secure. In the Army I was used to these strange situations, to spending two or three years at a time in that sort of peace, or this sort of peril; but for Helena, with her entire life before her, the borderline seemed tangible, terrifying, irrevocable.

'When I was wondering how we could get back into touch,' I said, 'it seemed to me that the most English place you could reasonably ask to visit was the English church in Kyrenia. That would not have alarmed the Demopoulous, surely.'

Helena sighed. 'They are very devout people; and they like me to go to the Greek church with them. Of course I go. If I showed signs of wanting to go to St Andrew's, they would simply assume I had joined the other side; even though I think all these Greeks have a great respect for the English Church.'

I laughed. What on earth is political about going to church?'

'Oh, Michael!' she said, exasperated. 'How can you laugh? Do you still think it is only the Greeks who use their churches for politics? Can you imagine any criticism of Britain in an English church? It must be very hard for you to see your society as it appears to others, and to apply the same standards to yourself as you apply to these poor islanders.'

She was a schoolmarm again; but I knew I had failed her, and looked for some way of covering my embarrassment. I slipped off the rock into the water, and called her to come and have a swim.

She looked down at me and shook her head, smiling like a mother with a naughty child. I paddled around for a bit, then climbed up to the top of the rock to scout around and make sure we were still alone.

'And Xenis?' I asked when I had returned to her side. 'Is he devout?'

'He didn't seem so in London; but here the priests are so much a part of the national struggle.'

'I haven't been to church of my own accord for years. How about you?'

'Me? Darling Michael, I'm a very wicked girl. At one time, Xenis was all I cared about: he, and his ideas. What one cares most about is one's religion, isn't it?'

'And now?'

She rested her palm against the side of my face. 'There's always someone you care most about; at first so much that there isn't room for God, and then later, perhaps, so very much that there is room, has been room all along.'

Her body was warm against mine. After a little, she was clinging to me, and whispering over my shoulder 'When will you return to England, Michael?'

'It depends. A few months at the most. Why?'

'You know why.'

'Yes, I know.'

'Perhaps we could go to church together.'

'That would be a political act.'

'Yes, it would; and why not? There must be joy even in politics.'
She disengaged herself, and spoke sadly. 'Joy, joy, joy. If only we
could have it without this, or some other, shadow. So much
perfection now, and yet across it the thought of what lies
immediately ahead, and is ugly.' Then she said something I can
never forget. 'We seek a deeper quality of life, all the time; but we
never find it until after the chance of savouring it is gone.'

'Sometimes,' I mused, 'perhaps it helps to remember that we are
animals, so that we do not expect too much.'

She looked at me almost resentfully. 'It is not so easy. I have
known what it is to be an animal; to eat and drink and make love. In
the end there is only the shadow of longing for something better.'

The sun was dropping towards the Kyrenia range, and the heat
was going out of it. We talked on for a bit, and settled our plan for
Tuesday. If anything went wrong, Helena would do her best to ring
me. In case that failed, we fixed two or three rendezvous which I
could visit in turn, in the hope that she had managed to reach one of
them.

The end came suddenly. One moment she was sitting swinging
her legs and looking at me. Then she had kissed me, and was in the
sea, moving at a fast crawl back to the cove. I sat there, watching her
movements in the water, until the rocks hid her from sight, and I was
sitting alone on the edge of the mad world, under an evening sky.
That wind was blowing again from the Anti-Taurus, and I felt
terribly cold.

XIX - THE TRAP

On Sunday there were alarums all over our area, and I was kept busy searching hillsides and houses with my troops. After the capture of three wanted men in the Troodos mountains, the Army felt the stimulus of success, and the terrorists that of failure. EOKA was thought to be anxious to reassert its mystique in the eyes of the Greek Cypriots.

On Monday the Colonel sent for me.

'I want to talk to you, Michael, for two reasons. We'll start with the official one. I believe you and Bob Atherton drive around the island quite a lot. Right?'

'Right,' I said.

'Fair enough; within limits, I'm in favour. But you'll see a new map in the Mess that restricts your movements quite a lot. The powers that be reckon some roads are safe and others are not. The main roads have plenty of military traffic, and any terrorists laying an ambush are asking for unforeseen opposition; but the minor ones, at least those with no Turkish villages near, are another matter. I want you two to make a point of keeping off those minor roads except when you're on duty. You'll see which they are.'

'All right, sir. We'll be careful.'

'Good. I'm sure you will. Now the other thing. Have you ever met my big brother - the intelligent one?'

'No, sir.'

'I didn't think you could have done. That's a picture of him on the shelf.'

I had often studied the two photographs in the double frame on the Colonel's shelf, particularly the right-hand one, which was of a strikingly dark girl in a cotton frock, pretty as paint and aged somewhere in the late teens. The left-hand picture was of a heavy moustached man, older than the Colonel, standing up self-consciously and rather precariously, looking benignly over his glasses.

'Is the girl your niece?' I asked.

'Yes. Her mother died when she was born. I've got a picture of her somewhere. She was a very beautiful girl, too.'

'One of the subalterns assured me the other day that the picture was of a girl you had broken your heart over in the days of your youth.'

'All in all,' said the Colonel grimly, 'my heart has remained comfortingly whole. I'm a soldier, not a bloody film star.'

'Is your brother a film star?' I asked innocently, aware to within an inch how far I could go with him.

'No, he's bloody well not, as I suspect you well know. He's a university teacher, and in the line of duty he has to visit the Middle East now and again. For the past month he's been in Athens. Now I don't pretend he's very predictable, but it does seem he's going to fly here for a few days' holiday, starting tomorrow. I wondered if you could help.'

'Willingly. How? Would you like me to meet him at the airport?' I had a momentary feeling this was being sent to mess up my plans for Helena.

'No, I should be able to do that. It's just that I haven't always the time to show guests the sights, especially at the moment. If I felt you could drive him around a bit when I'm tied up, I'd know there was someone who could stand up to him intellectually.'

'Of course,' I said. 'I'd be delighted. Will his daughter be with him?'

The Colonel laughed. 'I'm sure you truly would be delighted if she were; but no, not this time. These two are really all the family I have, Michael; and I'm very fond of them. Alistair is a very interesting person, though you may have to keep him in order a bit. He loves wandering around and talking to people, and of course his Greek is entirely adequate, with a touch of archaism which I understand makes him a figure of great respect. Have I got the right word?'

'What, respect?'

'No, you fool, archaism.' He always had to keep up a pretence of being ill-educated.

I approved the word.

'Right, then. If Alastair turns up when he says he will, I'll bring him into the Mess for a drink tomorrow night, and introduce you.'

By tomorrow evening, Helena would have gone, and I should no doubt welcome a diversion.

We planned to collect her from the Kyrenia school at the time she had suggested, drive her straight to a restaurant in the Turkish quarter of Nicosia, and take her on from there by taxi to the airport. This was stiff with troops and British security men, and although I thought it possible that Yiorgo or someone would be despatched to the airport when Helena's disappearance was established, I felt reasonably sure that he would be powerless to be more than embarrassing, which Bob and I should be able to cope with. In fact, once we had Helena in the car, using the safest roads in the island, we should have the game half-won.

On Tuesday morning I had duties in the camp. Bob went out with a company on training, but was due to return before midday. In case he was delayed I was to go down to Kyrenia and pick up Helena, calling for Bob on the road back to Nicosia.

I was summoned to the Mess telephone at ten o'clock. It was Helena, and she sounded breathless.

'Michael, I'm speaking from the village, and I have to be quick. There's no school today, and we're still here.'

'No school!' I said, surprised. As far as we knew, matters were normal in Kyrenia.

'So Yiorgo says. Some protest is going on. Anyway, we're not needed; but he's asked me to come over and visit the Elementary School at Stenokhori. Do you know Stenokhori?'

'Yes.'

'We're to be there at eleven, but I don't know how long we're staying.'

'Right. I'll try and be there from a quarter past eleven onwards. If you can think of an excuse to slip back to the road after that time, I'll be there to pick you up. If it doesn't work don't worry. We'll manage it another day.'

'All right,' she said rather weakly. 'Now I must go.'

'See you later.'

I studied the map on the wall. Stenokhori was a Greek village on the south side of the Kyrenia range, nearer our camp than to Ayios Iakovos, but in an area that fell under the new prohibition from whichever direction. I need not leave for another forty-five minutes. The question was how to use the time.

I strolled outside to think. The morning was cloudless over the Mesaouria, and the temperature was pleasantly like an English summer. The empty brown cornfields, studded with sparse trees, shimmered away to the horizon and the hazy shape of Mount Olympus. I was young, and of the three courses open to me I really only gave one a chance. To go to the CO and ask for official sanction was open to the old objections; to postpone the whole business, after what I had just said to Helena, was beyond me. It seemed absolutely necessary to take a risk, use the car, and just this once ignore the CO's warning.

If no one expected me, other than Helena, a solitary Englishman driving a car would attract no particular attention.

Officers of the various government departments, Forestry, Water, Antiquities, Education, were still able to drive around the villages in their normal line of business. There seemed to me no reason why anyone should be expecting me. Helena would have kept her counsel, and I was unaware of the ways in which the eyes and ears of this island could operate.

There was little chance that Bob would return before I left, so I scribbled an account of what I was doing, marked it urgent, and gave it to the guard on the camp gate; then I changed into mufti, walked down to get the car, and, in good time, drove down to where the rough road wound off along the south side of the range.

As I bumped along the narrow road I told myself there would be no problem in identifying the Elementary School. These Schools were Government buildings, and tended to look much alike, very foursquare and uncompromising, with Public Works Department marks on. The worst problem I anticipated was finding somewhere to put the car. In both the villages I had to pass through on the way to Stenokhori the important buildings were in the centre of the cluster of houses, near the church, and in one of these cases they included a school. For an Englishman to wait in a car in the middle of a Greek village would attract attention and might be highly dangerous.

However, when I approached Stenokhori I saw with relief that an architect with an eye for a situation had solved my problem. The school was slightly apart from the village, on a low spur in the direction from which I was approaching. I had to turn off the road I was on, to drive for about a mile towards the mountains. From the school the loop doubled back through Stenokhori village and rejoined the road I was just leaving only a quarter of a mile ahead.

I found I was able to stop the car behind a bend and out of sight of the school, yet only a few hundred yards from it.

I got out, and walked up the spur that barred my view. From behind an olive tree I could keep the door of the school under observation. It was a yellow-stone, grim affair of the conventional pattern, big enough for two or three classes. In the road below it were parked three cars, one being the ancient Morris.

I looked at my watch. It was ten past eleven, and I pictured coffee being served in the headmaster's office, preparatory to a tour of the classrooms. When they moved it might be a good time for Helena to excuse herself and go down to the car, but the lengthy ceremonial of the Cypriot coffee-drinking would go on for a bit yet.

At twenty-five past eleven Helena walked out of the door, carrying a large handbag, and picked her way down the hill towards the parked cars. As she reached them, I drove up and opened the nearside door. She smiled tensely, got in beside me, and I accelerated away through the village. It was as easy as that.

It was now only a question of driving to Nicosia. No one seemed to be about in the village, which lay peaceful in the sun. Beyond it were the folds and fields of the Mesaouria, and in the midst of them Nicosia, the city and the airport. There was another mile of rough road before I was due to rejoin the only slightly less rough road I had left. It would be a pity if we got a puncture. I looked at Helena, and put out a hand to pat her.

'All right?'

She was dressed in the yellow and white outfit, sitting unrelaxed and riding the bumps worriedly.

'I have a dreadful feeling,' she said, 'that somehow they know what's going on. We must just trust that all is for the best ... but I don't know why they've let me go ... if they know, I mean.'

They knew all right. The ambush was just short of the road junction. One moment we were slowing for a bend, and the next there was a vast percussion and a sort of giant hand that threw the car across the road, and doubled me up, trapped in a curiously twisted seat with my legs held and my head turned to fire the left. Almost at once the judder of automatic fire began to echo from the hills, and I watched a line of bullets stitch their way across Helena's still body towards me. The last of the burst hit something hard and whined away over me.

There was no pain at first, just numbness and a feeling of being at the mercy of some mighty event. Everything was very quiet, and though Helena's face was lolling over away from me, I knew she was dead. In this stillness I heard boots on the road, and saw a face looking down at Helena with a blank, hard expression. It was that of a young man, with a curious grey lock of hair. For a moment he gazed; then he screwed his eyes up, said '*Panayia mou!*'[11] and looked across the road at someone I could not see. He crossed himself in the Greek way, and his lips moved again, but I heard no words.

After that he looked at me, and saw that my eyes were open. The blank expression returned, with behind it a trace of weariness. As he unslung his carbine, he looked more like a boy with too much work to do than a man killing a hated rival. As I waited for the *coup de grace* the pain in my legs began to tear at me, distorting my sight and sweeping me into unconsciousness. The last thing I remember was the barrel moving towards me, and the clatter on the road as the gun fell from his hands. I never heard the shot that Sergeant Sempill fired to even his personal account; the shot which gave the battalion the glory of capturing a wanted terrorist. Nor did I see Bob, whose common sense had saved my life.

---

[11] Literally 'Holy Mother'; a common exclamation with many interpretations

XX - THE BEDROOM

The memory of the bright Mediterranean sun was fading, and I was in the darkness of an unlighted bedroom on a winter evening in the Midlands of my own country. The girl in the Colonel's photograph was my wife. Cyprus was independent, and a long way off. The ambitions and passions of Brink were my daily concern, and the world outside existed only as a voice on the radio, a paragraph in the paper, or an oblique reference in a letter. After fighting for a doomed empire, I had reached a point where the extent of my struggle was for the safety of a neighbour's cottage, the recovery of a volume of local history, the tidy state of the village graveyard. Friend and enemy were no longer two easily identified categories; I was now at the strange centre of an uneasy world where any hostility damaged the common cause of living together.

Alfred Towle sat hunched in the armchair, his elbows on the arms, his hands clasped in front of his mouth. Had I really told him the whole story or had I been rambling on under these kindly, drowsy drugs?

'Forgive me for talking so much,' I said.

He stirred, and spoke slowly. 'It is the historian's dream to lead someone else's life.'

'Some of the past is very dead.'

'I'm not sure about that. Certainly, the great ideas that move men's minds are never dead. That is why I spend my time on them.'

'I have taken part in no great idea.'

'There again, I'm not so sure. Did those people in the Black Hole of Calcutta believe they were settling British policy in India for decades, or did they just see it as a personal experience of suffering? Yet to a schoolchild now, a century later, the two views are inextricably linked. A Jew, saved from a Nazi prison camp, might say he had taken part in no great idea, just as you say it.'

'But the great ideas are the victorious ones. Only conquerors can speak of them. 'We won the struggle for India a century ago: we won the Second World War. I can only speak for a nation that left Cyprus with its tail between its legs.'

'Oh, dear!' said Alfred, in real distress. 'There's so much to be said in answer to a statement like that. Victory and defeat are not like that, really they're not. One of the amazing things about history is to see how apparently dead ideas come back to life and dominate men's minds. You can never rule a line, and do a final account. A hundred and fifty years ago there were men who said different faculties of men's minds originated in different parts of the brain. These men were apparently completely discredited. Yet now ask any brain surgeon.

'Then again, the conquered, as you call them, do hang on to ideas through great areas of time and space. The idea of freedom, even the idea of empire, has in the past survived centuries of oppressive rule.

'But even by your own definition you were the conquerors in your case. You shot and caught your terrorist.'

'He was only wounded.'

'Not hanged?'

'Xenis Demopoulos was sentenced to death after a trial conducted very clumsily, but in which, mercifully, I was not asked to give evidence. When British policy had changed, he was reprieved, and his sentence was commuted to life imprisonment. Eventually, he was released, and became a member of the new Republican government; which, as far as I know, he still is.'

'And you still feel ... what? Guilty? Indignant?'

'Oh, guilty. That's a mild word to express what I've felt. All my thoughts about those events have been so full of turbulence that to turn them over in my mind has come to seem a pointless repetition of pain; so I've regarded them as a part of my life that is best forgotten.'

'I wonder if any part of one's life is best forgotten. If I were to try to forget the events of my own childhood, I believe I should just be left with unexplainable and incurable symptoms.'

It was ungrateful but human of me to hope I was not to be expected to listen to him yet again on the subject.

'Nonetheless, what is here and now is most important of all,' I said.

'Yes; but what was it you quoted? We seek a deeper quality of life all the time; and never find it until after the chance of savouring it is gone.'

I had done his powers of attention an injustice.

'*Si jeunesse savait; si vieillesse pouvait*,' I said. 'The young run about and break things, and the old look back and only half regret the damage. But the old go on trying to find joy in each remaining minute of their lives. It is the fresh food they want, not the stale.'

'The question is whether anyone ever tastes fresh food.'

'Yes, indeed; that is what Helena was saying: that there is a sort of taste, but never the real joy, the deep satisfaction of which we seem to be capable. I have come to believe that we have to wait for that beyond the borders of our present life.'

'But ought we to admit defeat? The satisfaction may be there, if only we work for it; if only we look again and again at our lives, looking for their meaning as time gives us fresh insights, sharing our experiences as you have shared yours, seeing their reflection in other people's eyes. I do not mean that we should live in the past, only that the past is able to help us savour the present. Have you really not talked over these events before? Surely there was no secret about them at the time?'

'Not about the bare events. I was caught in an ambush with the English fiancée of a Greek Cypriot terrorist. She was killed; I was wounded. But the story was rewritten by the kindness of my Colonel. When Bob got back to the camp that day and found my note, he had the sense to see that I was in considerable danger. So he went straight to the C.C. and told him all he knew. Colonel Hardman authorised him to take a party of troops straight out, and to include me in it. This meant that my foolish venture was given official backing, and became a battalion terrorist-hunting operation. It also meant that I got the disability pension I hardly deserved. EOKA could have added a few details to the story, but at that time they were not writing the history books. The effect of all this was that the complete truth was put tactfully on one side. Bob Atherton knew it, and so did Colonel Hardman, but apart from one or two hospital visits I was soon separated from them. They are far away now, and time has moved on. My wife and father-in-law belong to a new chapter of my life.'

Alfred Towle pondered. I heard the front door bang.

'Well,' he said slowly, 'I think you have been neglecting to feed at one of the sources of life. If time has moved on, where has it moved to? How can you know what your journey is if you try to forget the names of the stations you have passed?'

The door opened, and a voice called 'Michael?'

'Come in, Father,' I said. 'Turn the light on.'

The bulb caused us to shade our eyes for a moment. Then I saw my two odd visitors, Father Morris in a cassock that looked as if it had been slept in, Alfred Towle illuminated cruelly, his angles uneasily held by the armchair. Each looked less than savoury.

'Have you two met?' I enquired.

Father Morris advanced into the room. 'We have not only met,' he said; 'we have argued. Mr Towle is a thinker, and he knows about games.'

'Games?' I repeated stupidly. It sounded very unlikely.

'Yes, games. After his efforts with the choir the other night I have booked him for the next parish party.'

This took some swallowing.

'Have you brought Antigone back?' I asked.

'No. She's still with Anthaea. I offered to come and make sure you'd had your tea.'

'Tea. I'd forgotten about it. Let's get some more cups, and brew up. Alfred, I'm sure you'd like a cup.'

Alfred unwound himself, and stood up. 'Thank you, no.' The priest's arrival had disconcerted him. 'But before I leave you, there is one thing I'd like you both to know. My book has been accepted provisionally by the University Press. It will be published next year, when I have completed the third and final part.'

He grinned rustily as we congratulated him.

'You told me it was about the idea of honour; but what is the title to be?' I enquired.

'It is about the whole system of chivalry in Britain from Edward the Third until as late as George the Third. I am calling it *The Flower of Courtesy*.'

He twitched another grin, and took his leave.

'And that man,' I said as he disappeared; 'that man of all men writes on courtliness.'

'Have your tea,' said Father Morris. 'You have been talking to a man who knows most of all men about party games. He has studied them single-mindedly, and can occupy a large roomful pleasantly for hours at a stretch.'

'For goodness sake how and why does that come about?'

'There is a large gap between his lonely island and the mainland of humanity. This is one of the bridges he is constantly trying to build. Generally, his bridges collapse, but not this one. Given a chance, that man can become everybody's Uncle Alfred.'

'Holy and Reverend Father,' I said, 'as usual, you are right. The fool sees not the same tree that the wise man sees. That particular tree has given me much to think about.'

Father Morris settled on a chair, and waited for the kettle to boil.

'It happened again, did it?'

'That? Oh, you mean my accident. Yes, it happened again.'

'Is the doctor happy about you?'

'I think so. He's drugged me. I'd like to stay drugged.'

'You should of course have taken my advice.'

'I should.'

'Has Towle tired you? You should have thrown him out. Antigone suddenly realised you might need rescuing, and sent me over.'

He made the tea, and waited for it to infuse. I did feel tired, but only pleasantly so. Certainly the first effect of the Towle therapy was good.

'I've done all the talking,' I said. 'Fetching out old things and looking at them.'

'The psychiatrist's couch?'

'That's right. Or the confessional.'

'Confession is to authority, and is met with grace.'

'Grace is not only available through the proper channels.'

He laughed. 'I'm not jealous, Michael. You're not all that ill, you know. You can still argue.'

'The trouble with confession seems to me to be that it encourages people to think their sins have gone away. When you've confessed a sin, you haven't changed the past. You can be assured of grace, feel forgiven, make amends as far as possible; but what has happened has happened.'

'That's inevitable. But even if you can't change the past, you can change the future. Confession places what you have done in the care of God, who can be trusted to dispose it in the complexity of Providence so that its worst effects are limited, and its best infinite.'

'Is that orthodox?'

'How pleasant to hear that old word after so many years! Listen. When Peter denied our Lord, he cheated to stay alive. What followed from his repentance? The life he had cheated to buy was used to found the Church, and he was allowed his delayed crucifixion later.'

I shivered. 'Lucky fellow!'

'You may not be as lucky as that. You may die in your bed rather than on a road in Cambridge or … Cyprus, was it?'

'I should have told you all about it before.'

'I doubt if it's necessary; though it may have helped Peter to tell other people what he had done. I imagine he never lost his horror at it; it was just that the horror was increasingly dwarfed by the wonder of what followed.'

He handed me a cup of tea. 'Now drink that, Michael, be at peace, and get some sleep. I'm going to read my evening office quietly to myself in your armchair, and leave you when Antigone gets back.'

With the warm tea inside me, I went out like a light, and awoke only when Tiggy brought me my supper.

XXI - ILLNESS

'That damned doctor!' said Tiggy. 'I'm going to get him back. Darling, it's no good brooding. You're not a mental case. You're a rather special person who's had an explosion and needs time to get better; but that doesn't account for your present state. I'd say you were either being a bit selfish or you're sickening for something.'

I said I favoured the first solution, but all she would say to that was that I must talk to Daddy when he came for Christmas.

My bruises were in the past, but I was finding it hard to stir myself out of sitting and gazing at the ceiling. Outside, the verge of Christmas had brought a cold wind that ranged over the Midlands, bringing gusts and deluges of whatever can descend from the English sky in a bad winter.

As it happened, Tiggy noticed two days later that the whites of my eyes had turned yellow, and carried out her threat of summoning Dr Churston. I began the lengthy business of being treated for hepatitis.

We went ahead with our not very complex plans for Christmas, even though I was back in bed, and dieting weirdly. Alfred Towle, finally back from Cambridge, was dragged from his typewriter for Christmas dinner, in recognition of his services. He and my father-in-law debated the plight of scholarship while Tiggy brought me tiny portions of forbidden food.

My father-in-law had not been entirely at ease with me. He regarded himself as to blame for my state, and spent worried sessions in my bedroom chair urging me to get everything in proportion. I tried to reassure him.

'You know very well,' I said, 'how much I owe to you and your brother, and of course your daughter. You happened to arrive in Cyprus, admittedly on the wrong plane and from the wrong direction, at the moment when my predicament was on everyone's lips. There was no obligation on you to visit me in hospital, repeatedly and often without your brother, merely because I would under better circumstances have been showing you round the island.'

'As far as I can remember, the best sites were on that piece of coast. Anyway, Jim was otherwise engaged most of the time. Some dubious venture - which was it?'

'Suez,' I said grimly.

'Ah, yes. Suez. The whole battalion struck camp and sailed away, suddenly. That large young man, too, the friend of yours. He went ahead of the rest.'

'Bob Atherton. Then you invited me to come and convalesce on Mrs Stamp's food at Oxford. You didn't have to do that.'

'The event has been propitious; up to the point where I started interfering. The important thing, my dear fellow, is not to let this latest mistake of mine weigh too heavily. You are comparatively young. Life is before you, and you have a great deal to offer. Your brain is keen, and your general physique, though small, is as strong as a horse - if you will forgive the comparison with a beast of which as far as I remember you are not fond. The Greek centaur ...' he said dreamily '... the ideal of the university teacher: the keen brain, the strong body. Had you never thought of teaching?'

'No,' I said firmly. 'I had not. The Greeks also invented satyrs, with the bodies of goats.'

'Oh? Do you think they invented them?'

'Invented them, or believed in them. I tend to see myself as one of them.'

The Doctor chuckled politely. 'You are too hard on yourself,' he murmured. 'That is a centaur's joke.'

'I mean that we are more than minds and bodies. We have emotions. I am too susceptible.'

'The family has been a disappointment?'

'No, of course not; but on that rather horrible occasion in Cyprus I let infatuation warp my judgment.'

'I hate that word "infatuation". Please don't use it. Were you not in love with the girl?'

'Yes, I was.'

'And you were young and wanted to help her?'

'Yes.'

'And she is at peace long ago now. For whom are you sorry?'

That was too difficult for me.

'That reminds me,' he added, 'to tell you about my brother, whose views on this matter I share. I have news that he is being posted to London as a Brigadier.'

'That's good news. I thought he'd resigned himself to coming out of the Service.'

'The matter is still in doubt. He tells me this may be his last job. It seems a pity, because I believe him to be a good soldier.'

'He's outstanding,' I said; 'but in the old bachelor way, with no interests outside his job, or none that take his mind off it, and little time for the upstarts that forge past him up the Army List.'

'Funny that you should refer to his being a batchelor, because at long last there seems some doubt about this. There is a lady in Germany …'

'Good Heavens!' I exclaimed. 'At his age!'

'He is, I believe, forty-five,' said the Doctor mildly.

'And the lady?'

'I am not clear; but younger by about ten years, I think. She has been working in Bonn.'

'What excitement. When shall we see him?'

'In the spring, I understand. I am preparing Ruby.'

The Doctor's house in North Oxford was generally my old CO's home when he was in England. Ruby Stamp, the housekeeper, had run the place since Tiggy was an infant, and was not likely to take kindly to the arrival of a lady with claims on the person she still called Captain Jim.

My father-in-law's Christmas stay was brief. He enjoyed above all wandering about Brink, talking to people; but at that time of the year the High Street was mostly empty, except for one or two resolute and muffled housewives, butting their way through wind and sleet to do their shopping.

After he had gone we saw few friends - mostly Juliet and Father Morris, and occasionally Alfred Towle, whose typewriter was in full spate. Juliet had settled into the duties of a chatelaine, and seemed to have her father eating out of her hand. Macready had taken to going up to London for two or three days together on what he called consultancy work, and would bring occasional weekend guests back to be entertained.

'Women?' I enquired of Tiggy.

'Not so far; just business associates. Juliet wouldn't allow women friends. In a way, I wish he deferred to her less; he's settling her down as a household slave.'

'Oh, do you think so? She does have plenty of time to enjoy herself. She's always going out somewhere. It's such a change from the days when the old man watched her every movement.'

'Yes, but just you watch till he has to face the possibility of losing her. He'll raise the hosts of hell.'

'She's a free woman. That was established when she walked out.'

'And was put in doubt again when she walked back in. If you ask me, those two have more in common than meets the eye.'

'In common! Between her and that loquacious bounder?'

'Darling, Juliet's his daughter. They quarrel because they recognise themselves in each other.'

'I cannot see any possible point of resemblance between them. Between that lovely girl and that toad, paddling his damned fingers over anything in female shape.'

'Thank you. I never thought of myself before as a Thing in female shape.'

'Now stop it, and be serious.'

'Very well, I will. We've talked about the way that rapturous encounter we witnessed before Christmas has flowered into a romance.'

'You mean between Juliet and Richard Bone? We certainly have. Richard's been in to see me at least twice on his way to the Denbury Road.'

'And what about Derek Major?'

'Poor chap. It's just bad luck.'

'Would it surprise you to know that Derek still takes Juliet out just as frequently?'

'He doesn't, does he?'

'He does. And do you realise that Alfred Towle is again a regular visitor at the Macreadys'?'

'Good God!'

'So finger-paddling may not be limited to Macready senior.'

'Oh, nonsense! The girl's uncertain, that's all. She's having fun while it lasts, though come to think of it, it can't be much fun with Alfred! She's making up her mind.'

'Maybe. I'm all for numbers when it comes to young men; but just bear in mind the possibility that your girl friend may be a tiny bit heartless.'

This fitted too well into the jaundiced thoughts which I was having at the time, and which continued through January without my having recovered much zest for life. It was a month spent half in bed, half in the study, unwilling to work, but unable to accept my own feeble state. The dreary weather continued into February, when I was at last declared free from jaundice. For a day or two I led a normal life, pottering up the High Street through pale sunshine as far as the shops; then a violent cold attacked me and sank within a few days to my chest. I was back where I was, and a burden again to my poor wife.

'Everybody's in a state at this time of year,' declared Father Morris cheerfully. 'But the flowers are budding. Rebirth comes after suffering. After Easter, we've decided to have a party, so big that the Parish Hall won't take it. If your committee will hire us the Victory Hall, the Church is going to strike that note of joy which is generally absent from our lives. We're going to have wine and music and dancing and games, and you know who's going to be master of the ceremonies?'

'Oh, no!' I protested. 'Not Alfred!'

'None other. You will see him at work on his home territory for the first time. I promise you he is the life and soul. He's going to join my choir too.'

'Will you stop at nothing?'

'Nothing whatever,' said Father Morris happily.

XXII - THE VISITOR

For once April was the kindest month, and the warm spell that commonly ends March continued with only a few interruptions right up to Easter. For day after day I had sat on the balcony and watched the world go by, pottering in to do some work as I felt the energy returning to my body. An early bud or two appeared on the climbing roses, and up and down the town the cherries and magnolias were rioting in the gardens.

One day I heard the telephone ring inside and stop as Tiggy answered it. After a conversation that must have lasted forty-five minutes, she came out to see me rather hesitantly.

'I've got a surprise for you,' she said.

'Who was it?' I asked.

'He didn't want me to tell you; but he's coming tomorrow to stay with us for a few days.'

'Oh, come on! Who is it?'

'I'd better tell you. It's Bob Atherton.'

'Bob! The uncommunicative old so-and-so! I didn't even know he was in England.'

'He came back from Hong Kong a week ago.'

Since our wedding four years before, when Bob was my best man, we had heard from him twice and seen him not at all. For most of the time he had been on a lengthy posting to a Far East HQ, and I imagined he was now due for a spell in the UK. It was good news that he wanted to come and see us.

I sighed and blinked in the sun. 'Will he be in time for the opening of the Fair?' I asked.

'Just about. He's leaving London after breakfast.'

The Easter Fair was an annual event that involved the whole town, causing differing degrees of anger and delight among the inhabitants. In the square in front of the church, the fair crammed itself for three days, blaring forth music that permeated the streets and drove the inhabitants of the houses around the square particularly frantic. One old couple with an upstairs sitting-room had to watch the seats on the Big Wheel carry their giggling cargo a few feet from the windows all day and half the night. Any person entering the lych gate had to thread his way between a coconut shy and a darts stall; but no vicar ever seemed to mind. It was an event that had always happened and would always continue to happen; so the Kingdom of God and the kingdom of this world settled down happily to work together for a few days.

Fred Stirling was Mayor this year, and it was his task to open the Fair on Easter Monday. This meant that he put on his robes, processed from the Town Hall with his Corporation, and having proclaimed the Fair open climbed on the roundabout for a free ride. The sight, I thought, must bring delight to the heart of a man who had just spent three years in Hong Kong.

'Good morning, Antigone,' said an unctuous voice below us.

I leaned forward so that he could see there was a husband to reckon with.

'Ah, Jeffries,' said Mr Macready. He never used my Christian name, and I think still disliked me for having caught him off balance at the time his wife and daughter ran away.

'I trust we shall be seeing you both on Friday,' he said, posing on the pavement below.

'Why, what's happening on Friday?' I asked stupidly.

'The Parish Party is on Friday. I believe it is very important that we should support these local affairs. I am bringing my daughter and two business friends from overseas who are spending the weekend with me.'

Antigone had evaporated and left me to face him.

'Yes,' I said. 'We shall be there.'

'Good. The Vicar must feel he can rely on people like us for support.'

I wondered what particular points of resemblance made Macready and myself two of a kind.

'Unfortunately,' he continued, I have to leave for London before the opening of the Fair tomorrow. However, Juliet will be representing me. There again ...' He went on to state all the unexceptionable principles which are better not stated.

Mrs Ellerman's Pip lay on the garden wall, against a background of flowering currant. As I watched him, he put his head back and opened his mouth in an enormous yawn; then he looked in my direction, and I saw his ears go back and his tail twitch.

Next day started misty, but by mid-morning the sun was shining warmly through. The Fair vehicles had been in the town since the previous afternoon, and the stalls had been unloaded into their traditional places. Fred walked by on his way to the Town Hall, and I cheered him on his way.

'Don't fall off your horse,' I urged him.

He stopped and looked quickly at me. 'I get sick, you see. It's funny, because I'm all right in a car; but put me on one of those beasts and I get this feeling in the pit of my stomach.'

'Have a stiff drink first.'

'You've got to be careful. Remember last time the dogs came.'

One of the Corporation had got in among the stirrup cups last time hounds had met in the square, and there had been recriminations.

Ten minutes after Fred had disappeared, a red sports car weaved up the street and came to a stop below my balcony. A very fit-looking Bob got out, stretched himself, and regarded me.

'How do I get up there?' he demanded.

I explained.

'It's good to see you,' I said sincerely, when he emerged on the balcony.

'Well, I thought we might ...' he began; but his voice trailed away, and he just shook his head and sat down.

'What's the matter?'

'The matter? You look like a bloody ghost, old boy. I can't get over it.'

'Do I?'

'You do. Where's Tiggy?'

'She's getting ready to go to the Fair.'

'Are we going to a fair?'

'We are.'

'Talk about being swept into a breathless whirl!'

Tiggy emerged from the study in her new spring dress and greeted Bob, who made a low purring noise.

'I hope the privileges of a best man still hold,' he said, kissing her without obvious reluctance. 'You don't look as if you've had a bad winter, my dear.'

Tiggy wrinkled her nose at him and said lightly 'It's been a bit of a worry at times, that's all.'

'You ought to get her out more, Michael. Let's take her up to London while I'm here. We'll do a sort of Mystery Tour.'

'London!' I said, startled.

'Yes, London. What on earth are you jumping like a stag for? We'll go to London, won't we my dear?'

'It would be nice, wouldn't it, Michael?' said Tiggy rather tremulously.

'But ...' I began, and stopped. Everything seemed different and possible with Bob there.

'We ought to go to the Fair now,' said Tiggy. 'The Mayor and Corporation will be coming soon.'

We walked along to the church, where a crowd was waiting for the opening. The stallholders were at their posts, looking rather self-conscious. Father Morris was standing chatting to the proprietor. The spring sun showed off the bright colours against the tall sandstone houses and the great church tower, with its spire stuck on as an afterthought.

Juliet and Derek Major detached themselves from the edge of the throng and came towards us.

'Tiggy darling, the dress is marvellous,' carolled Juliet.

We introduced Bob, who made that purring noise in his throat again. 'Michael's surrounded with beautiful girls,' he announced, and took on the pair of them.

I had not talked to Derek since that day coming back on the train from London. He made a point of saying how glad he was to see me out and about again, and we stood together watching Fred and his uneasy followers march down the High Street to perform their duty. Fred shook the proprietor's hand and read a proclamation in a sort of '*Hear ye*' English, then amid the applause and ribald comments of the townsfolk he mounted the back of a large green-and-yellow dragon, followed on to the roundabout by his Corporation. The music started, shaking the square with its gaudy organ notes, and slowly the roundabout began to move.

Bob and the girls had moved off, and I saw them rocking with laughter on the other side of the square, with Father Morris joining in.

'Come along,' I said to Derek; 'we're missing the fun.'

We carved through the crowd, close to the roundabout, which was now whirling round at full speed. A green-and-yellow dragon hustled towards me and away again, carrying a man with eyes tight shut and cheeks that matched his mount. Poor Fred was suffering the penalty of eminence.

When we reached the rest of our party, the laughter had stopped, and Bob was delivering a lecture to the girls, who contemplated me with solemn eyes. Only Bob remained at ease.

'I want to go up the tower,' he said. 'And the Vicar says he can lend me the key. Tiggy won't come with me because of her dress ...' (Tiggy shut her eyes and shuddered) ... 'Juliet won't come with me because of her dress' (Juliet looked mesmerised, as if she would have written off several dresses to go up a tower with Bob) ...'so you'll have to take me up, old boy.'

'Me?' I protested. 'I doubt if I could get up to the ringing chamber. Derek will go with you.'

Derek stepped forward and opened his mouth, but Bob raised a hand and cut him off. 'Derek has promised Juliet to take her round the fair,' he insisted. 'Tiggy is going with them to make sure they behave themselves. Ready to go, Vicar?'

I looked beseechingly at Tiggy, but encountered a stony gaze.

'The key's in the vestry, Michael,' said Father Morris. 'On the board. Can you find it?'

As we threaded our way to the lych gate I glanced back and saw the roundabout slowing down. A moment later Fred slid off his seat and tottered away, glazed in the eyes but with his ordeal over.

The inside of the church was quiet and cool, and the Easter decorations made a bower of the pulpit and screen. I fetched the key of the tower and unlocked the door.

'Now take it easy, old lad,' said Bob. 'Go first, and go at your pace. If you get breathless, stop and rest.'

I had only walked up and down the streets since my illness. I felt curiously frightened at this sudden task, as if I were being asked to nip up Helvellyn without warning. My leg made it slowish going, but I was surprised and pleased to find when we reached the ringing chamber that I was no more out of breath than Bob.

We paused there, and inspected the records of peals; then I moved to the door that led to the bell tower.

'I believe it gets a bit narrow now,' I said.

'You believe!' exclaimed Bob. 'You believe it gets narrow! Are you trying to tell me you haven't been up here before?'

'No, I haven't as a matter of fact. Not beyond the ringing chamber.'

'And how long have you lived here?'

'Four years, isn't it?'

'Four years, and you've never been up the church tower. Good grief! My dear old chap, what has come over you?'

'Well, you know how it is. When something's on your door- step ...'

'Been up all the other church towers in the county, then, have you?'

'No.'

'Been up one?'

'Actually, no.'

'Good grief!' said Bob again. 'I should never have trusted you on your own.'

We moved up the tower stairway, very slowly because of the darkness and the narrow stairs. The bell chamber was lighter, but full of twigs and dust. From the bells a wooden stairway ran up to a door which came out in the base of the spire. I clambered up, and threw open this door. The first effect was to turn up the volume of a selection of Scottish marches on the roundabout, but they were quickly followed by a wave of sweet spring air in place of the musty tower-smell. Bob joined me on the roof, and we leant against the spire to recover our breath.

Round the tower was a parapet, beyond which, in the distance, was what looked like white smoke, obliterating the horizon. I moved forward and peered over, to realise that our fine day was in fact a clearing in a mist. Above us was the midday sun; beneath and around us were the houses and roads and gardens of Brink; but beyond the northern verges of the town was mystery.

A few fields were visible, among them the Grammar School playing fields; otherwise only the town seemed to exist, in air so still that two weathervanes within half a mile of each other pointed in opposite directions.

Immediately below us, the heads of people were moving among the coloured sectors of canvas that filled the square. In the patches of garden behind the High Street one or two misanthropes were sowing vegetables. I looked for our house, but it was mostly hidden behind the buildings on the near side of the High Street.

'Worth a look, isn't it?' asked Bob.

'It's as if the whole of existence outside had stopped,' I said. 'There's only Brink under the sun.'

Bob looked at me cautiously through narrowed eyes. 'They say people who've been in mental hospitals for a long time can't bear to leave them,' he commented.

'People who've been in the world a long time can't bear to leave it, either. You get settled in any place, even a prison.'

'Well, you said it. I will admit this is a lovely town, though.'

The sun seemed brighter than it had been, and I looked out towards the Grammar School. Beyond it, more fields were coming into view.

'The mist's clearing.'

Both weathervanes were pointing the same way now, and a light wind fanned our cheeks. To the north, beyond the borders of the town, there were gleams, first from a bus moving along the main road, then from the greenhouse of a nursery, then from the windows of a farmhouse. Visibility grew until the black edges of the reservoir were uncovered. In the south, where we now turned our eyes, there was no mist at all. The sun dazzled over miles of hills and fields, woods and farms, out to the stacks and towers of the steelworks and the city beyond.

'We were made to learn a poem at school about the Midlands being sodden and unkind,' said Bob, putting his tongue out at a seagull on the parapet. 'Which reminds me I'm thirsty. Did I see a hostelry on the edge of the square?'

We climbed down and collected Derek and the girls. A party was just leaving one of the rustic tables outside the Volunteer, which Bob promptly commandeered. We settled there till lunch, soaking in the sun and the beer and the last American musical but two, until our pores were glowing with them. Tiggy looked at me rather nervously at first, but seemed reassured and sat contentedly next to Bob, gazing at the concourse and smiling dreamily at his stream of comment.

The next two days were lived at a pace I had forgotten was possible. Bob's energy was never-ending, reminding me of younger days, when every minute of our life was full of event. I sensed he was watching me carefully, to make sure I was equal to the demands he made; but he never slackened, and we spent much time in the new red sports car, picnicking, visiting local pubs and beauty spots, and even trying the evening rise on Lord Fifield's stream, the first time my trout rods had been out since I was married. Twice, Juliet came with us; her father was not returning till shortly before the Parish Party on Friday, and she seemed to have unlimited time and appetite for pleasure, treating Bob like a favourite uncle. At least, that was how I hoped she was treating him, Bob's unmarried state, despite his age and eligibility, depending on his skill in manipulating emotional temperatures.

On Thursday, after a late breakfast, Bob looked at me triumphantly, winked at Tiggy, and said 'Now, old boy, today we have a surprise for you.'

'We?' I repeated.

'Yes. Tiggy and I. I think it'll do, don't you, my dear?' Tiggy smiled and said nothing.

'It's time for that mystery tour to London. We'll have a light lunch and be off afterwards, eh?'

'I don't believe you've let me cook a proper meal for you since you came,' said Tiggy, who was having the time of her life.

'Look, my love, you've been cooking for this chap for four years. It's time you had a break and a chance to wear some pretty dresses. Have you got something special for tonight?'

It seemed she had.

They made me take it easy till lunch. Afterwards we piled into the car and sailed away, down the London road, on to the new motorway, and out of the Midlands for the first time since the autumn.

We stopped for a long picnic tea in the last service area, and entered the suburbs of London as the early traffic was beginning to leave. Neither of them would tell me where we were going. I was to sit back and enjoy myself.

It was half past five before Bob drove the car into a garage in Mayfair. We emerged into the crowded back streets of high rush hour, and for a moment I felt a stab of panic.

'Now,' Bob announced, 'we're going to have a walk and see the sights. Are you game?'

'I'm game,' I said. 'Where shall we go?'

'Let's have a look at the hub of the old Empire, shall we?'

'All right,' I said.

'After that, we're going to Sam Browne's.'

Sam Browne's was a club in St James's, mostly frequented by army officers and ex-colonials.

As we approached Piccadilly I asked myself if I had a headache, but was unable to raise one. It was one thing to walk through London looking for employment, and another to visit it for enjoyment's sake with my wife and friend. Life even in London seemed too exciting to be frittered away on headaches.

Piccadilly was in its usual state, noisy and uncaring; but it seemed no concern of mine. We crossed to the Ritz and walked up towards the Circus. Everything was as I had always known it, the list of preachers at St James' church, the appeal for funds, the shops; even the titles of the blue films seemed only a slightly different combination of the words 'Paris', 'virgin', and 'nude'.

'It was here that I made a fool of myself,' I said, and as I spoke I looked into the eyes of the newspaper-seller at the Tube station. It could have been the one who helped me: I was too far gone at the time to remember his face.

'Never again,' said Bob firmly, and stopped to consider the Circus. 'Ugh!' he exclaimed. 'What hope was there for an Empire centred on this hideous and dangerous little roundabout? Remember Paris, Rome, even Athens, where at least there's an orange grove in the city centre. Can this vulgar effort presume to challenge them? Do you blame the subject peoples for fighting?'

'There are other places in London,' I said. 'This is only the centre of cheap culture.'

'Darling,' whispered Tiggy, squeezing my arm, 'are you really all right?'

Bob swept us back down Lower Regent Street, and into Jermyn Street. 'No, of course he's not all right,' he snorted. 'He's disgusted by the whole business, like the rest of us; and like the rest of us, he's spotted that it's after six o'clock and time for a drink. Now, Michael, the surprises are about to begin. They're pleasant ones, but you'll have to keep your head and remember that a lot of water has gone under the bridges since 1956. You've had your troubles, and other people have had theirs. I don't exactly class my three years of opening car doors in Hong Kong as suffering, though it hasn't tended to settle me in my chosen career. Believe it or not, there are worse things than opening car doors. This is a hard world, just in case I hadn't mentioned it to you before.'

He rambled on until we turned in at the ladies' entrance of Sam Browne's. The lift to the club rooms on the first floor was taking up a smartly dressed woman I had glimpsed as we negotiated the swing doors. As we waited, Bob consulted the porter.

'That's right, sir,' said the latter. 'In the Milward Room. Mrs Andrelski has just gone up.'

'Andrelski,' I mused. 'That rings a bell. Wasn't there a Duncan Andrelski in that Merseyside regiment outside Nicosia? Nasty man, but I don't remember a wife.'

Bob nodded grimly. 'Very nasty indeed. He won't be here tonight.'

The lift returned, and took the three of us up. The Milward Room proved to be a light, pleasant writing room looking on the square, with two groups of leather armchairs. From one of these the large and familiar figure of my uncle by marriage emerged, advanced, and hugged his niece comprehensively.

'Hullo, Michael,' he greeted me, winking over her shoulder.

'Hullo, Colonel,' I returned. 'Sorry, Brigadier. So this is the surprise; and very pleasant, too.'

'I said surprises, in the plural,' Bob reminded me.

'Yes, indeed,' said the Colonel, settling Tiggy in a chair. 'I want you to meet my future wife, Barbara Andrelski.'

Behind us, a smart, tall, middle-aged woman had come into the room. For a moment, I did not recognise her; then she came forward and offered her cheek, and it was Barbara: an older Barbara with her fair hair greying and short, and with curiously tired eyes.

'Barbara I know,' I said; 'but Andrelski?'

Brigadier Jim advanced on her, and took her hand. 'It's a long story,' he said. 'Anyway, it'll be Hardman soon. Bob come and be reintroduced ...' Bob advanced and chastely kissed her cheek '... but Antigone my niece you're meeting for the first time.'

Introductions over, he continued 'We have one more member of our party, and I propose to give him till seven o'clock; then we shall eat, whether or not he's joined us. I know you three have a long journey back.'

We all sat down. I found myself between Bob and Barbara, trying to adjust my thoughts.

'There's a lot to say, isn't there?' said Barbara. 'Jim's brought me up to date with some of the news about you. The last I heard of you was at a Press briefing in Cyprus in 1956. You were pretty ill, and that poor child what was her name?'

'Helena.'

'Yes, Helena, who had done nothing, was dead. I went to the service at St Andrew's, Kyrenia, and met the parents.'

'I saw them in hospital. They came to see me before they flew back; but I was still a bit fuddled. So were they ... decent, fuddled people, all wound around with the pretences of death. Everybody was pretending, that Helena had been a member of the British community in the island, that St Andrew's was her normal place of worship, that there was no particular motive for her killing, that she and her parents were on good terms, and so on.'

'It certainly brought out the bad journalist in me. I told the little EOKA link man in the bar of the Ledra Palace that I was disgusted with the whole business. Of course, he shrugged and said he quite agreed with me, but what could he do?'

'Aren't good journalists allowed to be indignant?'

'Oh, yes; but not for personal reasons. Bob could never understand that, could you, Bob?'

'I forgave you,' said Bob.

'People don't really want to be forgiven; they want to forgive. It was I who forgave you, Bob. Remember how I let you come and see me just before Suez? That must have been the last time we met until now. I was really very fond of you in those days.'

'Fond enough to marry Andrelski two months after I left?'

'Oh, marriage. That seemed at the time to be quite another matter. You weren't for a girl to marry. Nor was Duncan, but you couldn't have convinced me of that at the time.'

'How long did you stay in Cyprus?' I asked.

'Till 1958, when the two communities started a shooting match. Duncan's battalion had been posted to Germany, and instead of leaving him then, I fooled myself he might change enough for us to carry on somehow in new surroundings. I stuck it for a year, then had a quiet breakdown and got a job in Bonn afterwards. At some point Duncan's CO, who was a pet, reintroduced me to Jim. I'd known him vaguely in the old days as the benevolent terror of your lives, and meeting him again made me feel there was something stable in life after all. I don't wonder you boys were fond of him.'

'What are you talking about?' enquired her fiancé.

'I'm saying I don't wonder these boys were fond of you.'

The Brigadier patted her and looked at Bob and me severely. 'They were a hell of a handful. Too intelligent for me. Now I'm marrying an intelligent woman, and I suppose I'll need a dictionary at my own bloody breakfast table.

'Anyway,' he added, 'if I'm in difficulty I shall send for Alastair. He'll keep you all in order.'

As if on cue, a club servant approached him. 'Brigadier Hardman? There's a message from your brother, sir. He's at the

Senior Naval and Military. He says he's met a friend, and will you excuse him if he's a little late?'

The Brigadier groaned. 'No point in waiting, then,' he said. 'Was there ever?'

Over dinner he looked thoughtfully at Bob and asked him what he was going to do next.

'London and the daily Tube,' said Bob gloomily. 'Then maybe out of the Service. Maybe not.'

'Is the choice yours?'

'Yes. On the one hand my next posting would probably be back to the battalion, which could be pleasant; on the other hand as you grow older there are too many of these office jobs in prospect. Furthermore, and speaking seriously for a change, that awful mess at Suez made me wonder what the hell we were all doing.'

'I'm with you there,' said the Brigadier. 'Many of us were doubtful about the whole business from the start. No good was ever likely to come of it, and moving all those troops from Cyprus handed the island to EOKA on a plate.'

'Yes, at that point I think we had EOKA beaten. Are you staying in, sir?'

'I don't think I shall. I've given half my life to being a soldier, and this for the first ten years meant being at the centre of important events. Since then I have been at the centre of plenty of trouble, but not at the centre of any war to speak of. I have felt that the important events are elsewhere. The question is, where are the important events, and how can one get in on them?'

'Well, where are they?'

'Maybe in industry. It might be that the other half of my life, Barbara's half, would be better spent as, say, personnel manager to an industrial firm.'

Bob shivered. 'You almost persuade me to stay in; but of course I haven't yet discovered a Barbara. At least ...' He seldom looked confused, but at this moment he was not far off.

'At least not since Barbara?' suggested the Brigadier.

Barbara herself came to the rescue. 'I think Jim's the sort of person who wants to feel he's contributing to some master-plan; and in Cyprus and Suez there never was one that would have worked. Enormous forces were operating in the world, which meant that even what you call "beating EOKA" would have been no more significant as a victory than reopening the Suez Canal would have been, in the long run. Events like this make scenes for personal drama, but they're almost meaningless on the larger scale. You could say that the events in the Middle East in 1956 existed to blow Michael out of uniform, to blow poor little Helena out of the world altogether, to get me into the trouble I deserved, to make a turning-point in Jim's life, Antigone's life, even Bob's life if I deduce from what he says that he's actually wondering where he's going. That would be new.'

'Ow!' Bob protested.

'But you can always talk like that,' said Antigone unexpectedly. 'Even in times that seem to be full of meaning, like the War, millions of people are at the mercy of enormous forces. Whether they're on the right side or the wrong side or no side at all, their main concern is that their wives have left them, their businesses are failing, their fathers are in prison. Somewhere, somehow, the enormous forces have to be met at the small person's level, and if there really is any meaning to anything you have to believe that in however tiny a way these forces can be ... what's the word I need?'

'Challenged? Modified?' I offered.

'Yes, that.'

'I'm not so sure,' said Barbara. 'When that Greek in the Ledra Palace shrugged and asked what he could do, I was inclined to agree with him and say "nothing". Whatever he did was unlikely to have any significance two years or even two months afterwards. You can bring religion in, of course, and use words like "faith"; but we're talking about what happens in this world, not in some other. On the other hand I'm sure there are times and places where you can have an effect on history. Jim's looking for a point where he can join a battle that has meaning. If he'd been free to look for it in 1956 he wouldn't have gone to Cyprus or Suez. A romantic journalist might say the world was turning round some hut in the Atlas Mountains, or a back garden in Budapest; but in sober truth it may have been turning round a group of politicians in some Western capital who saw what ordinary people at that moment no longer thought worth fighting for, or round some discussion between management and labour in London. It would have been worth being at the right place at the right time.'

Her intended looked at her proudly. 'What a lot you know, my love. Beautifully put.'

'No, Uncle Jim,' said Antigone; 'I think you're both wrong. We've all got to believe that what we do here and now has all the importance in the world, and is right at the centre of what you call history. Faith is exactly the word I would use about this. Even though everyone has personal stakes that seem much bigger than the political ones, we have to believe that our handling of them affects the way the world is propelled around. Even people like Odysseus or you, Uncle Jim, have to have this faith in the end, or accept that they're has-beens. Odysseus has come home. He's burnt Troy, outwitted everyone, and won back Penelope. Is it possible for him to be satisfied with a reputation as a wise governor of a small island, or at the worst a name as a portentous bore? His own past seems infinitely more important than anything that lies before him; but he has to go on living. Remember that most people haven't even past success to look back on. The ordinary man has lost his war, lost his way, lost his family, and hasn't even an island to govern.'

'I didn't lose my way,' said her father behind her. 'It's just that I met a man on the train. How are you all?'

The Doctor was welcomed, forgiven, introduced to Barbara, and allowed to join the meal a course behind.

'I interrupted an important conversation,' he said. 'What was it about?'

Antigone looked at Barbara, and smiled. 'I needed your help. It was about Odysseus and Uncle Jim.'

'Ah!' said the old man; 'the return of the legions.'

'There you are, Barbara,' said the Brigadier. 'That's mind, that is. Beat that.'

'The question is, Daddy,' said Antigone, 'what battle remains for each of us to fight. Or perhaps I should say for each man to fight, because I'm going to go where Michael goes, and do what he does, in a very old-fashioned way.'

'This is my fault, Alastair,' said her uncle. 'I'm wondering whether to leave the Army and go into industry, because I suspect that's where I'm needed. You and I grew up in a country which had outposts around the world. We felt we lived in a big country which had confidence in itself and demonstrated this to the world. But the country we grow old in will feel much smaller and may struggle to survive, to resist outside forces. That's my theory in a nutshell ... you see, Bob?'

Bob shook his head. 'I'm one of Tiggy's little men,' he said. 'My wars are little ones. As long as I can find friends and knock about a bit, I shan't be complaining. I can't operate at your level.'

The Brigadier laughed. 'You make me sound very portentous.'

'No, sir,' said Bob. 'You make me feel very trivial.'

Barbara had sat back in her chair and relaxed, looking peaceful and elegant. Now she laughed to herself and said 'On Antigone's definition I'm one of the little women. I've lost most of my battles. Perhaps that helps, because it makes you keener on the future. I really feel at the moment I just want to be Aunt Barbara, Uncle Jim's wife. Like Bob, I've discovered the things that look important aren't worth fighting for.'

'I don't believe I said that,' Bob protested.

'Like me, you've been blown up, Barbara,' I said. 'When the shock is over, you may see things differently.'

She looked at the Brigadier tenderly. 'If this is shock, I'd like to stay in it. But tell me, Michael, how do you see things?'

'It's difficult to say, because one only really sees them at all now and again. I'm beginning to view people more dispassionately and less superficially; including myself. Trying to achieve anything is less of an obsession and more of a cheerful effort. Most of the time I don't seem to be getting anywhere or doing anything or fighting any battle; then suddenly one has a brief glimpse of truth and sees that one fits into an enormous pattern of good and evil. Life seems rather like a marriage; it offers years of self-discipline and growing-up, only relieved by the steady gleam of affection and lightning flashes of real ecstasy. I can't look at it all as the Brigadier does, because I don't believe man can gain control over his destiny. What's more, I'm glad he can't, because he's too dangerous. His causes become obsessions, and innocent people suffer. What sort of person does one most admire? The one who is dedicated to a cause, or the one who is open to them all, and apart from them all?'

I looked at my father-in-law, and saw he was directing at me a glance of such real approval and affection that I remained very quiet for the rest of that happy evening.

XXIII - The Parish Party

Bob left us on Friday, and we were back to our ordinary lives, feeling very flat. As Tiggy had said, Troy was burnt, the voyaging past; the humdrum affairs of Ithaca remained. The prospect of seeing friends and family now and again cheered both of us somewhat. Barbara had seemed frightening to Tiggy, but she trusted her uncle's judgment; as for Bob, her brief encounter with him at the time of our wedding had not prepared her for such a devoted ally.

'After the last few days,' she said, 'the parish party tonight is not exactly going to seem a wild debauch. I don't believe the entire population of Brink would be able to summon one tenth of the air of carnival Bob brings to having his breakfast.'

'I wonder who will escort Juliet,' I mused.

'Probably no one. She'll be coming with her father's nasty weekend guests.'

We presented ourselves shortly after eight o'clock, and found the Hall decorated with spring flowers and greenery. The stage was occupied by a music stand, backed by the set of the last production of the Brink Amateur Theatre. This group had wisely avoided the conventional title of the Brink Amateur Dramatic Society, without avoiding the standard the initials would so brutally have suggested. The scene-painting for the Christmas production of *Aladdin* was horrifyingly crowded with oriental pillars and jewels.

The Morrises greeted us and guided us to the coffee urn, where we found the Arbuthnots. I asked after the progress of Cyril's history of the school.

He shook his head. 'Terrible. Even in the holidays there's never enough time. We're busy fighting a battle for the school at the moment, and that takes up a lot of energy.'

'A battle?'

'Yes. They want to treble our size and change our name. If they succeed, it will give my history an end at least.'

So there were echoes of wars even in Brink. We found a table and sat and chatted, while the Hall filled up. There was no sign yet of the Macreadys.

At half past eight, Father Morris climbed on to the stage and told us what was going to happen. This was to be a joyful occasion, when we could be ourselves and enjoy each other's company. There would be dancing, and singing, and games, and a running wine and cheese buffet. The Master of Ceremonies would be Mr Alfred Towle, who at that point climbed up and assumed station at the music stand, his eyes glittering with what at first looked like terror, but which proved to be a mordant and infectious amusement.

The English will dance cautiously, but the idea of singing or playing games has them reaching for their coats. I can only say that Alfred had ways of presenting these activities which removed their sting and left his audience relaxed and cooperative.

He knew the words of every song and the rules of every game. He knew to whom to appeal for help. Everyone shared his obvious pleasure at being allowed to run a party, and there was no time to stop and wonder at that strangely gawky figure nodding and gesticulating in the great hall of Aladdin's palace.

We had just finished a group of old music-hall songs when the Macready party arrived, consisting of the old man, Juliet, and two foreign-looking guests. Tiggy waved to Juliet to bring folding chairs over and join our table.

There was sufficient of a hiatus in the activities for Macready to be able to do his introduction act.

'I want you to meet,' he said impressively, 'the two Trade Commissioners of the Cyprus Republic in London. Mr Spirou ...' I shook hands with a dark plumpish moustached man of forty and Mr Demos. Mr and Mrs Jeffries.'

The grey had spread to most of his hair now, even in his late twenties. He was clean-shaven, with dark, handsome eyes, upright, and alert.

I stood up. 'Demos?' I said. 'Demopoulos, isn't it?'

He looked at me closer. 'Demos is easier. Jeffries. Yes, of course. How do you do?' He held out his hand, smiling, and waited. I hesitated, then shook it.

'You know each other?' enquired Macready.

'Yes,' said Xenis. 'We met in Cyprus.' He moved on to shake hands with Tiggy, and to be introduced to the Arbuthnots.

Juliet settled into a chair next to me, and whispered 'Generally, I don't go much for Daddy's guests, but this one really is rather a lamb.'

'The fat one?' I enquired.

'No, silly; the one with the beautiful eyes. Mind you, he's a bit of a wolf.'

'Perhaps he's a wolf in lamb's clothing.'

'Now you're being beastly.'

My brain swam as I watched the lamb who had murdered Helena take a chair on the other side of me, and contemplate me calmly.

'These are better days, eh, Captain Jeffries?'

The fiddle and piano struck up before I could reply. Alfred had found a group of older townsfolk who were prepared to sing their hearts out, and he had the music-hall technique of feeding words to an audience. It was *John Brown's Body*, and the volume was tremendous.

'This I know,' shouted Xenis, conducting with one hand and leaning across to me. I sat dumbfounded, watching this multiple killer singing about a body mouldering in the grave.

After the song we were promised some dancing shortly. Xenis leaned towards me again. 'Truly, Captain Jeffries,' he said, 'I am sorry for what we did to you. I did not like to see that your leg hurt you when you stood up.'

'There were others that you killed,' I said. 'Decent people. You killed Helena.'

He shrugged. 'It is a long time ago. It gave me very great pain, believe me; but what could I do? Truly, it was necessary at the time. The struggle of the Cyprus people had to be won. Now it is possible to forgive. We harbour no ill feelings towards you and your people.'

'Thank you,' I said shortly.

'I understand. You do not like to be forgiven; but it is for myself and my people that I must speak. Come and visit us now, and you will see that all is changed.'

There was a chord of music, and Alfred announced that if we would take our partners for the *Sir Roger de Coverley*, he would lead us through the dance. Xenis immediately stood up, and bent over Juliet. 'This I do not know perfectly,' he said; 'but you will teach me.' He bore her away, grinning and excusing himself to me.

Tiggy detached herself from the adhesive Macready, and moved into Juliet's seat. 'Are you all right, darling?' she enquired. 'Who's your attractive friend?'

'My attractive friend,' I said between my teeth, 'is the EOKA terrorist who blew me up in Cyprus.'

She laughed. 'Not the very one, I imagine.'

'It is, I tell you!'

'But he looks so nice.'

'Does he? Well, he says he's been nice enough to forgive me for getting in his way.'

She was examining me with concern now.

'Do you want to go home?'

'What, leave my own parish party for him?'

'Darling, it's only this once. You don't have to go through anything you don't want to, just because this nasty old man chooses his guests badly.' A thought struck her. 'You don't want to fight him, or kill him, or anything, do you?'

Gloomily, I considered these possibilities. 'I haven't got anything to kill him with.'

'I suppose you could borrow a sharp knife from one of the church ladies in the kitchen, as long as you promise to let them have it back. I don't think Father Morris would approve of the idea.'

'Stop being so silly. I don't want to kill him.'

'I just don't want you to feel I'm stopping you from doing what you must. It would be nice if just for one evening the lion and the lamb could lie down together.'

'The wolf,' I said mechanically.

The *Sir Roger de Coverley* was going well, and was acquiring recruits for a second time round.

'The what, darling?'

'Oh, nothing.'

Macready leaned over. 'Mr Spirou thinks he has mastered the dance,' he said to Antigone, 'and wonders if you would partner him,'

She looked worriedly at me. 'All right, darling?'

'Yes, of course. I'm not against Cypriots, you know. They're all right as people.'

When they left, Macready came and sat next to me, and explained how important he considered it was to show visitors from overseas our customs and dances. He ran on until the music was ended and the dancers were returning to their seats.

'To show Greeks an English dance is like showing Spaniards a British sherry,' I said savagely. 'They have the Kalamatiano.'

Xenis, returning to his seat with Juliet, caught the last word. 'Ah!' he said; 'you know the Kalamatiano?'

'Slightly.'

'It is a good dance; but this one is interesting. It is like your Scottish dances.'

He resumed his seat without embarrassment. 'You know, it is strange, meeting you here like this. You are in the Army still?'

'No. I live here and bind books.'

'Ah. You enjoy this?'

'Sometimes.'

'You have a very beautiful wife.'

'And you? Are you married?'

'Not yet.'

'You work in London?'

'Not exactly. I visit London a lot.'

'And you enjoy life?'

'Sometimes. Since the fighting there is less excitement; but we have the task of building our country, and there are many problems still.'

'And Yiorgo?'

'Yiorgo? He lives in my village and works for the school. He is not ambitious, that fellow.'

Alfred was splitting us into groups for a game, and I found myself back with the Arbuthnots and Tiggy. Cyril was happy to do most of the work, and I had time to think. Curiously, I was tempted to envy Xenis. He had fought and won his battle, by whatever means; now he was able to follow up and build on his victory. Knowing the frustrating hollowness of what passed for a constitution in Cyprus, and the speed with which it was breaking down into civil war, I could see that Xenis would not be short of more battles in the future. Unless he met the fate he had meted out to others, he would have the luxury of a cause for many years to come. I wondered what sort of business he was doing with Macready, and who was getting the better of whom.

I was tempted again, this time to hope that it was Xenis who got the better of Macready.

After more games I looked up and found him standing over me.

'Captain Jeffries,' he said.

'Mr Jeffries,' I corrected him.

'I apologise. Mr Jeffries, I have to go now. You understand, we are with Mr Macready. Truly, I mean what I say about visiting Cyprus. Bring your wife, and we will arrange a party, isn't it?'

'No,' I said. 'I shall never come to Cyprus again. There is too much about it that I wish to forget.'

'A pity. Think about it. What is past is past. We can be friends now.'

I shook his hand, not because I wanted to be friends, but because he would not have understood any other reaction.

After the Macready party had gone, I felt an access of impatient energy.

'Come on,' I said to Tiggy, standing up; 'let's go home.'

'I can't come yet,' she said. 'I promised to help the ladies clear up. Are you tired, darling? Your terrorist has gone, hasn't he?'

'No,' I said, 'I am not tired. I have never been less tired. I just want to get out of here before Alfred gets us all playing Acting Clumps. I choose life, not drama.'

'Ooh!' she exclaimed. 'Life, is it? I'll get away as soon as I can, and come and help you. You go off.'

I walked out of the Hall, and made for home. It was warm enough for people to be dawdling in the street. One or two couples were hanging about experimentally up side alleys, and in a parked car I saw the gleam of a woman's face, with the shadow of a man bending over it. The night air was full of the sweet smell of balsam poplar.

For an hour I sat in the study, and thought. For all I had said, one strove after joy, after ecstasy, seeking to harness the earth and draw it after one. No man could be content to sit and wait for ecstasy to descend, however well he knew that could be the manner of its coming. I had striven after the joy that was Helena and lost her in the explosion of my world. Then, without raising a finger, I had been given Antigone and a new world.

What was this new world, that I had been so fearful of exploring? Certainly, it held a second chance of enjoying what one had seemed to lose for ever. Father Morris had said that most of us needed a big explosion. He himself had been blown from commuter to priest, Richard Bone from planter to librarian, I from soldier to bookbinder. With Mrs Macready, Alfred Towle, Barbara, and many others, we were in our worlds of second chance, where the leaves are greener with the remembrance of the lost leaves of innocence. We must at all costs make the most of these worlds. Some people, like Tiggy and Bob, seemed to need and enjoy only the one life; the rest of us needed the big bang.

Over an island I would never see again, that wind was blowing from the Anti-Taurus, over Helena's grave and the graves of others who had died in a battle that had never been important. Xenis, trapped in a dream of strife, was happy to dream on, unhurt yet by his own cruelty. We who had fought against him walked in the clear light of truth, listening for the faint sounds of battle on some more fruitful field.

Our way was pleasant, our air invigorating, our hunt companionable. There was love and faith, and spring still came to the earth. In fifty years, we should have joined Helena, victims of some event only comprehensible in God's infinite wisdom.

Meanwhile I wished Tiggy would come back from the party, while my precarious faith held.

I went out on to the balcony, and breathed the night air again. As I stood there, Tiggy's hand slipped into mine, and I felt her warmth at my side.

'Limping winter,' I said. 'It's over, thank God. Is the party over, too?'

'It's over,' she murmured. They said they could manage without me.'

'That's as well, because I can't.'

'Is there something I can help with?'

I looked at her, and marvelled at the curve of her cheek where it was touched by the light from the study.

'Just to get rid of the last of this limping winter.' Out of the corner of my eye, I saw Alfred Towle stalking along the street.

'*Look to behold this night,*' I declaimed, '*Earth-treading stars, that make dark heaven light.*'

Alfred stopped, and thought. Then he got it:

'*Such comfort, as do lusty young men feel*
When well-apparell'd April on the heel
Of limping winter treads.'

'Right?'

'Right,' I said. 'Congratulations on a triumphant evening. Goodnight.'

He hesitated, then padded on and went into his cottage.

Tiggy's arm stole round my neck. Her eyes danced.

'Now what about this ecstasy you talk about?' she whispered.

I remember her head thrown back, her shining dark hair over the pillow, and her lips parted. Then the front door bell rang, and with shut eyes she murmured 'Bread. I promised him some bread. Give it to him, darling.'

I threw on my dressing-gown, rushed down to the kitchen, and opened the front door. He was standing there, with bent head.

'I ...' he began; but I had thrust the bread into his hands. He nodded, and twitched, and swallowed. 'Thank you,' he said. I shut the door, and went back.

Tiggy was as I had left her, with her eyes still shut. For a moment I thought she was asleep. Then she murmured 'For a moment, I was afraid it might be your ... terrorist.'

'It was one of my terrorists,' I said. 'They're all over the place. But wherever we go, my darling - as in good time we must go - we must be patient with our terrorists, and loving with our friends.'

'Not forgetting our wives,' she said; and she opened her dark eyes and looked at me. 'As for going, whither thou goest I will go.'

So we went together.

AFTERWORD

The *Wall of Winter* was Paul's first novel, written sometime in the late 1970s soon after he retired as headmaster of Aldenham. The novel deals with the difficulties associated with forgiveness and reconciliation which were very real for him.

Paul spent his early twenties in the 14th Army, facing the Japanese in Burma during World War II. Here his fellow officer and best friend, David Butler, was killed by a sniper.

During the Cyprus troubles of the late 1950s, he was headmaster of a multi-national school holding together a community of young Greek, Turkish and other nationalities. Two of his staff were shot by terrorists and some of his pupils were arrested. One former pupil was even hanged for murder, a theme he returned to in *A Slippery Isle*.

Once peace was declared in both the Far East and Cyprus it was necessary to put away former animosities and live with new peacetime realities. Being Paul, he could forgive but not forget, and his sympathies were always with those who were not there to enjoy the benefits of peace. His contempt for those that personally benefitted from conflict or sought to subvert its reality for their own ends knew no bounds.

Running a language school in Cambridge in the late 1970s, he was famous for his love of all nationalities and especially their various quirks which, while often politically incorrect by today's standards, were wittily perceptive and produced much amusement amongst the students themselves. Again, he picks up some examples of these in a later book.

The illustration on the front cover is of the Queen's window at St Hilarion Castle, a key location in the story and a place of great tranquility. When he was writing this novel, the castle was out of bounds having been taken over by the invading Turkish army. It is now open to all once again.

As with his other books, the *Wall of Winter* only existed in typescript at his death. I have converted it to an electronic form and corrected any obvious errors. Those that remain are my fault.

I am grateful to members of the wider family, to Joris, and Stilvi Vreede and to Derryth Ridge for their help and advice.

I feel sure that Paul would have dedicated this book to my mother Felicity, and to Cypriots of all origins, languages and faiths who seek a peaceful co-existence in Aphrodite's isle.

JPG

ALSO BY PAUL GRIFFIN

Autobiographies
Changes and Chances
The Lost Battalion
A Noisy Isle/A Charming Terror
Off Games
Beyond Teaching

Novels
The Wall of Winter
A Slippery Isle
Green Belt
A Line to the Sea

Uncle Raymond books
A Degree of Uncle Raymond
All Greek to Uncle Raymond

Religious
The Other Six Days

Poetry
Hums
More Hums
Sing Jubilee
Nearly Funny Poems
Songs about Suffolk
Going Away
Lighthearted Lines
The Sound of Violins
Diamonds for Aphrodite